A lad

Thomas's good opinion of her would quickly change if he knew the truth. As would the opinions of those in Treasure Creek who had befriended her in spite of her standoffish attitude. Tears clogged her throat. She wanted so much to draw close to them all, to be a true friend to them, but friendship meant questions and confidences that she dare not invite.

Guilt, sorrow and regret formed a heavy weight in her chest, pressed down on her already aching heart. She did not truly belong with these good people. Certainly not with a man of faith and integrity like Thomas. She could only live on the fringe of their friendship, returning what help and service to them she could in exchange. She blinked the film of moisture from her eyes and stole a sidelong look at Thomas from beneath her lowered lashes. Perhaps she could help him with his missionary work in some way. Perhaps that would help atone for her past.

ALASKAN BRIDES:
Women of the Gold Rush
find that love is the greatest treasure of all.

Yukon Wedding—Allie Pleiter, April 2011
Klondike Medicine Woman—Linda Ford, May 2011
Gold Rush Baby—Dorothy Clark, June 2011

Books by Dorothy Clark

Love Inspired Historical

Family of the Heart
The Law and Miss Mary
Prairie Courtship
Gold Rush Baby

Love Inspired

Hosea's Bride
Lessons from the Heart

Steeple Hill Single Title

Beauty for Ashes
Joy for Mourning

DOROTHY CLARK

Critically acclaimed, award-winning author Dorothy Clark lives in rural New York, in a home she designed and helped her husband build (she swings a mean hammer!) with the able assistance of their three children. When she is not writing, she and her husband enjoy traveling throughout the United States doing research and gaining inspiration for future books. Dorothy believes in God, love, family and happy endings, which explains why she feels so at home writing stories for Love Inspired Books. Dorothy enjoys hearing from her readers and may be contacted at dorothyjclark@hotmail.com.

Gold Rush Baby

DOROTHY CLARK

Love Inspired

Special thanks and acknowledgment to Dorothy Clark for her contribution to the Alaskan Brides miniseries.

Recycling programs
for this product may
not exist in your area.

TM LOVE INSPIRED BOOKS

ISBN-13: 978-0-373-82871-5

GOLD RUSH BABY

Copyright © 2011 by Harlequin Books S.A.

www.LoveInspiredBooks.com

Printed in U.S.A.

And Jesus looking upon them saith,
With men it is impossible, but not with God,
for with God all things are possible.
—*Mark* 10:27

This book is dedicated to editor Emily Rodmell,
who skillfully walked me through the process of
writing a book in a continuity series.
Thank you, Emily, for your patience and good humor
in answering my many questions. And to the other
authors of this Alaskan Brides continuity series,
Allie Pleiter and Linda Ford...what can I say?
You are both very talented and gracious ladies.
I count it an honor to have worked with you.

"Commit thy works unto the Lord,
and thy thoughts shall be established."
Your word is truth. Thank You, Jesus.
To You be the glory.

Chapter One

Treasure Creek, Alaska, August, 1898

Her heart pounded. Her lungs strained for air. Viola Goddard ignored their screaming need, held the hem of her long skirt out of the way of her feet and ran on. Impervious to bumps and shouts, she dashed around and through the press of prospectors and townspeople on the board walkway, driven forward by the horror of the note crushed in her hand. *The baby! Goldie's father had trusted her to care for his baby and now— Please, God, let Goldie be all right! Please keep her safe until I—* "Oh!"

She crashed into a solid, lean body, bounced off and staggered back, trying to get her balance. Strong hands clamped around her upper arms, steadied her. Viola wrenched her shoulders, pushed against a hard chest. "Let me go!"

"Steady, Miss Goddard."

Miss Goddard? Who... She looked up. The handsome man staring down at her frowned, tightened his grip on her upper arms.

"Are you all right, Miss Goddard? You seem distressed." His green eyes darkened. "Is it the baby? Has her health taken a turn for the worse?"

Goldie's health? A memory flashed. Thomas Stone. Yes, that was his name. He was the missionary who had brought the injured stampeder into the clinic, when she took Goldie in to be examined.

"You're trembling, Miss Goddard. Please, tell me what's wrong. Perhaps I can help."

The concern in his voice squeezed at her throat. "It's Goldie—" Fear choked off her words.

"Goldie?"

She took a gulp of air, nodded. "The baby. She— she's been kidnapped!"

"What?"

People near them on the street stopped, stared. A low murmur started, hummed against her ears.

Confusion leaped into the green eyes looking down at her.

"I found this in her cradle." She bit her lip to stop a rush of tears, and shoved the ransom note at him. "Do you know where Mack Tanner is? He's not in his store and I have to find him. He has—" His hand slid down her arm, tugged. Her heart sped. "What are you *doing?*"

"Taking you to the sheriff."

The murmur grew louder.

"Let me *go!*" Viola dug in her heels and pulled at his strong hand gripping her elbow as he ushered her down the street. Her resistance was no match for his strength.

A roar of laughter went up from a group of prospectors, who split to allow them passage on the walkway. "You show the little lady who's boss, mister!"

Viola caught her breath. *I can't have you running away, Viola. You will give my other girls ideas. I warned you. Now my men will have to show you Richard Dengler is boss.* She shuddered at the memory, yanked against Thomas Stone's grasp.

He shot her a look and tightened his hold. "I am trying to help you, Miss Goddard. This is a dangerous situation for both you and the baby. You need the sheriff, not Mack Tanner, even if he is the mayor of Treasure Creek." He opened the door of the new log building that served as the sheriff's office and jail, and tugged at her elbow, urging her to step inside.

She shook off the memory, grabbed the door frame and tried once more to resist. "I do need Mack! He has the *gold.*"

"Gold?" The sheriff's growl stopped her struggle. "What's going on, Viola? Is this about Goldie again?"

She looked at the giant man leaning back in his chair, with his booted feet propped up on a desk he made look much too small, and the last of her strength deserted her. She stepped inside. "Yes, she—"

"Don't people ever give up!" Ed Parker shook his head, motioned her closer. "Who's been trying to claim the baby and get their hands on those gold nuggets this time?"

"No one. She—" Her throat closed on the words.

"The baby has been kidnapped, Ed."

Hearing Thomas Stone say the words made it worse… more real. She sagged, felt him grip her elbow again, support her.

"Kidnapped!" Ed Parker's feet hit the floor with a thud. "Close that door."

There was a click behind her. Her knees wobbled as the missionary led her to the only chair in the place. She sank onto the hardwood seat and fought for composure as he laid the crumpled paper on the sheriff's desk.

"That's the note the kidnapper left her."

Ed Parker smoothed out the paper and read it, his broad face darkening into a scowl. He fastened his gaze on her. "Start at the beginning and tell me everything."

Viola tightened the grip of her folded hands in her lap, digging her fingernails into her palms to keep from crying. "Goldie has been fussy, and I have been up day and night with her. She developed a fever today, so I took her to Dr. Calloway's clinic this afternoon. I was afraid she had come down with the cholera that spread through the Indian village. Teena Crow examined her and told me Goldie is…is teething and her gums are inflamed. She gave me an herbal balm to…to take away the pain." *She would be in pain. Oh, Goldie, baby, I'm so sorry!*

She swallowed hard, squared her shoulders. "The balm worked. Goldie calmed and fell asleep. Hattie insisted I go to her room and catch up on my sleep while she watched over Goldie, and—" *And it's all my fault! I should have stayed with her.* She took a deep breath and pushed her fingernails in deeper. "When I woke, I went to my bedroom to check on Goldie. Hattie was asleep in the rocker and…and the cradle was…was empty, except for that note. I ran to Tanner's store to find Mack Tanner and get the gold nuggets he is keeping safe for Goldie, but he wasn't there. I was running to his home when I collided with Mr. Stone—" she shot him a look that let him know how little she appreciated his interference "—showed him the note and he brought me here."

She rose, bracing herself, lest the missionary try to push her back down on the chair. "Sheriff Parker, please—I will answer all of your questions later. Right now, I have to find Mack Tanner and—"

"I'm here."

Viola whirled toward the door. Mack Tanner stepped into the small office, pulled the door closed and fastened his gaze on her. "Harold Goodge came to the schoolhouse to get me. Said he was on the street and overheard you tell Thomas you were looking for me because Goldie has been kidnapped. Said he saw Thomas bringing you here." A frown creased his forehead, his gaze shifted to the missionary, then returned to her. "Is it true about Goldie being kidnapped?"

She caught her breath, nodded.

"I suppose, like all the other greedy louts who have tried to claim her for their child, they are demanding the gold nuggets Goldie's father left for her care?"

"Yes."

"It's always about gold!" Mack's face tightened. "On the way here, I heard a couple of men talking about the Tlingits being behind the kidnapping. Any truth to that?"

"The Tlingits?" Ed Parker scowled. "You didn't tell me that, Viola."

"I cannot tell you something I do not know, Sheriff. The kidnapper did not sign the note." She took a breath, smoothed the asperity from her voice and held out her hand in entreaty. "Could we please stop talking and—"

"The kidnapper left a note?"

The sheriff nodded at Mack Tanner and snatched up the paper on his desk. "Got it right here. It says… 'Leave the gold at midnight at the creekside entrance to the fenced-in cemetery. If you do, you'll find the baby soon thereafter. If you don't, the baby dies.'" He rubbed his big hand over his long chin, looked back over at Mack. "Nothing there makes it sound like the Indians."

"No, but some people believe the baby is Indian, because of her dark hair and those moccasin booties she was wearing." Mack scowled. "I knew those booties were going to be a problem the day Viola brought the baby to me and told me how she'd been left on her doorstep. And, of course, it's common knowledge that the Tlingits are angry because Teena Crow is working at the clinic with Dr. Calloway. And with the cholera having hit their village so hard and the town being spared…" Mack turned toward the missionary. "Your work is with the Tlingits, Thomas. What do you think? Would they—"

"What does it *matter* what he thinks?" Viola shoved the words out of her constricted throat. She was beyond caring if Mack Tanner was the founder and mayor of Treasure Creek and the keeper of Goldie's gold nuggets. He was wasting time. "Goldie is in danger. We cannot simply stand here *talking* about it! The note says—"

"Calm down, Viola." Ed Parker's voice was kind, but firm. "There is time to meet the kidnapper's demands. And we can do that best if we know what we're up against." He looked beyond her. "What *do* you think about the Tlingits being involved, Stone?"

She might as well be invisible! Viola glanced up at the missionary, found his gaze on her. She was not invisible to Thomas Stone. A shiver slipped along her spine. He looked calm and decisive. And strong. She lifted her hand and rubbed the spot where he had gripped her elbow as he'd propelled her along the street. *All those forceful men at Dengler's had—* He glanced down at her hand. She froze and he looked back at the sheriff.

"I think the rumor is ridiculous, Ed. The Tlingits are honest traders. Kidnapping a baby for gold or revenge is not their way. And no Tlingit would use the wording in that note. But Teena Crow would know for certain. Why not ask her about this?"

Yes. Decisive and strong was the perfect description of Thomas Stone. But not calm, as he appeared. There was a little muscle jumping along his jaw. A sure sign a man was angry. She knew all the signs. She turned, using the movement to create more space between them. "Sheriff Parker, I don't *care* who the kidnappers are. It doesn't matter if they are white men or Tlingits. I only want to get Goldie back." She whirled and took a step toward Mack Tanner. "Could we please go get the gold nuggets now? I have to take—"

"Not you, Viola."

She whipped back around to face the sheriff. "But I *must!* I—"

"Nope. It's too dangerous. The note just says 'leave the gold', it doesn't say who should take it there."

"But—"

"No arguing. You go on home and let us men handle this." Ed Parker pulled a gun belt from a drawer, strapped it on and came around the desk. "I think Stone's got the right idea. Let's go talk to Teena Crow, Mack. You come, too, Stone. We'll see if she agrees—"

"I am not going home."

The men stopped at the door, turned their heads and frowned at her. Viola drew her shoulders back, lifted her chin and faced their displeasure. "Goldie was left on *my* doorstep, along with a note from her father asking me to care for her until he returns from the gold fields. *I* am responsible for her, Sheriff Parker. And I am going with you."

"Now see here, Viol—"

"Her point is a valid one, Ed. And there is no danger to Miss Goddard at the clinic." The missionary's quiet words interrupted the sheriff's growl.

Ed Parker scowled but said no more, simply snatched his hat off a hook on the wall, slapped it on his head and opened the door.

A group of men clustered on the walkway looked up. "What's goin' on, Sheriff? We heard—"

"You men go on about your business now. There's nothing here that concerns you. If I need help, I'll come find you." The sheriff stepped outside, using his giant size to force the men to move. Mack Tanner followed.

Thomas Stone took a step back. "After you, Miss Goddard."

Viola stared at the missionary. Why had he argued in her defense? Why had he insinuated himself into this situation in the first place? She had not asked for his help. A shudder traveled through her. In her experience, men always had some nefarious motive for their actions. And it was usually costly for a woman. But she hadn't time to concern herself with that now. Saving Goldie was what mattered.

She stiffened her spine and swept by the man, out onto the plank walkway, and hurried to catch the sheriff and Mack Tanner. If Thomas Stone did have a base motive, if he thought he could collect some personal "favor" for helping her, he was very much mistaken. Richard Dengler and his thugs were back in Seattle. She had escaped his grasp and was through with a life of prostitution forever. And no man...*no man* would ever touch her again. Not even to save Goldie. She would listen to their plans and then she would find another way. One that kept her at a distance from Thomas Stone. She did not like the hint of admiration she saw in his eyes, though at the moment, she was grateful for his tall, muscular presence beside her, blocking her from the crowd forming in their wake as they walked toward the clinic at the other end of town.

Thomas strode beside Viola Goddard, close enough to protect her from the crush of the swelling crowd following them, but far enough to maintain a respectful distance. A safe distance. He had felt a drawing, a *connection* to the woman when their gazes had met earlier at the clinic, and he wanted nothing but the most distant and casual of relationships with her. He had vowed to himself, when his wife and baby died, he would never love or marry again. And he'd felt no interest in any women for the past three years. But there was something about Viola Goddard....

He glanced down, swept his gaze over the sacklike thing covering her hair, that was gathered in a mass at the back of her head, studied her pale, tense face. She was staying strong in insisting she have a part in the kidnapped baby's rescue, but her strength was born of desperation. There was a vulnerability in the depth of her eyes that tugged at him, made him want to help her, to protect her. An odd thought. It was the baby who was in danger.

The anger born when he'd learned of the baby's kidnapping surged again. He'd been helpless against the pneumonia that had claimed his baby's life, but he could fight the kidnapper that was endangering this one. He clenched his jaw, focused his gaze on the sheriff. He would ask Ed Parker to deputize him. That would be best. But one way or another, he would help get the baby back alive.

"That is…it's…*untrue*." Teena Crow's dark eyes shadowed with hurt. "What have my people ever done to the whites of this town that they would say such a thing?"

Viola moved over to stand beside her friend. "People do not always deserve what is said about them, Teena. But—"

"But what, Viola?" Teena turned toward her, her dark braids and the small strings of beads dangling from her ears swinging from her quick movement. "Are you saying your heart believes my people have taken Goldie from you?"

"I did not—"

"What's going on, Teena? I could hear voices in the other room."

Viola jerked her gaze from the soft smile of delight that warmed Teena's face, to the doorway. Dr. Jacob Calloway stood there wiping his hands on a towel and scanning the room. A frown line appeared between his dark brows. "I thought I heard your voice, Sheriff." He looked at her. "Is this about the baby, Viola? Mavis Goodge told us she had been kidnapped. Have you found her injured? Do you need—"

"They think some of my people have taken Goldie."

Viola shook her head. "That is not true, Teena. None of us have accused the Tlingits. We only came seeking your opinion of the note—though why it matters is beyond my understanding." She lifted her hands and rubbed at the throbbing in her temples. "I don't care *who* kidnapped Goldie. I only want to get her back. And we are wasting time with all this talking!"

"You are right, Viola. To save baby Goldie is what is important." Teena gave her a quick hug, then crossed to the sheriff. "There are good and bad in all peoples. I will speak the truth. What do the words on the paper say?"

Dr. Calloway stepped behind Teena and gently rested his hands on her shoulders. It was a loving, protective gesture. Or was it? Perhaps it was possessiveness. Viola looked away. The sight of a man's hands made her stomach queasy. She stared at the floor and tried not to think about Goldie being hungry or afraid or hurt, while the sheriff read the note.

"Those are not words my people would know to use."

Ed Parker nodded. "That's what Stone said."

At last! Now perhaps Mack Tanner would get her the gold and she could go to the cemetery as instructed. Viola glanced up. Thomas Stone was looking at her, compassion in his eyes. But again, that hint of admiration lurked in their depths. In the world she'd come from, that meant only one thing. She straightened, refusing to reveal the twinge of fear that streaked through her. Fear revealed weakness, and the men she had known grew meaner and more demanding when they sensed fear.

"I agree with Teena and Thomas about the note. And the Tlingits I have met are not dishonest. Nor do I think they would threaten harm to a child. I suggest you look for a white man, Sheriff." Dr. Calloway's voice was strong with conviction.

Viola shifted her gaze, saw Teena look up at Jacob, her dark eyes wide and soft with pleasure. *Oh, Teena, don't trust him. Never trust a man.*

"And I suggest you step outside and tell that to the crowd. It's getting larger." Thomas Stone jerked his thumb over his shoulder toward the window behind him.

"Confound it! I told those men to go home. I was afraid something like this was gonna happen." Ed Parker jammed the note into his pocket and looked over at her. "You stay here with Teena, Viola. It might not be safe for you to be walking home alone now, with the crowd thinking about gold. And we men have got things to do."

Viola stiffened. But before she could reiterate her intentions of taking the gold to the cemetery, the sheriff was barking out orders.

"Mack, the people in this town hold you in high regard. You come outside with me while I send this crowd packing once and for all, then go get the gold nuggets and take them to the cemetery at midnight, like the note says. Thomas, when the crowd clears, you get to the woods by the cemetery and find yourself a good hiding place. I want you there just in case there are some Tlingit involved. And if you see a good chance to grab the baby, do it. No telling what this guy is planning. I want you there, too, Doc. If there's any shooting…"

Shooting! Viola didn't wait to hear more, she slipped out of the room and hurried toward the back door. Soft footfalls whispered on the floor behind her.

"You are going home?"

"No. To the cemetery." She turned. "Don't tell them, Teena. Please. I cannot sit here and wait. Goldie may—" she swallowed back the fear pressing on her throat "—she may need me."

Teena nodded, her gaze solemn. "I will not tell them you follow your heart." She glanced over her shoulder, stepped closer. "Go to the back of the school, then beyond the cabins to Dunkle's farm—where the goats are penned. Walk straight to the trees on the mountain. There is a path in the woods my people use to go to the waterfall. You will not be seen."

"Thank you, Teena." Viola gave her a quick hug, then opened the door and stepped outside.

"I will pray." The door closed.

The soft words brought comfort, hope. She walked through the back lots toward the school, slipping in and out of the dusky light as the shadows of the buildings covered her. The sound of the sheriff's voice, the mumblings of the crowd trailed after her. She shivered, wished for a jacket, though the night was not cold. The chill was inside her.

At the school she paused in the shadows, swept her gaze over the cabins, then stepped out into the fading luminance and crossed the open area toward the Johnson brothers' cabin. There would be no eyes gazing out of windows there. Last week she had mended a rent in Uriah Johnson's tent so he could take it with them on their trek up the Chilkoot Trail to the gold fields. She kept to the left side of the cabin, using it as a barrier to hide her from the Tucker cabin. If Frankie looked out a window and saw her, she would come to investigate. And she could abide no more delays. She moved on past the Monroe home, and once beyond the cluster of cabins, quickened her steps to the Dunkle farm.

The goats gamboled over to the fence to greet her. Tears clogged her throat. Goldie's feeding bottle was at home. How would… She forced down her imaginings and ran to the edge of the woods at the foot of the mountain, then stepped into the welcome darkness. Silence pressed in on her. *Help me find the way, Lord.* She moved forward slowly, searching through the dim light for the Tlingit path. The feel of forest loam pressed firm beneath her feet, assuring her she had found it. She turned and followed in the direction of the waterfall.

She had to reach the cemetery before the sheriff and the others arrived. Before the kidnapper came.

Chapter Two

The water roared over the mountain ledge in a silver deluge that washed the face of the layered rock, foamed over and slithered through the piled boulders, then whispered its way into the creek flowing toward town.

Toward the cemetery.

Viola shivered, studied the deep shadows beneath the towering firs. She spotted no one lurking in the depths, and moved forward until the woods opened onto a small clearing and she could see the fence. And the gate.

She should have stayed and made the sheriff listen to her. What if the kidnapper was expecting a woman? What if he saw Mack coming and sensed a trap? Bile burned its way into her throat. She leaned back against the massive trunk of a tree, its branches laden with yellow leaves, and closed her eyes. *Please, Lord. She's a helpless little baby. Please protect her.*

A violent shaking took her. Tears stung her eyes. She took a deep breath, blinked them away, and opened her eyes and stared at the gate. If there was one thing her past had taught her, it was that tears never helped. The light grew dimmer, slid toward deep purple. Twilight back home. Nearly midnight here.

A figure emerged out of the shadowed distance, strode across the cemetery and stopped by the gate. She watched Mack Tanner sweep the woods with a long, searching gaze, willed him to hurry and do what the kidnapper asked. He pulled a small bag from his pocket, held it aloft, then bent from the waist and placed it on the ground at the foot of one of the gate posts, turned and walked off the way he had come.

It was done. Now they had only to wait. Where were Thomas Stone and Dr. Calloway and the sheriff? She scanned left and right, saw nothing but trees and rocks and shadows. Where was the kidnapper? What if he didn't come? What if he'd seen one of the men? Or her? What if he left with Goldie? The shaking took her again. She shouldn't have come. She should have listened to the sheriff and stayed at home. Maybe…

Movement at the edge of the woods caught her eye. Her heart jolted. Was that *him?* She stared into the shadowy gloom formed by the thick growth of trees, made out the blanket-wrapped bundle the man carried, a gun in his other hand.

Lord, don't let him see me. Keep Goldie safe.

She pressed back against the tree trunk, felt the rough bark bite into her palms and back, the pulse throbbing at her temples and the base of her throat. Footsteps neared, turned away, stopped. *Where was he?*

She strained against the silence, broken only by the sibilance of the creek flowing by. Her ears failed her. So did her lungs. They were as frozen as the glaciers atop the high mountains. She inched her head to the left. He was there, crouched behind a pile of huge rocks, looking toward the cemetery.

Time stopped. She dug her nails into the bark to hold herself from running to him and snatching the baby away. She stared at the bundle. It was quiet…still. Why wasn't Goldie moving? Or cooing? She loved to wave her little fists in the air and chatter her baby talk. Fear seized her, dropped like a rock into the pit of her stomach. Rage burned away the ice in her lungs. She took a deep breath, clenched her hands. If he had hurt the baby…

She jerked, yanked her head back. He had glanced her way. Had he seen her? She checked to make certain her long skirt was hidden, inched her head to the right and peered around the opposite side of the tree trunk. What was he *doing?* Heart pounding, she watched as the man rose to a half stoop and moved toward a dead tree beside the pile of rocks. He placed the bundle in the hollow base of the tree, gave another scan of the area, then, gun raised, stepped into the small clearing and walked toward the cemetery.

She held her breath and waited. *I'm coming, Goldie. Oh, baby, don't be afraid. I will get you as soon as he is far enough away that I can get across the clearing.* No! She jerked her gaze toward the movement on the right, saw a man slipping through the trees toward the stones. Toward the bundle. They had set a trap. There were two of them! They had never intended to return Goldie. Could she reach the baby first?

She grasped her skirts, lifted the hems, then let them fall and leaned back against the tree again. The distance across the open area was too great. She would follow the man. She glanced toward the kidnapper. He was opening the gate, reaching down for the gold. When he turned back, she— Her thoughts froze, focused on the sheriff who was edging around the small building in the middle of the cemetery.

A stone flew out of the woods and crashed against the pile of rocks. She jumped, gasped.

The kidnapper looked up, spun around and raced back toward the stones.

The sheriff shouted and gave chase.

Goldie! She had to get her! Viola whirled, saw a man break from the woods and sprint toward the rocks. *Thomas Stone!*

The kidnapper stopped, raised his gun.

"*No!* Don't—"

The report of a shot slammed against her ears, echoed off the mountain. Thomas Stone lurched, ran forward, grabbed the bundle and ran back into the woods. *He had saved Goldie!* Joy flooded her. She grabbed her skirt, lifted her hems. Another shot rang out. The kidnapper staggered, fell. She turned and ran. Shouts, grunts and curses followed her to the woods.

Thomas Stone was sitting with his back to a tree, the unwrapped baby in his arms. He smiled when she skidded to a stop, dropped to her knees and reached for the baby. "She's all right."

Viola nodded, clutched Goldie to her breast and looked at him. "Thank you, Mr. Stone. I—" She stared. The left side of his shirt was soaked with blood. "He shot you." The whispered words brought a crooked grin to his face.

"It appears so." He tried to rise, grimaced, sank back and closed his eyes. The blood stain spread.

Her heart clutched. "Don't move, Mr. Stone. I'll get the doctor." She put Goldie on his outstretched legs, lurched to her feet and ran.

* * *

"He's coming around, Viola. He's going to be all right."

Her lungs emptied in a long sigh. "Thank You, Lord." She fought back grateful tears and brought up a smile. "And thank you, Dr. Calloway."

He shook his head. "You were right the first time—thank the Lord. If that bullet had been a little closer to…" He stopped, smiled. "But it wasn't. I was able to extract it safely." The smile morphed into a frown that knit his brows together. "The problem now is his recovery. He lost a lot of blood before we got him here to the clinic, and more during the operation. He's going to be as weak as that baby you're clutching as if you'll never let her go. And he won't be able to move for a few days, and not use his left arm normally for weeks. He's going to need constant care. I don't know where we will find that for him. The clinic is full. And there is no place—"

"He's not married?"

"No. And it's certain he can't go live in that hut of his on the Chilkoot Trail." Jacob Calloway shook his head, sighed and massaged the back of his neck. "I'll keep him here in the clinic overnight of course, but then I'll need the room for other surgical patients." The frown returned. Then he gave her another tired smile. "Why don't you go home now and get some sleep. Morning will be here soon, and when the laudanum that thug gave Goldie wears off, she is going to be demanding a lot of attention." His smile widened. "You can put her down, you know. She's safe here."

"Not yet. It's for my sake I'm holding her." Viola kissed the baby's silky, dark hair, squelched the war raging inside her. It was clear what she must do. "You said Mr. Stone is 'coming around.' May I see him?"

He studied her for a moment then nodded. "All right. He keeps muttering about a baby. It will likely do him good to see you holding the baby safe in your arms. But you can't stay but a minute. Like I said, he's lost a lot of blood and needs rest."

"I understand." Viola rose, and hugging Goldie close, followed Jacob Calloway through his small surgery, to the tiny room where his surgical patients recovered, her steps reluctant but determined. She smiled at Teena Crow, stepped to the bed and looked down at Thomas Stone. Her heart almost stopped. She had never seen anyone so pale. Only his eyebrows gave his face color. Even his blond hair seemed to have paled.

"I didn't realize he was so… I will thank him tomorrow." She took a steadying breath, looked up at the doctor. "You said Mr. Stone will need care and a place to stay, Doctor. I have room. Please bring him to my cabin when he recovers and—"

"No."

Viola glanced down. Thomas Stone had opened his eyes. Though his voice was weak, the look in those green eyes left no doubt that he meant exactly what he said. The tension left her. She had offered to care for him. Her obligation was satisfied. It was not her fault the man refused. Still, she stood rooted to the spot, unable to walk away. The man was in dire straits and most likely not fully aware of his situation. "This is no time to stand on pride, Mr. Stone. I am in your debt for saving Goldie, and Dr. Calloway has said you will need constant care—until you are recovered. Staying at my cabin is the sensible solution. I live close by, and the doctor will be able to come visit you daily."

"No." His voice was weaker this time, but the tone just as adamant. "Woman…repu…ta…tion…" His eyelids closed, fluttered, but refused to open.

"You'll have to leave now, Viola. He needs to rest."

She nodded, stared at Thomas Stone's pale, still face. Surely, he hadn't meant he was concerned for her? Of course not. It was his own reputation as a missionary he was concerned about. "No one's reputation will be sullied, Mr. Stone. Hattie Marsh lives in my home and will help me care for you. Now, rest well. And I will see you tomorrow." There was no response. She must have put his worries over his reputation at rest.

She looked up at Jacob Calloway. "As I was saying, Doctor, please bring Mr. Stone to my cabin when he is sufficiently recovered. I will have a bed ready for him." She glanced at Teena, mouthed "thank you" and left the room.

"No."

"Don't be foolish, Thomas. If you don't go to Viola Goddard's, where will you go? You need care."

Dr. Calloway sounded decidedly exasperated. Too bad. He was not going to spend a couple of weeks under Viola Goddard's care. He wouldn't do it. In spite of what she said, there was her reputation to think of. And there was the baby. Thomas mustered what little strength he could find and opened his eyes. "I'll go to…my hut."

"That's ridiculous, Thomas. You're too weak to even lift your head off the pillow. How do you expect to— Stop that!"

Jacob gripped his good shoulder and held him pinned

to the bed. He hadn't strength enough to push the restraining hand away, let alone sit up with one arm. Not that he wanted to try again anytime soon. The agony that shot through his upper chest at his movement was enough to hold him still.

"I told you not to try and move, Thomas. Any strain could start that wound bleeding again, and if that happens, I doubt I could save you. Here, swallow this, it will help with the pain." The doctor held a spoon to his mouth. He swallowed. "Good. Now, stay quiet. I am keeping you here the rest of the day. But this evening, Sheriff Parker is coming to help me move you to Viola Goddard's cabin. There is no choice here. You need care."

He had no strength left with which to argue the matter. Time enough for that tonight, when he would be stronger. He closed his eyes and waited for the knife-like pain to subside. Felt the darkness slip over him....

"Here is the quilt from my bed, Hattie. The coverlet is fine for me." Viola rushed from her bedroom into the living room, the quilt overflowing her arms. "If we double it, you should be nice and warm here on the settle."

Hattie stopped tucking the sheet around the thick, feather tick that padded the seat of the long, wood settle, faced Viola and fisted her hands on her ample hips. "Stop fussin', Viola! I been takin' care of myself for close to seventy years, and I reckon I can do so now. This mattress we've fixed up here on the settle will make as fine a bed as any I've e'er slept on. Now, go on with fixin' up that bed for Mr. Stone, and leave me get my work done."

"You are a pure gem, Hattie!" Viola hugged the short, round woman, then dropped to her knees beside Goldie, who was lying on her back on the braided rag rug, waving a rattle and cooing. "And so are you, little Miss Goldie." She grabbed the baby's free hand, kissed the tiny palm and then kissed her way up the pudgy little arm to her round, rosy cheek. The baby squealed, laughed and kicked her feet.

A knock on the door stopped the play. "That must be Mr. Carson to pick up his mending." Viola rose and shook out her long skirt, brushed back a curl that had escaped her snood, and went to answer the door. "Oh, Mr. Foster. I was not expecting you until tomorrow."

"I know I'm early, Miss Goddard, but I got a chance to join up with three other men going up to Dawson today. Heard tell there's been some new sites opened up, where the gold is just laying on the ground waiting for someone to scoop it up. I aim to be that someone." The wiry little man grinned. "I'm hoping I don't have to go without those shirts you was mending for me. That blue one is my lucky shirt."

Viola nodded and stepped back to let him come inside. "Your lucky shirt is ready. As are the rest. I'll get them for you."

She walked to the large wardrobe where she kept her sewing work, and pulled out the shirts tied up in a neat package. "Here you are, Mr. Foster. I hope your blue shirt works for you."

"It will." The man took the package, glanced up at her. "Having you sew it up will make it doubly lucky, Miss Goddard. Tell you what— When I strike it rich I'll give you half!"

Viola stiffened. She wiped the smile from her face

and cooled her voice by several degrees. "Fair payment for the mending is all I want, Mr. Foster."

He nodded, looked down. "I reckon I know that by now, Miss Goddard. My payment is in the scale." He made a little bow. "Good day to you. And to you, Hattie Marsh." He walked away whistling.

"And to you, John Foster! You old *fool*." Hattie's voice was rough with hurt. "Go on and join the others who risk their lives o'er and o'er, just cause some miner gets drunk and starts spinnin' tall tales about gold just waitin' to be claimed." The elderly woman snapped the quilt through the air, folded it and jammed one side down between the mattress and the back of the settle. "Old fools ne'er learn! But at least that one doesn't have a wife to leave behind, lonely and grievin' when he don't come back."

"Oh, Hattie." Viola rushed over and put her arm around the plump woman's shoulders. "Your husband never meant to leave you."

"I know. None of them do. That's why they're old fools! And him no better than the worst of them. Sellin' all we had to outfit hisself for minin' gold. Then dyin' up there. And me left with no one to care about me, nothin' in my pocket and nowhere to go. It was a blessin' when you took me in and gave me a home, Viola Goddard. A true blessin'." Hattie patted her hand and smiled up at her. "You're my family now. You and little Goldie. Now, go put the dust from the scales in your poke, and get back to work on that bed. No tellin' when Dr. Calloway will be bringin' your patient."

Chapter Three

Pulsing pain pulled him out of the darkness. Thomas tried to move his left arm, gritted his teeth at the sudden stabbing anguish in his chest. He gathered his strength against it, opened his eyes and stared up at the rough board and beam ceiling. A soft cocoon of warmth held him. A hint of roses, coming from the bedding, encouraged him to breathe deeply, to capture more of a distant memory of his mother sitting on the lawn, doing needlepoint while he played at her feet.

The dusky light of a midnight sun cast an ambient glow over the room, softening the edges of the rocks on the chimney climbing the opposite wall to the ceiling. He slewed his gaze left, toward the window that ceded entrance to the purple and gold twilight. Curtains softened the hard lines of the frame. Where was he? He frowned, willing the fuzziness away.

A rustle of fabric, soft footfalls interrupted his effort, cleared his head. He didn't have to look their way, didn't want to look their way. He knew who was there.

Viola Goddard stepped into his line of vision, glanced down at him. The connection he'd felt the first time their gazes met burgeoned. "You're awake, Mr. Stone. Would you like some water?"

What he would like was to be in his hut. But judging from the pain and the weakness in his body, that wouldn't happen anytime soon. "Please. My mouth... dry..."

She turned away.

He closed his eyes, summoned physical strength for the effort to lift his head and drink the water, and inner strength to resist the pull of his emotions toward this woman caring for him. He'd never felt so helpless. For an ungracious moment, he wished the kidnapper was miserable. There was a clink of glass, a small gurgle.

"I shall have to give you the water from a spoon."

He opened his eyes, stared up at her.

"Doctor's orders. You're not to move."

He couldn't stop the frown.

She didn't comment, merely held a napkin against his chin and offered the spoon. He fought back the urge to turn away and parted his lips. She parted her own and leaned forward. The spoon touched his mouth, water moistened his tongue. He felt the soothing coolness trickle toward his parched throat and swallowed, tried to keep his attention focused on the sensation. It was an abysmal failure. When half the glass was gone, he gave up the fight. He'd had enough. Not of the water, but of the sight of Viola Goddard leaning over him, her violet-blue eyes warm with sympathy. He closed his eyes, heard the soft rustle of her dress as she straightened and moved away, the soft clink of the glass as she set it down. *Help me, Lord. Help me to fight this sense of connection, and feel nothing but gratitude for this woman. You know I made a vow to never—*

"Mr. Stone, please open your mouth once more. The doctor instructed me to give you a dose of this medicine as soon as you awoke. It will ease your pain."

He considered feigning slumber, but the agony in his chest and shoulder overruled the idea. He opened his eyes, took the medicine and closed them again. There were soft footfalls, the creak of caning in a chair and the whisper of rockers against the floor. He tried to will away the image of Viola Goddard's beautiful eyes, fringed with dark-brown lashes so long and thick they looked like velvet, her full, rose-colored lips and the wisps of dark red curls brushing against her forehead. He failed, and slipped into oblivion, wondering if her porcelain skin was as soft and smooth to the touch as it appeared.

Viola smiled and lay her sewing aside. Goldie had rolled over again, and one shoulder and pudgy little arm were uncovered. She rose from the rocker and stood a moment, looking at the adorable baby face, the tiny button nose and the small rosebud mouth moving in and out in little sucking motions. Tears welled in her eyes. She leaned down and moved Goldie back to the center of the cradle and tucked the covers around her, blinked the tears away and brushed the back of her finger over the baby's silky, brown hair, her warm, rosy cheek. She blinked again, straightened and turned away, shaken by the strength of the love that filled her.

What if she had lost her? What if the kidnapper had harmed her? No. She would not dwell on that. She shuddered, wrapped her arms about herself and waited for the trembling to pass. It would. And every day the memory would become more dim, the trembling would lessen, and someday she would be able to look at Goldie and not think of what could have happened. Or remember that it would have been her fault.

The thought set her stomach churning. How would she ever have explained to Goldie's father? She looked out the window, studied the shadows of trees clouding her yard. Where was Goldie's father? Would he ever return? The selfish part of her hoped not. The unselfish part prayed he would. Girls needed fathers to shelter and protect them.

As she would have been sheltered, had her father and mother not died in that carriage accident. If her father had lived, she never would have been forced out onto the streets of Seattle by foreclosure on their home. And Richard Dengler would never have found her sitting on that park bench crying.

Oh, how innocent and trusting she had been! Believing Dengler when he told her she reminded him of his dear dead daughter. And that he was lonely and it would please him if she would allow him to provide for her, that she could stay in his dead daughter's bedroom until she found work by which she could support herself. How shocked she'd been when he presented her with a bill for her room and board and made her that oh, so magnanimous offer to allow her to work off her debt in his house of ill repute, knowing full well she had nowhere else to go, no one to turn to for help and no skill with which to make a living.

Her chest tightened. Sickness washed over her—the same sickness she felt that day she succumbed to the circumstances and agreed to work for him. The day she sold her innocence and youth to pay for her keep.

She clenched her hands into fists, forced air into

her constricted lungs. One thing was certain. If Goldie stayed in her care, she would make provisions for her. She would never leave the child without means. But neither would she ever marry. *Never!* The very thought of a man's hands on her again revolted her.

Viola whirled from the window, fighting the memories pushing to the surface, took a slow, deep breath to ease the churning and knotting in her stomach, the tightness now inching up her neck into her face. Her gaze lit on Thomas and the knotting and the tightness increased. Had she gone *mad,* having the man in her home? He was weak and helpless now, but what about when his strength returned and he still needed care because of his disabled arm? He was strong. Very strong.

She shivered, rubbed her elbow where his hand had gripped her. When he was stronger, she would give his care over to Hattie. He had saved Goldie, and in gratitude and thankfulness, she would shelter and nurse him. But she would not be a victim of a man's wants again. Not ever again.

She walked back to the rocker, pulled a blanket up over her shoulders and leaned her head back and closed her eyes, fighting for breath. *Almighty God, cleanse my mind of all the bad memories, I pray. Take them from me and cause me to forget....*

"Got the oatmeal fixed, Viola. I'll sit here with your patient, whilst you eat."

Viola took the empty bottle from Goldie's mouth and set it aside. "I'm not hungry, Hattie. I'll stay with him." *I owe him that much.* She dabbed a drop of the sweetened goat's milk from Goldie's little mouth and handed her a wooden dog to play with.

The elderly woman frowned and stepped to the bed. "Handsome one, ain't he? Even if he does look like death is just a-waitin' to claim him." She chuckled. "Guess I don't blame you for wantin' to stay with him."

If you only knew the truth. "Do you realize he might wake and hear you?"

Hattie turned from the bed, the wrinkles in her face deepened by a wide grin. "Which part don't you want him to hear? The part about his bein' handsome and death waitin' to claim him…or the part about you not wantin' to leave him?"

"All of it." It came out sharper than she intended.

Hattie's grin died. "Wouldn't hurt you none to take an interest in someone, Viola. It ain't right, a beautiful young woman like you being satisfied to do nothin' but work and spend her time with an old woman and a baby."

"I'm not." Viola summoned a cheeky grin, offered it as penance for her sharp tone. "I go to church, too."

"Hmmph." Hattie stepped in front of her and held out her arms. "Leastways, let me take this one and feed her some of the oatmeal. Lest you want her growin' up to be a slender slip of a thing like you." She lifted Goldie, propped her on her round hip, grabbed the bottle and headed for the door. "It wouldn't hurt you to put some flesh on them bones, you know. Men like somethin' they can get ahold of." The parting comment floated over her round shoulders as she walked away.

"Which is exactly what I do not want!" Viola pressed her lips closed on her vehement whisper and lifted her hands to rub her fingertips across her gritty, tired eyes.

Since moving in with her, Hattie had become aware of her lack of social life and was beginning to probe as to the reason. And the woman was not satisfied with her casual answers. She was pushing harder.

She rose and crossed to look out the window, absently rubbing at the scar on the outside edge of her left hand. The one where Dengler had cut her with his knife the last time she had run away. Perhaps it had been a mistake to take Hattie in. But she couldn't simply ignore the woman's homeless state when her husband had died. *Please help me, Lord. Please give me the right words to say to satisfy Hattie's curiosity. You know I can't tell her the truth of my past, nor can I lie to—*

"How's our patient doing?"

She gasped and spun toward the doorway.

"Sorry, Viola, I didn't mean to startle you." Dr. Calloway smiled. "I knocked, but the door was open, so I came on in. I thought you must have heard me at the door."

"No. I—I was thinking." And remembering. She forced a smile. "Come in, Doctor." She stepped back to allow him ample space to pass her in the narrow room. "I'm afraid Mr. Stone is still sleeping."

"I'm…awake…."

She jerked her head toward the bed, looked into those penetrating green eyes. How long had he been awake? Had he heard Hattie's comments? And her whispered retort? *What if she had prayed aloud?* Her body went rigid. She looked away. "I'm going outside for some fresh air while you examine your patient, Doctor. I shall return shortly. If you need anything meanwhile, Hattie is in the kitchen." She turned and walked out the door.

The doctor stared after her a moment, then looked down. "That is one beautiful woman. But I guess you've probably noticed."

"A man would have to be…blind not to." Thomas frowned. What had caused that flash of fear he had seen in Viola Goddard's eyes before she turned away?

Jacob grinned, set his bag on the end of the bed and lifted the edge of the covers. "Feeling a little grumpy, are we?" He pulled his watch from his vest pocket.

"Grumpy?" Maybe he had imagined the fear. He gave a snort, winced. "I'm feeling downright surly. And…uncomfortable." The doctor's fingers closed around his wrist.

"The pain is bad?"

"Beyond bad. But it's the weakness that aggravates me." Thomas scowled up at Jacob. "And your betrayal. I told you I did not…want to come here."

"Ah! That is a problem." The doctor chuckled.

Thomas turned the scowl into a glare. "It's not funny, Jacob. And I promise I will take that smile off your face…as soon as I can stand." He sagged into the mattress, all strength gone out of him from the long speech.

The doctor tucked his watch away and pulled his stethoscope from his bag. "All right, Thomas, you shall have your chance to do so when you recover. But that recovery depends on good care. And *that* is what you will receive from Viola." He put the earpieces in place and leaned down, listened, then straightened. "I want you to drink a lot of water, Thomas. You need to get your fluids built back up. And above all, no movement! Now, tell me about the pain." He put the stethoscope away and began to check the bandages.

* * *

"Hey, Viola."

Viola dragged her thoughts from the past, spotted Frankie Tucker, hammer in hand, gazing at her from behind the picket fence she was building around the churchyard. An undertone of melancholy in the woman's usually hearty voice made her abandon her walk and cross the road. She recognized loneliness when she heard it. "Hello, Frankie." She smiled, placed her hand on top of one of the pickets. "You've done a good job. The fence really dresses up the churchyard."

"It'll be finished today. Except for the painting. Burns was going to do it, but he and his dog left for the gold fields. I just have to fancy up these end posts—round the tops off a mite. Mack didn't want no gate. Says he's not trying to keep folks out, just lead them in and corral them once they get here." Frankie smiled, then frowned and ran her work-roughened hand over the taller square post at the edge of the stone walk. "Should of been finished with this job last week. Been kinda slow without Lucy and Margie helping me much. But Lucy is helping to keep Caleb's books now. And they've both been busy…setting up their new homes and all."

So that was the cause of the unhappiness in Frankie's eyes. She should have guessed. Even in the short time she had been in Treasure Creek, she'd learned how close the Tucker sisters were. And how adamantly opposed to marriage the three of them were until Lucy had fallen in love and married. It must have been a shock for Frankie. Especially when Margie followed their younger sister's example a few weeks later. She nodded, tried for the right tone of sympathetic understanding. It wasn't easy. She was as opposed to marriage as Frankie, though for very different reasons. "It must be difficult to get used to both of your sisters being married in such a short time."

Frankie snorted, jammed her hammer back into her leather belt, bent over and grabbed a tool from a bucket at her feet. "Never thought I'd see the day a Tucker girl would marry." She slammed the tool against one corner of the post and shoved down on it, repeated the movement over and over. A blade bit off thin little bits of wood that made a small pile on the ground. "Pa must be spinning in his grave." The shavings grew longer, wider, curled. The corner now sloped from the center of the post to the outer edge. "He raised us to be able to take care of ourselves, not need some *man* to do for us!"

Viola nodded. It was the best she could offer. She had nothing good to say about men or marriage.

Frankie stopped working, waved the tool in the air. "You won't find me getting yoked up to no man." She scowled, then started shaving away at the next corner of the post. "I'm gonna be a deputy, soon as I can convince that stubborn sheriff of ours I'm as good or better than them men he takes on to help him out when there's a need."

There was hurt lurking behind Frankie's bravado. Her heart went out to the unhappy woman. At least in this, she could offer some comfort. "I'm sure you would make a fine deputy, Frankie. But what will the people of Treasure Creek do without your building skills to call upon?"

Frankie paused, fastened her blue-eyed gaze on her. "Guess I hadn't thought about that." She squinted at the post, ran her hand over the two sloping corners and moved on to the next. "I'll still keep building things for folks. Being a deputy is only when there's a need. And it seems like Sheriff Parker ain't a very needful man." She stopped, looked at her. "Been talking only about me. How's Goldie? And how's the preacher doing? He mending all right?"

She gasped. "Mr. Stone! I forgot all about him." Guilt shot through her. She stepped back from the fence. "I have to go, Frankie. I told Dr. Calloway I would be right back." She lifted the hems of her long skirt, ran across the road and hurried back to her cabin.

"No movement. And no solid foods for Thomas today, Viola."

She nodded and walked the doctor to the door. "What would you advise for his sustenance?"

"A good, strong beef broth will help build his blood back to strength. If none is avail—"

"Ha!"

Viola laughed at the satisfied grin on Hattie's face. "Hattie has already prepared a beef broth, Doctor. She was quite certain it was what you would request for him. Is there anything else?"

"No. Just keep him warm and quiet, and continue the pain medicine. Give him the broth as often as he will take it. And water. He lost a lot of blood, he needs to replace the fluids he's lost." Jacob Calloway reached for the door latch. "I will return to check on him this afternoon. Meanwhile, if he develops a fever or other problems, please come for me. And if he moves and that wound starts to bleed, come *immediately*."

"I shall, doctor. Please give Teena my regards." Viola closed the door, made the smirking Hattie a little bow, then took Goldie into her arms.

"Would you please bring Mr. Stone some broth, Hattie? I'm sure he must be hungry." She turned and walked into the bedroom. Thomas Stone's eyes were squeezed closed, his mouth was pressed into a tight line and his face looked more wan than ever in the full light of day. She stared at him, feeling sick to her stomach. If she had stayed with Goldie instead of napping to catch up on her lost sleep, the kidnapping would not have happened. Thomas Stone would not have been shot. He would not be in this pain. If only there was something she could do to make him feel better. Perhaps... She whirled around, to Goldie's gurgling delight, and hurried to the kitchen.

"Hattie, keep the soup on the warming shelf. And please watch Goldie for me. I think, perhaps Mr. Stone might feel a little better if I wash his face and comb his hair." She handed the baby into Hattie's arms, then hurried to the tiny bathing room off the kitchen, draped a washcloth and towel over her shoulder, threw a comb and a bar of her soap into a washbowl and went back to the stove to ladle hot water out of the reservoir on the side.

The hot water felt wonderful on his face. The hint of roses hovered, even after she rinsed the soap away. Thomas thought again of his mother, focused on the past to keep from thinking of how soft Viola Goddard's hands were. Or about the ache their gentle touch brought to his gut. He hadn't known, until now, how much he missed the touch of his wife's hands.

The softness of a towel absorbed the moisture from his skin, dragged across his whisker stubble. He had a flash of vanity, wished he was clean-shaven and looking his best.

"I'm going to wash your hands now, Mr. Stone." Her voice sounded different, sort of tight and small. Her fingers brushed against his neck, slid beneath the edge of the covers.

"Wait!" He forgot, tried to grab the covers. White heat streaked through his shoulder and chest. He broke out in a cold sweat. "Shirt…cut…off me." He closed his eyes, silently cursed the weakness, the bullet that had put him in this bed.

"You mustn't move, Mr. Stone. I will do it."

The blankets lifted, cool air washed over his right shoulder and arm. He opened his eyes, looked up at her. Her face was taut. She turned to the washbowl, wrung out the rag and soaped it. He held his breath, fought the sickening throbbing in his shoulder.

"You are quite covered in bandages, Mr. Stone. I'm so sorry for your pain." She lifted his hand. The warm, soapy rag slid over his skin. Her hands were trembling. He saw her catch her lower lip with her upper teeth, turn to the washbowl and rinse out the rag, and swallowed hard against the churning in his stomach.

"I haven't had the opportunity to properly thank you for saving Goldie." She wiped the soap from his hand, took a little shuddering breath, put down the cloth and dried his hand with the towel. "I'm so very grateful." She smiled, but there was something in her eyes…. He tried to block out the pain and nausea and concentrate.

"Your left arm is bound to your chest. To keep it still, I suppose. I shall not wash that hand." There was relief in her voice. She pulled the covers back over him and picked up the washbowl. "You rest now, Mr. Stone. I shall take care of these things and be back in a moment with some broth for you."

Thomas closed his eyes, yielded to the weakness. She had tried to cover it, but Viola Goddard had been upset by his bandages. There had been a fear, a vulnerability deep in the depths of her beautiful eyes that belied her cool demeanor as she washed him. A vulnerability that made him want to take care of her. He clenched his hands into fists, caught his breath at the pain that knifed through his chest and prayed for a quick recovery before falling asleep.

Chapter Four

Viola stared down at Thomas Stone's pale, sleeping face, placed the spoon in the bowl, lifted the napkin off the quilt and carried them to the kitchen.

Hattie glanced at the bowl and frowned. "He didn't eat but half. How's he doin'?"

She shrugged and placed the bowl of broth on the warming shelf. "All right, I suppose. At least that's what Doctor Calloway said. But he looks frightful to me." She stepped to the end of the stove, out of Hattie's way, and stood absorbing the warmth. Her growing weariness was causing an inward chill. "If only he had some color in his face. And that horrible weakness. Oh, Hattie, he hasn't strength enough to even *talk* without stopping and gasping for air. And it's my fault."

Hattie stopped stirring and looked at her. "*Your* fault? How'd you figure that?"

"I should not have napped. If I hadn't—"

"I told you to get some sleep whilst I watched over Goldie." Hattie spooned soup from the pot into a bowl. "Guess the way you figure it, I'm the one to blame. I'm the one shouldn't have gone to sleep."

"Oh, Hattie, no! That's not true." Viola hurried to the elderly woman and put her arm around her shoulders. "I don't blame you, Hattie. Please don't think that. Goldie's father left her on *my* doorstep. His note asked *me* to care for her until he returned. She is *my* responsibility, not yours. I meant only that. Do not blame yourself."

"I don't." Hattie scooted out from under her arm and plunked the bowl onto the table. "Sit down and eat whilst Goldie and Mr. Stone are sleepin'. You're lookin' a mite peaked your own self."

Viola shook her head, brushed back a curl that fell onto her forehead. "You go ahead and eat, Hattie. I'm not hungry. My guilt over Mr. Stone, and Goldie, and, well, this whole situation, has stolen my appetite."

"Fiddlesticks! You ain't to blame for what happened any more than I am. That kidnapper is. And I don't need two sick grownups and a baby to look after. Sit down and eat."

She sat. "All the same, I should have been with Goldie instead of napping."

"Why? So you could have been hurt or worse when that man snuck in here to take the baby, so's he could get his hands on them gold nuggets the father left for you to use to pay for Goldie's care?" Hattie turned and walked back to the stove. "It's likely there was two of them, you know. 'Cause that man wasn't expectin' to find us sleepin' that time of day. I figure God worked things out for the good."

Two of them. Viola stared at Hattie's back, her nerves tingling. With all that had happened, she had forgotten about that stone thrown from the woods. It had been a warning. The kidnapper had a partner. What if he decided to sneak into the cabin and… She shivered, gripped her hands and waited for the nervous chill to pass, took a breath to remove any tremor from her voice. "I don't see how you can say that, Hattie. Mr. Stone is lying in that bedroom too weak to even lift his head off the pillow. How is that God working things out for good?"

"He could be dead."

"Oh. Yes. He could…" Viola placed her hand on her roiling stomach and drew another deep breath. She couldn't understand faith like Hattie's. She had experienced too much of evil. Bitterness rose like bile, formed a metallic taste on her tongue. "If God was involved, why would He have let all of this happen?"

"I don't figure He did." Hattie carried her bowl of soup to the table and bowed her head. "Bless this food, Almighty God. Use it to keep us healthy and strong and to help heal Thomas Stone. Amen." She lifted her head, scooped up a piece of beef with her spoon. "The Good Book says there's good and evil in this world, and because of that, bad things are gonna happen. But it also says God'll take the bad and turn it to good for His children."

By allowing a helpless young girl to be forced into choosing to make her living by prostitution? And then, after she escaped that life, by forcing her to bring a man into her home? By placing Thomas Stone here, in his helpless condition, where he could be killed if someone broke in again? Viola laid down her spoon, swallowed to hold back the bite of onion and peas that did not want to stay down. "Forgive me for disagreeing, Hattie. But I do not see the good in this situation."

Hattie scooped up a piece of potato and broth, looked up and smiled. "It ain't over yet."

That is what I'm afraid of.

* * *

Viola looked up from her sewing as Hattie carried Goldie into the bedroom and sat her down on the rag rug. "This one's all fed and dry and ready to play." She straightened, glanced at Thomas Stone, then looked her way. "I'm gonna take me a walk down to Tanner's store. I'm all out of licorice drops. You need anything?"

"Yes." Viola handed Goldie the wooden spool she'd just emptied. "I need another spool of blue thread, and another packet of horn buttons." She smiled at the baby and looked up. "And ask them to please order me another five yards of tent canvas. I've used the last of mine. Oh! And shaving supplies for Mr. Stone. He will probably want them when he is sufficiently healed to move his arms."

Hattie nodded and started out the door.

"Hattie…"

The elderly woman turned.

Now what was she smiling about? Viola stared at her friend, then gave a mental shrug, kept a casual tone in her voice. "Please leave word that I would like Frankie Tucker to come see me."

"What do you want with Frankie?"

"I have some work for her to do."

Viola watched Hattie amble away, then turned and glanced at Thomas Stone to see if they had disturbed him. He was sound asleep. The pain medicine she had given him after the broth was working. She stared at his face, watching his eyes to make certain. The loose-fitting shirt she was making him out of soft cotton needed no measurements, but for the sleeves. But she did not want to ask him, for she was certain he would refuse the shirt.

She looked at the covers over his chest, watched the even rise and fall of his breathing and set aside her sewing, picked up her tape measure and hurried to the bed. As stealthily as she could manage, she lifted the edge of the covers until she could see his free arm. She measured the length from shoulder to wrist, then inched the tape around his wrist for the cuff measurement, trying her best not to see his hand. She knew well the punishment a man's hands could inflict, and she knew the strength in his from his firm grip on her arm.

She shuddered and backed away, but could not leave his shoulder and arm uncovered. His breathing remained steady and even. She glanced at his face, stepped close and drew the covers back in place, then hurried back to her chair. He looked younger in repose. And handsome. But she had seen handsome turn to ugly very quickly.

She dropped her tape on the table and went to her knees beside Goldie, to wash away the dark memories with the sight of the baby's sweet face. Goldie dropped the spool and grabbed for her feet, tugging at her moccasin booties, letting out a howl of frustration when they did not yield. "Shhh, little one, you'll wake Mr. Stone."

Viola gave her back the spool, lifted her into her arms and carried her to the chair. The rockers whispered against the floor as she cuddled the baby close and exorcized the remembered cruelty of hard, rough hands with the silky touch of the baby's cheek against hers.

Thomas opened his eyes, drawn out of the darkness by the warm, musical laugh of the woman who gave him such cool, remote smiles. He slewed his gaze toward the rocker, saw Viola playing pat-a-cake with the baby and shut his eyes against the ache that filled his chest—an ache that had nothing to do with the bullet wound in his shoulder.

Louise, I am so sorry. So very sorry.

He opened his eyes and stared up at the rough wood ceiling to block out the image of his infant daughter in his wife's arms when he had buried them. An image seared into his mind. He had buried them together so they would never be apart. He clenched his jaw against the memory he couldn't stop from invading his thoughts. He was over the ravaging grief, but the guilt remained. He never should have given in to Louise's pleas that they marry before he answered his call to minister to the Alaskan natives. And he should have stayed strong and refused when she begged to come along. He hadn't known it then, of course, but living conditions in the Indian villages had proven too primitive and harsh for his city-bred wife. And then he had gotten her with child. All selfish acts that had cost Louise and tiny little Susan their lives. If he had known...

A soft gasp broke into his thoughts. Instinct drew his gaze toward Viola Goddard. She was peering closely at the baby who was standing on her lap, supported by her hands around her small chest. "Goldie! Oh, baby, you have two *teeth!*" The hushed words floated toward him on a ripple of quiet laughter that spoke of surprise and delight. The baby waved pudgy little arms, babbled sounds that made sense only to her infant ears, then gurgled out laughter.

The ache in his chest sharpened. His baby girl would never— Thomas yanked his gaze back to the ceiling, clenched his hands and set himself to battle the guilt in his heart. *Forgive me, Louise, for my weakness and selfishness.*

How many times had he thought those words over the past three years? How many more times would he utter or think them before the guilt went away? *Would* it go away? Or would he live with the shadow of his selfish acts clouding his life forever?

This time he didn't fight the darkness that rose to claim him, but yielded to the weakness and the medicine, and welcomed the oblivion that blotted out all thought.

Viola leaned down, picked up the rattle Goldie had dropped, then straightened. "I want strong locks put on my doors, Frankie. I thought perhaps you could do that for me?"

"Sure I can, Viola." Frankie Tucker's blue eyes gleamed with excitement. "You figure someone else will try to break in here and kidnap the baby, now that the idea's been planted in people's heads? I told Sheriff Parker I thought that might happen, and asked him if I could help him watch your place. I mean, I know he shot the kidnapper dead, but what if he had a partner or something?" Frankie sighed and tucked a lock of her short, curly, dark hair behind her ear. "He refused. Like always. I don't know why he doesn't think I'd make a good deputy. I'm smart as any man. Smarter than Henry Duke for sure! And he uses him sometimes."

The hurt in Frankie's voice tugged at her heart. Viola set aside the fear that had surged at Frankie's mention of the kidnapper's partner, and searched for some sort of balm she could offer—remembered that awful moment when she saw the blood spreading across

Thomas Stone's shirt. "Being a deputy can be dangerous, Frankie. Look at what happened to Mr. Stone. Perhaps the sheriff is afraid you will be harmed in a gun battle, or—"

"Ha! I can outshoot any *man*." Frankie's blue eyes flashed. "Our pa took us girls hunting as soon as we were strong enough to heft a rifle. And he taught us to use pistols, too. Lucy and Margie are good shots, but I'm the best. I don't miss. And the sheriff knows it. I challenged him to a shooting contest tomorrow, just to show him. Figure that ought to make him look favorable on me as a deputy."

That would be amusing, if she weren't envious. Viola caught Goldie's baby hand before she could grab her hair, kissed its pudgy palm. "I wish I knew how to use a gun. Things would have been much different." She bit off the bitter words, afraid she had revealed more than she intended.

Frankie grinned. "That would have surprised the kidnapper for sure." Her face lit up. "I could teach you if you want. I got time. No reason for me to be home, with Lucy and Margie gone."

Viola stared, shocked by the offer, then intrigued. She would never have to be afraid again. Not of Dengler and his thugs, the kidnapper's partner, any of her male customers or any other man. She would be able to protect herself. She curved her lips in what she was afraid was a rather grim smile. "I would like that, Frankie. When Mr. Stone is recovered, I shall buy a pistol and you can teach me how to use it."

"Good. You let me know when. Now I'll go down to the smithy and check with Duncan. If he's got a couple good, sturdy locks in stock, I'll come back and put them on your doors tonight." Frankie opened the door, paused. "If not, I'll have him make you some. It won't take him long, if he's not busy. And if he is, I'll see to it he gets to them fast as possible."

Viola nodded. "Thank you, Frankie. You have relieved my mind a good deal." *More than you can possibly know.* "Tell Mr. MacDougal to put the locks on account. I will stop by and pay him as soon as Mr. Stone is well enough for me to leave him." She closed the door, lifted Goldie into the air and smiled up at her. "There, sweetie. Now you will be safe…and so will I." She lowered the laughing baby to her chest, held her close and hurried to the bedroom to check on Thomas Stone.

"How are you feeling, Thomas?" Jacob Calloway set his black bag down, then pulled back the covers. "That light-headedness and nausea any better?"

"Somewhat. It's not a problem so long as I don't try to…lift my head." Warm fingers circled his wrist. Thomas slid his gaze to the watch in the doctor's other hand, waited. The watch was tucked back in a vest pocket with no information offered. "Well?"

"Steadier and stronger. It should be back to normal soon, as long as you follow my instructions and drink plenty of water and take broth often."

"And I'll be able to get out of this bed then?"

"It's going to be a few days, Thomas. Aside from the weakness due to your loss of blood, you need to limit movement and give this wound time to begin to heal. I put in some deep sutures to stop the bleeding, but only a few loose ones at the surface. You'll have quite a scar, but any infection will be able to ooze out." Jacob leaned down, peered closely at the bandage on his shoulder.

"Hmm, we've got some seepage here. I'll cleanse this and apply a new bandage." He turned his attention to removing the bandage.

Thomas sucked in a slow breath, gathered his strength to talk against the pain. "Look, Jacob, I respect your skill, but—"

"No buts, Thomas." Jacob delved into his bag, splashed liquid from a bottle onto a clean white cloth. "Hold still now."

The cloth touched his shoulder, cool and moist. And then the burning started. He gritted his teeth, willed himself not to flinch away.

"There, that's got it. Now for the bandage…" Soft cloth covered his wound. Jacob's fingers brushed against his sore flesh, secured the bandage in place. "You will stay flat on your back in that bed until I say you can move, Thomas. Unless you want to rip that wound open and make everything worse. Now, let's take care of your personal needs, then I will go back to the clinic. I'll come check on you again tonight."

A few more days until he could get out of this bed. And then, how long before he could go home to the solitude of his hut? How long must he be here with the baby? And with Viola? The woman pulled at his emotions in a way he had never experienced before, not even with Louise. She was eye-catchingly beautiful it was true. But it was something else. Something he couldn't put a name to. But it was there all the same. When he'd first looked into her eyes he'd felt that sudden, sure connection. And it hadn't gone away. It had gotten stronger.

Thomas pulled in more air, set his jaw and stared at the chimney stones against the opposite wall. It didn't matter how long he stayed, or how strong the draw he felt toward Viola Goddard. He had made a vow to never again subject a wife to the primitive living conditions necessary to his missionary work with the Tlingits and the men swarming up the Chilkoot Trail to the gold fields. He intended to keep that vow. Being the cause of Louise's and Susie's deaths was enough guilt and regret to carry.

Chapter Five

"Sorry. So sorry…"

Viola started, opened her eyes, blinked and stared into the darkened room. Who was Thomas speaking to?

"I'll carry them— Auugh!"

"Mr. Stone, no! Don't move!" She threw off her blanket and rushed to the bed, placed her hand on his good shoulder to stop him from trying to rise. "Lie still. You will injure yourself!" His eyes opened, his good hand lifted, clamped around her wrist. She jerked, grabbed for his fingers. "Let go of—"

"Don't try to stop me, Seth. That's my wife and child. I'll bury them myself."

He was dreaming. Viola's panic died. She stopped pulling at his fingers, stared into his unseeing eyes. The reflected, low flame of the oil lamp gleamed in their green depths, revealed shadows of pain.

"Do you want me, Viola? I thought I heard you call."

She jumped, glanced over her shoulder at Hattie standing in the doorway in her rumpled nightgown, her gray hair hanging down around her plump shoulders, and shook her head. "Thank you, Hattie, but no. Everything is fine. Mr. Stone was dreaming."

"Night, then." Hattie yawned and padded off into the other room.

Viola took a calming breath and turned back. Thomas Stone's eyes were closed, his mouth parted slightly in slumber. She tugged gently at his fingers. His grip tightened. She fought back resuming panic, the queasiness rising in her stomach. The man was sleeping. He didn't know what he was doing. No matter, he was injured and Hattie was near. She was safe. She took another breath, tapped his check. "Wake up, Mr. Stone." He blinked, stared up at her. She held her voice steady, tapped his hand. "Please let go of my wrist."

His gaze dropped. He stared, frowned. "What…" He sucked in a breath, pressed his lips into a tight line.

"You were dreaming. And thrashing about a bit, which has probably increased your pain. I'll get the medicine." She pulled at his fingers, slipped her wrist from his grasp while he was still confused. His hand dropped to the bed.

Viola stepped back, moved to the window and pulled the bottom of one curtain back a slit. A narrow streak of midnight sun spilled down the wall and washed over the commode stand. *Please, Almighty God, don't let him have hurt his shoulder. Please don't let it bleed.* She opened the bottle, filled the spoon and turned back to the bed, on his wounded side. She would not make the mistake of standing by his good arm again. "Here is your medicine, Mr. Stone."

He opened his eyes, fastened his gaze on hers. "I'm sorry for…whatever happened, Miss Goddard. I hope I didn't hurt you."

His voice was tight with pain. She shook her head. "You were dreaming, Mr. Stone. And I am fine."

His eyes darkened. "No, you're not. You're trembling."

The words came out from between his gritted teeth. She looked down at the quivering medicine in the bowl of the spoon. *Never admit fear.* "I guess I am more fatigued than I realized. You had better take this before I spill it." She held the spoon to his mouth. He swallowed. "I will get you some water in a moment. But first I must look at your bandage."

"No. That upsets you."

How did he— Oh, when she had washed his hand. Viola stared down at him, uncertain of how to respond to his concern—if that's what it was—then turned and laid the spoon on the medicine tray. "I cannot deny that is true, Mr. Stone. But this is no time for such foolish weakness." She turned back, reached for the covers.

"Please, don't." He slid his good hand toward her.

She jerked back, caught herself and leaned forward. He could not reach her unless he turned onto his wounded shoulder. "I'm afraid I must. The doctor warned me that if you moved you could cause your wound to begin bleeding again. If that happens, I am to go for him immediately." She braced herself and lifted the covers, let out a relieved sigh. "There is no sign of bleeding."

"You're brave…"

His words were halting, slurring. "Don't go to sleep, Mr. Stone. You must have some water. Doctor's orders." She replaced the covers, poured water into a glass and picked up the spoon. She managed to coax half of the water into him before sleep overcame his will. She gazed down at his face, taut with pain even in slumber, then slid her gaze to where his hand rested on top of the covers. Had he really tried to stop her from looking at his bandage because he had noticed it bothered her? She could not remember a man ever showing concern for her feelings. Not even her father. He had been only a distant figure of authority.

She put down the glass, stared at Thomas Stone's bared arm. She had to cover it. From the other side of the bed. His good side. The queasiness returned to her stomach. She rubbed her wrist, erasing the feel of his grip, strong even in his weakened state, and studied his face. It would be all right. He had slipped into a deep sleep. She tiptoed to the other side, lifted his hand enough to free the covers beneath it, pulled them over his arm and shoulder and hurried back to her chair. He hadn't even blinked. He would sleep quietly until the medicine wore off.

She picked up the blanket off the floor, shook it out and covered herself, leaned back and closed her eyes. So Thomas had a wife and child who died. What had happened to them? Odd that he had never spoken of them. Of course, they were only acquaintances because of the circumstances, and they weren't exactly having conversations. He was sleeping most of the time.

She turned her head and studied his face, shadowed by the low light of the lamp. Is that why he had helped her when Goldie was kidnapped, because he had once had a child? And had he refused her offer to come to her home and let her care for him because he felt it was a betrayal of his dead wife?

She huffed out a breath, closed her eyes again. She, of all people, should know better than that. Many of her repeat customers at Dengler's "house" had been married men. And marriage vows had not kept them from their pleasure—not even in the beginning, when she had begged and cried.

The familiar tightness clamped around her chest, inched up her neck into her face. She forced herself to relax, to slowly pull in air. Simply because Thomas had been considerate of her feelings over the bandages was no reason to ascribe him high motives for everything. No. He may have shown consideration for her feelings now, when he was weak and needed her to care for him. But she must stay wary and watchful, and be very careful. His strength was beginning to return.

Viola bent, picked up a bright red leaf and twirled it between her finger and thumb. "I'm sorry Mr. Stone was sleeping when you stopped on your way to the clinic to check on him, Teena. But I'm glad you suggested a walk. The fresh morning air feels wonderful." A worm of guilt squiggled though her. And that fear that never quite left her made her glance back at her cabin. "But I shouldn't go too far. I want to be back before Goldie or Mr. Stone wakes." *Or someone comes.*

"We will go only to the woods that hide my village from the town, and then return."

Viola nodded. She would be able to keep her cabin in sight the whole way. She took a deep breath and glanced over at her friend. Teena looked as calm and serene as ever, but there was a new, happy glow in her dark eyes.

She sniffed at the air, enjoying the blended scents of the towering firs, the moist, grassy undergrowth and the dirt path they trod. "The air here is so fresh and untainted by the smells of the campfires and trash of the swarms of stampeders." She frowned, twirled the leaf faster. "Everywhere you go in the area around town, from the harbor to the mountains, the land is covered with the garbage and discards and the broken equipment of the miners. Why is it clear here?"

"Most of the whites do not travel the path to the Tlingit village. They stay far from my people." Teena glanced over at her. "There are only a few who come. And they are respectful of our ways and our lands."

The happiness was in the soft lilt of her voice, the gentle tilt of her lips. The picture of Teena looking up at Dr. Calloway the night of Goldie's kidnapping flashed into her head, and she knew. Her stomach knotted. She tossed down the leaf and looked back toward the cabin, searching for a way to put off her friend's confidence. "Like Thomas Stone?"

Teena Crow's long black braids glistened in the sunlight as she nodded. "Yes. Like Thomas Stone. He is good to my people. And he is good *for* my people. He leads them to God, so their hearts may be healed." Teena paused at the edge of the woods and turned toward her, her face aglow. "And like Jacob." The name was a soft whisper of love and hope and trust. "Jacob helps heal my people when they are sick, as I help him heal his people when they are sick." She smiled, held up her hands and clasped them. "Our two hearts have become one. We are to go to Skaguay and marry. I wanted you, my friend, to know."

Viola sucked in air, dared not speak. Teena was so quiet, so serene standing there, bathed in her happiness, she refused to destroy it with the truth of what men really were. *Please don't let him hurt her.* She dredged up a smile, hugged her friend and forced joy into her voice. "I'm so happy for you, Teena. I pray you will find every happiness your heart seeks."

"It will be so." Teena gave a soft laugh, stepped back and placed her hand on her chest. "My heart knows this."

She nodded, turned and started down the track toward town, searching her tumbling thoughts for an appropriate change of subject. She did not want to talk about the false hope of love. "Will you live at the clinic, or in the house with your people?"

"My father is with his ancestors. My brother will bring his bride to the house to live with our people one day. It is right that he does." Teena smiled. "I will go where Jacob wishes to be. For that is right, also." She gave another soft laugh. "You see, already I find that the hearts of our peoples are not far apart."

What had Hattie said? There is good and evil in the world, and bad things happen because of it. It was no doubt the same with the Tlingit people. Hearts are the same in all people. Was there no place to hide? To be safe? She smiled as they reached the point where the road divided and Teena would continue on toward town. "Thank you again for stopping to share your news, Teena. I will tell Hattie as soon as I get home. I know she'll be delighted for you." She turned toward the faint path that led to her cabin, looked over her shoulder and smiled. "Come again soon. I enjoyed our walk."

"Much better, Thomas."

"I feel better." Thomas watched the doctor put his stethoscope back in his bag and pull his watch from his vest pocket. "I can draw breath easily. And I can speak an entire sentence without gasping. So when can I get out of this bed?"

"Ah, it's always a good sign when the patient becomes impatient and starts complaining. Of course, in your case, that does not apply. You have been complaining since you awoke after surgery."

"Very funny." Thomas looked from Jacob Calloway's grinning face to the fingers circling his wrist. "Well?"

"Back to normal."

He waited, frowned. "And?"

"And now I check the bandage." Jacob lowered the covers to his waist. "More good news. There is no seepage."

He fought the urge to grab the doctor's shirtfront and shake an answer from him. As if he could. "Which means?"

"Which means I must speak to Viola and see if she has more pillows I can use to prop you up a bit. *If* you give me your word you will not try to lift yourself higher, sit up or move about."

"Fine."

The doctor's left brow lifted toward his dark hair. "That sounded a little sour, and came a bit too quickly, Thomas. I will have your word as a man of God."

Perhaps twisting Jacob's shirtfront and choking him would be more satisfactory than merely shaking him. Thomas took a breath, nodded. "All right. I give you my word."

"Excellent. Now let me go and find Viola and see about those pillows."

Thomas watched Jacob go out the door, tried not to envy him the freedom of movement. There was finally some progress. Not as much as he would like. But it would be good not to have to lie flat on his back and… *In everything give thanks: for this is the will of God in Christ Jesus concerning you.* The scripture flowed into his thoughts, brought him up short. He closed his eyes and opened his heart. "Forgive me, Lord, for murmuring and complaining. I thank You for Your care. Please heal me quickly, so I am not a burden to Miss—"

"These pillows will work perfectly, Viola."

Thomas opened his eyes, slid his gaze toward the door, listened to the footsteps approaching. Surely Jacob was not bringing Viola Goddard in here. His bandages! He braced himself for the pain he knew would follow and groped for the covers, froze when Viola, carrying a pillow, entered the room followed by Jacob Calloway, his arms wrapped around more pillows.

Viola looked his way, her steps faltered, he looked at her eyes, followed her gaze to his uncovered chest, and clenched his hand on the edge of the blanket. Choking was not fit punishment for Dr. Calloway. He would have to think of something more dire.

"You stand there, Viola—" the doctor dropped the pillows on the bed and indicated the spot next to his wounded shoulder "—and I will go around to Thomas's good side and lift him. When I have his head and shoulders high enough off the bed, I want you to place the pillows—two beneath his head and one beneath his shoulders. Thomas—" Jacob looked down at him, no longer friend, but all doctor "—do not tense your body, and do not try to help. All right, everyone ready? I shall lift on three. One…two…three."

Pain sliced across his chest, drove the air from his lungs. Thomas gritted his teeth and set his jaw, fought down a swirl of nausea. His vision blurred, then cleared to reveal Viola leaning over him, her teeth clamped down on her full lower lip, her violet-blue eyes gentle with sympathy. The soft warmth of her hands touched his back as she placed the pillows beneath him. "All right, Doctor."

He stopped himself from tensing as Jacob lowered him and withdrew his arm. The softness of feather pillows in rose-scented cases embraced him. Cold sweat chilled him. He shivered, closed his eyes, drew a breath. The nausea ebbed.

"He can have solid food now, Viola. But I want him to continue to drink a lot of water. And he may begin moving his good arm a bit now. But only up and down slowly."

"All right, Doctor."

The covers were pulled up over his chest and shoulders. Soft hands tucked them under his chin—*her* hands, with that same faint hint of roses clinging to them.

"Give him the pain medicine with his meals, even if he says he doesn't want it. He's a stubborn cuss. But if you appeal to his godly side, he will come around."

"I shall remember that, Doctor. Now, if there is nothing further, I will go and tell Hattie she does not need to fix any broth for Mr. Stone, that he will share our dinner."

Thomas opened his eyes, watched Viola walk from the room, then fastened his gaze on Jacob Calloway. "You have a lot to answer for when I get out of this bed, Doctor. I do not want Viola subjected to such tasks again."

"Threats? Tsk, tsk." Jacob smiled and picked up his bag. "Remember your profession, Pastor Stone. Brotherly love and all of that."

"No need to concern yourself, Jacob. If you do not ask Viola to do any more nursing tasks all will be well. And if you do, I will love you the whole time I am pummeling you."

"You're not smiling, Thomas."

"No. I'm serious, Jacob. The sight of my bandages upsets Viola. I do not want her subjected to that again."

"I see." Jacob narrowed his eyes and studied him. "Methinks thou doth protest too much. The question is…why?" He lifted a hand in farewell and walked out the door.

Why?

The question hung suspended in the empty room, bald and begging to be answered. Thomas closed his mind to its challenge. He looked out the window, lifted his gaze beyond the trees in Viola's backyard, to the mountains that enfolded the town of Treasure Creek, and thought about the prospectors climbing the Chilkoot Trail in search of gold. How foolish those men, thinking happiness rested in possessing the precious metal or the things it could buy.

Viola slipped the bottle from between Goldie's lips, blotted away the sweetened goat's milk pooled at the corners of her tiny mouth and rose from the rocker. She knelt on the floor, kissed the warm, soft cheek and laid Goldie in her cradle. The baby's eyelids fluttered, opened, slid closed again. Viola smiled, drew the blankets up, then sat back on her heels and looked at the handmade cradle. Goldie would soon be outgrowing it. As soon as she could leave Thomas to Hattie's care, she would go to Tanner's and look through the catalogs and order a crib for the baby.

She glanced toward the bed to check on Thomas, found his gaze on her and suppressed a shiver. "I didn't realize you were awake."

"I didn't want to say anything. I thought I might wake the baby."

There was sadness in his quiet words. And in his eyes. Or was she imagining it because she knew about his child? She rose, shook out her long skirt and crossed to the bed. "Goldie sleeps quite soundly for a baby…I think. I've no experience with babies."

"From what I've seen, you're very good with her."

"Thank you." She reached up and tucked a lock of hair Goldie had pulled free back under her snood. "Would you like some water? Or perhaps some bread and butter? It will be a while until supper, and you must be hungry after having only broth since you were… wounded."

"No bread and butter. But I will have some water please. And no spoon. Now that I am permitted to move my arm, I can handle the glass myself." He grinned, chuckled. "Foolish of me to feel that is such an accomplishment. I've been feeding myself for years now."

She stared at him, taken aback by the deep, rumbly sound of his chuckle, the warm, fluttering response in her own chest. Dengler, and the men who visited her in his house, never laughed in a pleasant way. Nor did his thugs. Their laughter was cruel. The urge to smile died. She poured Thomas's water and handed him the glass— hovered nearby while he drank it, lest he start to spill.

"Thank you." He held out the glass.

She stared at it, empty now, with nothing to spill if he grabbed her wrist.

"Is something wrong?"

She glanced at him, met his gaze and shook her head. "No, nothing." She snatched the glass, drew it away from his hand. "Would you like more water?"

"Not now. What I would like is for you to sit down and rest." His gaze swept over her face. "You look tired. I'm afraid you're exhausting yourself caring for me."

"I'm fine." She turned away from him, uncomfortable and tense. Why did he say things like that? She put the glass on the table and reached to close the curtains.

"Would you leave the curtains open please?"

She lowered her hands, looked at him. "You do not want them closed so you can sleep?"

He shook his head. "No, I have slept enough, and I like looking outside. It makes me hopeful. There is nothing like God's sunshine to cheer you up."

His smile was warm, friendly. It increased her discomfort. Thomas did not act like the other men she had known, which made her very uneasy indeed. She didn't know what to expect from him. She went to the rocker and picked up the jacket she was mending for Ezra Paine, freed the threaded needle from the fabric, where she had stuck it for safekeeping and took another neat stitch in the row, repairing the slash in the sleeve. A knife slash. Now she understood that. She glanced at the ridge of scar tissue on the edge of her hand. She was familiar with things like knife cuts and bruised flesh. But not with a man who considered a woman's needs. How was she to respond to such remarks from Thomas Stone? What was she to think…to believe?

"How long have you had Goldie?"

She jerked, pricked her finger—not hard. There was no blood. She resisted the urge to put the stinging fingertip in her mouth and took another stitch. "It will soon be two months."

"I'd heard she was left on your doorstep, but figured it was just a rumor."

"No. It's quite true." She stilled her hands, looked down at Goldie. "There was a knock on my door one night, but when I opened it no one was there. Only the cradle on my stoop, with Goldie wrapped in her blanket fast asleep, a bottle, a few items of clothing, the small poke with two gold nuggets and a note from her father asking me to care for her until he returned."

"So her father is a friend."

She glanced at him, then looked down and resumed sewing. "No. I was only newly arrived in Treasure Creek at the time. I had no friends."

"You had one."

Did he doubt her word? She frowned, looked up.

He smiled. "God chose you to watch over the baby."

You wouldn't say that if you knew my past. She shook her head, as much to rid herself of the thought as to deny his statement. "I hardly think it was God."

"I'm certain it was." His gaze held hers. "The Bible says, 'When my father and my mother forsake me, then the Lord will take me up.'" He smiled. "God is simply using your heart to love Goldie, and your hands to care for her."

It was a lovely thought. One she might even believe, if she hadn't been forsaken. Of course, God's word might not apply to a fifteen-year-old girl cast penniless and helpless onto the streets of Seattle when her parents died. Bitterness rose, soured her stomach. "Perhaps you are right, Mr. Stone. But if that is true, the Lord will have to help my unbelief. Now, I must go see how Hattie is coming along with supper." She set her sewing aside, checked to be sure Goldie was sleeping and hurried from the room before he could ask another question about her past.

Chapter Six

"Here's dinner."

"Hattie, I told you to call and I would come get his food." Viola put down her sewing, rose and reached for the plate. "You didn't have to carry this in."

"I wanted to see how your patient is doin'." Hattie ignored her outstretched hands and walked to the bed.

Viola flexed her empty hands, frowned and hurried after her. Hattie was so outspoken and unconventional, there was no knowing what she might say or do. And the way she had been smiling...

"You're lookin' some better, Thomas." Hattie tipped her head, studied him. "Seems like you might even live."

Thomas grinned, gave an audible sniff. "I think I might—once I get whatever you're holding that smells so good in me."

Hattie gave her pleased chuckle. "It's beef stew. Beef'll help you get your strength back fast."

His stomach rumbled.

Hattie laughed, looked up at Viola. "Better feed this poor man afore he perishes."

A frown wiped the smile from Thomas's face. "I'm sorry I can't feed myself, Miss Goddard."

"I'm certain you will soon be sitting up and doing so, Mr. Stone." She reached for the plate. It was pulled back. She jerked her gaze up to Hattie's face.

"Well ain't you two all niminy-piminy!" Hattie snorted, looked back to Thomas Stone. "What's wrong with you two calling each other Thomas and Viola is what I'd like to know?"

Viola stiffened, stared at Hattie's artless expression. So that was what she—

"Nothing at all, Hattie. If Miss Goddard agrees."

A smug expression, quickly erased, swept over Hattie's aged face.

Viola masked her displeasure, met Thomas's gaze and gave him a polite nod. "That will be fine." She reached out and took a firm hold on the plate. Hattie relinquished it with a sweet smile.

"I'll take Goldie out to the kitchen with me, Viola. So's you won't have to worry about her whilst you're feedin' Thomas." The elderly woman turned to the baby, scooped her up and marched out the door.

Viola watched her leave, wishing she had never come and that the past few minutes had not happened. Thomas and Viola. So cozy and friendly. Well, she had no intention of befriending Thomas Stone. And now, thanks to Hattie, it would be difficult to resume that polite distance she had so carefully maintained. She put down the plate and spread the towel over the quilt, careful not to meet Thomas's gaze, then lifted the plate.

"I think I can manage the bread."

She nodded, handed him the piece of bread and butter

resting on the rim of the plate. "I apologize for Hattie's comment, Mr. Stone. We—"

"Thomas." He took a bite of bread.

She took a breath. "As I was saying, we do not have to use our given names."

"Mmm, real food. Tastes good!" He looked up, met her gaze, held it. "No we don't. But continuing to use formal address seems rather foolish in these circumstances."

"Yes, but—"

He shook his head. "No 'buts,' Viola. You agreed."

A tingle skittered through her at the soft way he spoke her name. It intensified when he smiled. She looked down at the plate, confused by the reaction.

"You don't want to get us in trouble with Hattie, do you? She strikes me as a lady to be reckoned with."

"So I am learning."

He chuckled, and that odd, warm little flutter happened again in her chest. She pushed at a piece of meat, held her face expressionless. She was a master at that.

"How long has she lived with you?" He took another bite of bread, then lowered his hand to rest it on the bed.

More questions about her past. She held back a frown. "Since her husband died." She stabbed the bite of beef and held it to his mouth. "It's a little over a month now." She chose carrot and potato for his next bite. Swiped it through the rich gravy. When she looked up from the plate, she found him studying her, his face sober.

"Did you know Hattie before you came to Treasure Creek?"

"No. I met her at church." Her words were curt, her

tone cool. She offered him the bite of vegetables to stop him from talking.

"So you had only just met when she was widowed?" He accepted the bite, chewed slowly.

"Yes." She stabbed another piece of beef, uncomfortable with his steady perusal.

"Yet you took her in."

There was something warm in his voice…approval? Whatever it was, she didn't want it there. She nodded, gave him a cool look. "I only did what anyone would do." She added onion and held out the piece of meat, wishing she could leave the room.

He nodded, fastened his gaze full on hers. "That's good to know. Who else offered?" He took the beef.

She stared at him, feeling as if she had somehow walked into a trap. "Well—"

"I can answer that…no one else offered to take me in."

Viola stiffened. Had Hattie been eavesdropping? She turned, shamed by her thought, as Hattie stepped through the doorway with Goldie parked on one well padded hip and a plate in her other hand.

The elderly woman glanced up at her. "I know you don't like me talkin' about your kindness, Viola. But it's true just the same." She came and stood by the bed, looked at Thomas. "The others in the church were talkin' about what to do…about takin' up a collection so they could help me pay my week's rent at the boardinghouse. Then Viola just up and offered me a home with her. It was a real blessin' when she took me in. Me bein' penniless and all, I'd soon have been on the street."

"Hattie—"

Scraggly, gray locks of hair dangling from her disheveled bun swayed as Hattie shook her head, jutted her chin out. "I ain't gonna hush, Viola, 'cause it's true and you know it. I ain't sayin' the others don't have kind hearts, 'cause they do. But you…well…you showed me real Christian love, and I ain't forgettin' it. And I ain't gonna keep hushed about it neither!"

Hattie cleared her throat, plunked the plate down on the stand and swiped her freed hand across her eyes. "That there's berry pie for when you're through with the stew, Thomas. Hope you like it." She hitched Goldie higher on her hip and hurried out of the room.

Silence.

Viola stared down at the plate in her hands, the fork with the last bite of potato and carrot impaled on it, uncomfortable, and uncertain. She was accustomed to censure, not praise. She slid the fork through the last of the gravy and held it out to him, careful not to meet his gaze, hoping Hattie's interruption had put an end to his questions.

"You need a bigger cabin, Viola." He took the bite into his mouth.

She drew back the empty fork, relieved that he had broken the awkward quiet. "A larger cabin?" She set the empty plate on the stand, picked up the one that held his pie and turned back to the bed. "I'm afraid I don't understand."

"Goldie…Hattie…and now me." His eyes held hers, something warm and unknown to her in their depths. "You've taken us all in when we needed care and a place to go, Viola. You need a cabin as big as your heart."

Viola stood at the window watching the light fading to purple. It was normally nightmares that kept her from restful sleep, but tonight it was—what? She curved her lips in a wry smile. If she knew the answer to the question she would be able to sleep. She let the curtain fall back into place and looked down at Goldie. The baby was sleeping so soundly it wouldn't be fair to pick her up, but she wanted something familiar, something she understood, to hold on to. She glanced at her sewing basket, but was too restless to sit and sew.

You need a cabin as big as your heart. She frowned, glanced toward the bed. Why did Thomas say such things? Why had he looked at her that way? Warmth stole through her at the memory. She frowned, rubbed her palms against her long skirt. She wanted him to stop. It made her nervous. But she could hardly tell him she didn't want him being nice to her. But was he? Or did he use charm instead of abuse to get what he wanted from a woman?

She shivered, massaged the scar on her hand. He was so different from any man she had ever known. Tears smarted her eyes. If only she could believe him. But she knew better than to do that. Oh, why had she ever offered to take care of him? She wanted him out of her house. And out of her life. He made her afraid in a way she had never been afraid before. In a way she didn't understand.

She wrapped her arms about herself and stepped closer to the bed to study him. There was no danger of his waking. The medicine made him sleep soundly for at least two hours after he took it.

She skimmed his features. He truly was a handsome man, more so when he was clean-shaven. She looked at his mouth, slightly open in slumber. She had never seen it tight and ugly with anger. She stared at the left side, the one that raised more than the other when he smiled, which was often, even through his pain. His crooked smiles made her want to smile back. They reached his eyes. Those expressive green eyes. She looked up at them, closed now in slumber, his short, thick brown lashes resting on the weathered-tan skin stretched across his cheekbones. She had watched carefully, but had never seen cruelty in his eyes. Only pain, and kindness and—and that…warmth.

She spun away from the bed and walked over to settle herself in the rocker. It was time to stop her nonsense and get some work done. With the care of Thomas taking her time, she was falling behind in her sewing and mending for her customers. And since she had spent most of her back wages, that she had taken from Dengler's desk when she left, to buy the cabin and furnishings, she had to earn enough to take care of Goldie and Hattie. But first she must finish the shirt she was making for him. Hopefully, he would need it soon. She pulled the shirt from the basket, then threaded her needle. She had only to make the buttonhole and sew on the button and his shirt would be finished. She slid on her thimble, stared at her wrist. When he had gripped her wrist he had frightened her. But he had not hurt her. Not even when he was dreaming. And he could have. He was strong.

Thomas woke to a dull throbbing in his shoulder and discomfort in his whole body. Every muscle was aching from his lack of activity, screaming at him to get up and move. He would…if it weren't for Viola.

He frowned, stretched the muscles in his legs and drew large circles beneath the covers with his feet. He could cope with the pain in his shoulder. It was his growing admiration for Viola, his increasing attraction to her that held him rooted in bed. That connection he had felt when he first looked into her eyes was getting stronger, and he dare do nothing that might result in a prolonged stay in her company.

His frown deepened to a scowl. It wasn't that he was weak willed. Not at all. He was a man of strong faith and moral integrity. But he was still a man. And Viola…

Thomas sucked in a long breath, gave in to what he'd been wanting to do since he woke, and looked at her. She was asleep in the rocker, her head leaning against the high back of the chair, her face turned toward him. The dim light from the turned-down wick of the oil lamp on the table beside her made dark smudges of the long, thick eyelashes that rested on her alabaster skin; warmed her high, perfectly molded cheekbones with a whisper of gold and created a soft shadow beneath her full lower lip.

His pulse quickened. He'd never seen a woman as beautiful. But it was more than her beauty that drew him. It was the mystery of her. She appeared so confident and controlled, yet there was that shadow of fear, that vulnerability in the depths of her eyes that made him want to take care of her. And there was the warmth and sympathy in her care that put the lie to her cool smiles and demeanor. He was drawn to her by everything he knew, and everything he was learning about her.

He looked at the oil lamp, turned low so it did not bother his rest, pulled close so she could see to work. *Her candle goeth not out by night.* The line of scripture from the Book of Proverbs slipped smoothly into his head. How perfectly it described her considerate and unselfish nature, working at night because caring for him took up her days. He lowered his gaze to her hands, resting on the blue shirt she'd been sewing when she fell asleep. *She seeketh wool, and flax, and worketh willingly with her hands.* How tireless she was in earning a living for herself and for others. *She stretcheth out her hand to the poor: yea, she reacheth forth her hands to the needy.*

Thomas sucked in a long breath, looked at the baby asleep in her cradle close to Viola's chair, glanced at his medicine on the stand beside the bed and listened to Hattie's snoring from the other room. Something akin to fear gripped him. *Who can find a virtuous woman? For her price is far above rubies. The heart of her husband doth safely trust in her, so that he shall have no need of spoil.* What man would ever need the riches of gold, if he had a wife like Viola?

He looked over at her, jerked his gaze to the ceiling and clenched his hands into fists. "Don't let it happen, Lord. You know I answered Your call to minister to the Tlingits and the men on the Chilkoot Trail. And You know that means I cannot marry. I will never again subject a wife to those harsh living conditions. I'll not be the cause of another woman's and child's deaths. Keep me strong, Lord. Keep me strong, I pray. Don't let me fall in love with Viola Goddard."

He prayed the words. He prayed them sincerely. But, even as he whispered them into the night, his heart was telling him it was already too late.

Chapter Seven

"Here is your mending, Mr. Stewart." Viola watched him drop his payment into the bowl on the table, then stepped forward to close the door behind him. "Good luck in your search for gold."

She started to close the door, caught a glimpse of a familiar figure in loose-fitting work pants, leather belt adorned with tools and a billowing red plaid shirt turning onto her path from the road. "Hello, Frankie. Have you come to put in my locks?"

The shake of Frankie's head set her cap of short, black curls flopping. "MacDougal's had some pressing business. Says he'll get at them soon as possible."

"I see." She hid her disappointment, stared down at Frankie, who stopped at the edge of the stoop. "Thank you for coming to tell me. Would you like to come in?"

The black curls flopped again. "I have to get back to the church. Got some work to do so the bell tower will be ready when that bell gets here, if it ever does." Frankie slapped at a spot of dirt on her trousers, brushed her hand against her thigh. "Seems like it's been forever since Mack told us he'd ordered it."

"Yes, it's been a while." She stopped, unsure of what to say in the face of Frankie's odd behavior. The fearless, self-confident woman was acting…nervous. She glanced at Frankie's dry, work-roughened hand, now toying with the hammer handle that protruded from the wide leather belt that slung down onto her hip, heard the huge breath Frankie inhaled and blew out, and raised her gaze.

"You busy caring for the preacher, or you got time to step out here and talk a minute, Viola?"

"Dr. Calloway is with him. But…are you sure you don't want to come in?"

"Nah, this is private like." Frankie lifted the hammer, let it fall back into place. "I don't want anyone overhearing what I got to say. Thought maybe we could step over to them trees."

"Of course." What had Frankie so discombobulated? She held her face impassive, closed the door, lifted the hems of her long skirts and followed Frankie into the shadows beneath the towering firs that grew close to her cabin.

"I got me a problem, Viola. And I don't rightly know what to do about it." Frankie locked a scowling gaze on her. "Remember the other day, I said I was going to challenge the sheriff to a shooting match?"

"Yes."

"I *missed!* And I ain't missed a shot since…well, since I can't even remember, it's been so long."

Viola stared at her. What did Frankie expect her to say? She knew nothing about shooting a—

"I can't figure what happened, less it's because I was

all trembly like, with Ed standing so near and all. I couldn't seem to make my hand stop shaking a mite, and it threw off my aim."

Oh. "I see." *Not Frankie, too.*

Frankie grabbed hold of a dead branch, broke off a small piece and pulverized it between her palms. "I get like that when I'm around him. Get upset some in my stomach, too. I mean, I guess it's because I want to be a deputy so much." The expression in the blue eyes fixed on her changed to one of appeal. "You figure that's what it is, Viola? That I just want so much to be a deputy? I mean, it couldn't be…" the expression turned fierce, challenging "I don't…*like* him or nothing."

Her heart sank. How could *she* help? All she wanted to say was, *"Run, Frankie, run."* But she had to say something. "I'm sorry, Frankie, but I can't help you. I've never…*liked* a man. I don't know how that feels." Memory of the soft, warm, fluttery feeling in her chest whenever Thomas chuckled popped into her head. She shoved the absurd thought away. "Perhaps you should ask Lucy and Margie—"

"Willikers! I can't ask them, Viola!" The words roared out of Frankie's horrified freckled face. "They'd laugh 'til they was sick. They're all the time telling me, 'Just wait until it happens to you. Just wait until you go all weak-kneed and trembly when *you're* around your special man. Just wait until you fall in love!'" The appeal flashed back into Frankie's blue eyes. "It can't be that, Viola, can it? It *can't* be that!"

She had nothing but her bad experiences with men from which to form an answer. But she had to offer Frankie some sort of help. "Well, do you want to be around him often? Do you want him to like you?"

"Well sure. But I thought…" An appalled look swept over the freckled face. "Willikers." It was a soft whisper this time. Frankie sagged back against a tree trunk and looked at her. "What am I gonna do, Viola?"

At least with this she could help her. "Well, to start, you could perhaps change those baggy trousers for a divided skirt like your sisters sometimes wear. And you could get some shirts in different colors, like blue to match your eyes, and in a smaller size that will fit you better. And you could ask Sheriff Parker to help you when you have something too heavy or difficult for you to do alone."

"You mean act like a *girl.*"

She bit her lip to hold back a smile and nodded. "At least a little, in the way you dress and such, Frankie. I think it's the only way you will find out how you really feel about Ed Parker. And how he feels about you."

"Perhaps tomorrow, Thomas." Jacob Calloway put his stethoscope back in his doctor's bag. "I don't want to hurry things. I know you're feeling stronger, now that you are eating and drinking and sitting propped up in bed. But that wound is not even close to being healed. Any false move could tear it open again."

"All the more reason for you to help me, Jacob." Thomas fixed an unwavering gaze on the doctor. "No more waiting. I am getting out of this bed today. If you don't help me, then I will do it myself, after you leave."

Jacob frowned, snapped his black bag closed. "What's gotten into you, Thomas? I've never known you to be foolhardy. Give it another day. Tomorr—"

"Today. One way or the other."

Jacob studied him. "You're serious?"

He dipped his head.

The doctor's brows lowered. "You leave me no choice, Thomas. But you must do exactly as I say."

"Agreed."

"I'll go get a chair. If you get weak or dizzy on me, I can't sit you in that rocker."

"Jacob." The doctor stopped, looked at him. "Help me into my pants before you go. Then bring a towel to cover my chest. I don't want Viola in here while I am sitting in a chair, clad only in my long drawers and bandages."

The doctor grabbed his pants off a hook on the wall, slipped them on him and left the room.

Thomas watched him head for the kitchen and took a deep breath. It was done. All he could do now was hope he was making the right decision. And ask God for strength. He closed his eyes. "Almighty God, You know my frame and You know my heart. I cannot stay here longer, Lord. It is painful seeing the baby every day, knowing I am guilty for my own wife's and child's deaths. And last night laid bare the growing feelings I have for—"

"There is no need for a towel, Doctor. I have made him a shirt of a loose design that will fit overtop of the bandages."

Thomas opened his eyes, looked toward the door. His heart gave a small kick as Viola entered. She was followed by Jacob Calloway, carrying a slat-back chair.

"The shirt is right here by the rocker."

Thomas tensed. It couldn't be.

Viola went to the basket on the floor by the rocker and pulled out a shirt.

It was.

Thomas stared, then looked away from the blue shirt in her hands. The shirt she had been working on when she fell asleep last night. The shirt she had been staying up late to make for him. He clenched his jaw. How could he wear that shirt? Every time he looked at it, every time he felt it against his skin he would remember the way she looked last night. But how could he not wear it? How could he refuse her gesture of consideration and generosity? By telling her he didn't want the shirt because he was falling in love with her?

"All right, Thomas, let's get you out of this bed. I have to get back to the clinic. Watch closely, Viola." Jacob came to the edge of the bed and leaned toward him. "We will do this in stages. First, I am going to help you sit up straighter, then, without twisting your torso, I want you to slide your legs, one at a time, over the side of the bed. After that, I will help you turn. Now put your arm around my shoulder. Ready? Here we go."

Jacob's arm tightened. Thomas braced himself, completed the maneuver and found the pain bearable, but his head was woozy. He sat on the edge of the bed, hung his head and took a deep breath.

"Dizzy?"

"A little. It's getting better."

"Rest a moment, then we'll get you on your feet. Viola, where's that shirt?"

"Here."

"Put it on him."

"No. You do it, Jacob." The bile pushing at the bottom of his throat kept him from protesting further.

"I have to steady you, and it's all part of nursing, Thomas. Come ahead, Viola."

Thomas swallowed, watched Jacob's brown shoes and trouser legs move to the side, and Viola's long, green skirt take their place. There was a rustle, a softness brushing against his ears. Dark blue fabric fell in front of his face, shutting off his view. A soft, warm hand brushed against his bare right shoulder, eased in his arm. The fabric moved, slid down to cover his back and fell away from his face. He caught the faint scent of roses and lifted his head, looked up into Viola's eyes. "Thank you."

She nodded, finished adjusting the fabric across the top of his shoulders and stepped back.

"Ready to try and walk, Thomas?"

There was a small, swift intake of breath. He gave Viola a quick, reassuring smile and shifted his gaze to Jacob. "I'm ready."

"All right. Rest your arm on my shoulder, but do not use it to lift yourself. Use your legs. I will steady you. And don't try to walk. Stand still until you feel steady and strong enough to move. If you get dizzy when you stand, tell me and sit back down. Ready…stand up."

Help me, Lord. Thomas leaned forward, straightened his knees, then his body. Pain shot from his shoulder into his arm and chest. He clamped his jaw tight, fought a surge of light-headedness. The sharp pains subsided to a heavy throbbing. He drew in a long breath and looked at Jacob. "Let's walk."

"I-if you no longer need me, Doctor, I will go finish feeding Goldie."

Thomas looked at Viola, read sympathy and fear in her eyes. Was she concerned for him? He frowned at the conceit embodied in the quick rush of pleasure that thought gave him. Viola had a tender heart. She was concerned for everyone. He settled that thought firmly in his head and took his first step as she hurried from the bedroom.

"So how'd he do?" Hattie gave Goldie another bite of mashed egg. "Is he walkin' by hisself?"

"I don't know. The doctor didn't need me after I helped put Thomas's shirt on him, so I came back to finish feeding Goldie." Viola rubbed her palms against her long skirt. "He was standing up when I left."

Hattie squinted up at her. "Well, mayhap *you* should sit down. You look a might peaked."

"I'm fine. It's only... It bothers me to see people in pain." *Like one of the girls, when Dengler's men had finished beating her as punishment for some infraction of his rules.* She drew a breath and stepped to the table. "I can finish feeding Goldie now. You can go back to your knitting."

Hattie spooned another bite into the baby's mouth. "The egg's almost gone. I'll finish. Whyn't you make yourself a cup of tea and rest a bit?"

Viola shook her head, brushed back a curl that escaped and tucked it into her snood. "As long as Thomas or Goldie doesn't need me, I think I'll go outside for a minute and get a breath of fresh air." She turned away from Hattie's curious gaze, walked to the door and stepped outside. She didn't need any questions.

A breeze caressed her face, played with the wispy curls at her temples and forehead. She walked out into the yard, sniffed. There was a hint of rain riding the breeze. She turned and looked toward the harbor. Dark clouds were gathering. In Treasure Creek, just as in Seattle, the storms came from the direction of the water.

White light flashed across the sky in the distance. She stood and watched the flickering brightness, heard a distant grumble. She liked thunderstorms. In Seattle they meant fewer customers. Here, in Treasure Creek, it seemed as if God was washing the earth clean.

The wind picked up, fluttered the puffed fabric at the tops of the long, tight sleeves on her white shirtwaist, rippled the dark green tweed of her long skirt. She lifted her face to the sky, felt the moisture, more mist than rain, as the wind blew the storm closer. *Wash me, God. Wash me clean and make me forget.*

Thunder rumbled louder. The mist gathered into drops and pattered against the dry, colored leaves littering the ground at her feet. Lightning snapped. Close this time. The back door opened.

"Viola, Doctor Calloway is fixin' to leave. He wants to talk to you."

"All right, Hattie. I'm coming." She sighed, turned and walked back to the house, still carrying the guilt and shame of the past on her damp shoulders.

Chapter Eight

Viola took a breath to steady her voice. "Is there anything more, Doctor?"

Jacob Calloway pulled open the door and shook his head. "No more instructions as to his care. I wanted him to take another day of just walking a bit with my help, but Thomas is mule stubborn and insisted on sitting up today. However, I do not want him sitting in that chair for more than a quarter hour this first time." He gave her a concerned look. "I have patients waiting and cannot stay. Thomas is a gentleman and will not want you helping him. But that wound is only beginning to heal, and cannot be strained, you *must* help him back into bed, Viola." He stepped through the open door and hurried off toward his clinic.

She closed the door, sagged back against it and closed her eyes, the doctor's words ringing in her head. She couldn't do it. She could not offer herself as support for Thomas. He would have his arm about her shoulders. A shudder shook her. Perhaps Hattie could—no. Hattie was too short.

A sharp rap echoed through the room, vibrated the

wood behind her shoulders. She gave a startled yelp, jerked erect. The door opened, slammed against her as she turned. "Ugh!"

"Viola?" A narrow boot was jammed between the door and the frame, followed by a red clad shoulder and a mop of short, dark curls. "You all right, Viola?"

"Frankie?" Viola pulled the door fully open, stepped back and rubbed her banged elbow. "You startled me."

"Well I'm sorry I pushed in like that. But I thought something was wrong when you yelled out." Frankie grinned, lifted a paper bag she clutched like a weapon. "I was ready to knock any owlhoot over the head with your locks." Her gaze shifted. She smiled and nodded. "Hello, Hattie. Good to see you up and around, Preacher."

Preacher? Viola whirled. Thomas stood just outside the bedroom doorway, his face pale, his mouth pressed into a tight line. He looked about to pass out. "Thomas! What are you *doing?* You're not supposed to get up." If he fell… She ran to him, grabbed his good hand, ducked, then straightened with his arm draped across her shoulders, her free arm behind his back. "You must get back to bed. Are you able to walk?"

"Yes." A tremor moved through his body, his arm tightened around her shoulder and he stepped forward.

"I'll help you, Vi—"

She darted a thankful glance toward Frankie, saw Hattie grab her by the arm and give a quick shake of her head. Frankie stopped, gave the elderly woman a quizzical look, then turned back to the door.

Anger lent Viola courage. She braced herself and steadied Thomas, moved beside him into the bedroom, vowing to speak to Hattie about her interference the moment she got him settled. He slowed, halted short of the bed. Oh, no! She shot a quick look up at him.

"I'll sit here in the chair until Jacob returns." The smile he attempted turned into a grimace. "I'm not sure how to get back into bed. It's awkward with my arm tied down. And I hate to admit it, but…I'm not as strong as I thought."

She caught her breath at the exhaustion on his face and took a firmer grip. He was too heavy for her, and if he fainted and broke open that wound— If he hadn't already! She snagged her lower lip with her teeth, judged the distance to the bed. "You need to lie down. I'll help you."

"No. I'm too heavy for you. Just steady me until I get in the chair." His voice was losing strength, but determination shone in his green eyes despite the pain shadowing them.

"It will be as easy for you to sit on the edge of the bed." She moved slightly, to block him from sitting in the chair, looked at his set jaw and her worry escalated. The man was stubborn indeed. "Please. I will not be able to hold you if you faint."

He frowned, gave a curt nod. "All right. Help me sit on the bed then. But I will manage from there." He edged backward until the backs of his legs touched the mattress, then tightened his arm around her neck. She leaned forward and he sat down, released his hold and used his arm to brace himself. "Thank you. You can let go now."

She shook her head, kept her arm around him. "I'm going to help you lie down. Doctor Calloway said you're not supposed to strain. Not even with your uninjured arm."

"Jacob is not here. And I don't want you hurt." He lifted his hand, touched her arm. "It will be all right. Let go, Viola."

The caring in his voice touched a place deep inside her that had been closed off long ago. She swallowed, forced firmness into her voice. "No. And it will do you no good to protest further. I, also, have a stubborn side. Please lie down before weariness overtakes you." Their gazes locked. The tiny gold flecks in the green of his eyes darkened. He looked away, sucked in air and leaned to his right.

She moved with him, supporting him as best she could as he eased onto the propped-up pillows. He lifted his legs onto the bed and she helped him shift over onto his back, then slid her arm free.

"Thank you." He closed his eyes, but the tension around his mouth betrayed his pain.

She hurried to the other side of the bed and lifted the hem of his shirt.

"Don't—"

"I need to check your bandage, Thomas. I have to make certain you didn't open your wound." *Please, Almighty God…* "It's all right—there's no blood." Anger soared on the wings of relief. "Whatever made you get out of that chair by yourself?" She tugged his shirt back in place, grabbed hold of the covers at the foot of the bed and pulled them up over him. "It was a foolish, *dangerous* thing to do." She willed her hands to stop shaking, opened the bottle and poured out his pain medicine. "Here, take this."

He frowned, looked up at her. "It wasn't as dangerous as what could have happened to you if that kidnapper's partner had come to try for the gold again." He opened his mouth, swallowed the medicine. "That possibility has been on my mind. And when I heard you cry out I thought…" He grimaced, closed his eyes. "Some protector I turned out to be."

Protector? Of *her?* The anger drained, leaving her trembling and unsure.

His eyebrows drew down, he opened his eyes, couldn't sustain the effort, they closed again. "I need a gun… I'm sure…of no account…without one…"

The grumbled words trailed off. His brow smoothed, his breathing evened out into the rhythm of sleep. She stood looking down at him, an odd sensation, rather like curling up in a soft, warm blanket on a cold night, spread through her. Had he really risked tearing open his wound to get out of that chair because he thought she was in danger? That couldn't be. She must have misunderstood him. Yet no other explanation made sense. He had risked his life for her. But how could such a thing be true?

She turned to the window, wrapped her arms about herself and watched the rain sluicing down the small panes. Something inside her was changing. Her head, every bit of experience she'd had with men, told her not to, but she believed him. That warm, comfortable feeling swelled. The icy, hard and frightened place inside her began to soften and melt. She touched the spot on her arm where Thomas had rested his hand, felt again the warmth of it, the caring in his touch. How could a strong man's hand be so gentle?

A burst of laughter came from the other room. A spate of baby babble and gurgles brought her back to reality. A reality that contained dangerous men who had kidnapped Goldie and shot Thomas. Her world righted

itself. The spell was broken. She shook off the linger-
ing feeling of wonder, smoothed back the curls that had
come loose during her effort to help Thomas into bed
and walked into the other room to see how Frankie was
coming with the locks.

"Doctor Calloway was not pleased."

Thomas looked up, ignored the kick in his pulse as
Viola entered the bedroom. "So he said. He'll get over
it." It didn't help the state of his pulse when she seated
herself in the rocker. His chair was so close he could
reach out and touch her. Not that he would. He still
fought to forget the feel of her holding him that morning, as she helped him into bed.

"He said you were not trustworthy, and I was not to
leave you alone again."

She would be helping him into bed later. His pulse
kicked the pace up another notch. "Jacob takes too much
on himself. You are a busy woman, with a baby to care
for and customers to serve. You do not need to stay here
in this room watching over me. Besides, it was not de-
liberate disobedience." He frowned at the defensive note
in his voice. But it irked him that she looked upon him
as a charge. He decided not to examine too closely the
reason that was so.

She leaned down and lifted a pair of trousers out of
the basket on the floor. "It's no hardship. I am perfectly
able to do mending right here." She plucked a threaded
needle from a pincushion on the table and set to work.

Thomas studied her. Something had changed. It was
nothing he could put his finger on, but it was there.
Some subtle difference in her tone, or... He shoved his

musings aside. He spent too much time dwelling on thoughts of Viola Goddard.

He looked out the bedroom door, but couldn't see much. Straight ahead a settle, with a lamp stand beside it, faced a fireplace on the far wall of the living room. There was a hoop-back Windsor chair sitting against the wall at the end of the fireplace, a lamp shelf and sampler above it. "*With men it is impossible, but not with God, for with God all things are possible.*' That is an excellent verse to meditate on." He let the words settle into his heart, glanced back at Viola. Her head was bent over her work. "Did you work the sampler?"

"Yes. I…enjoy needlework."

"It seems as if most women do. I can remember my mother doing needlework. I used to play at her feet while she worked." He brushed his hand over the prickly stubble on his face, wished he could shave.

"Does your beard bother you?"

Not as much as the soft sound of your voice. He looked back at her and nodded. "I'm not used to it, and it itches some." He frowned and scrubbed his hand over his jaw again. "I need to shave. If this stubble gets much longer, it's going to be a job to get rid of it."

Her gaze dropped to the level of his chin. "I'm afraid I know nothing about such things. How could you shave one-handed?"

"Clumsily, no doubt. But I could sure make a good try of it. Probably nick myself up some." He curved his lips in a wry smile. "I'd ask Jacob to bring me shaving equipment, but, mad as he is, he'd probably use the razor to slit my throat."

She laughed. A musical ripple that made his gut tighten. He allowed himself the pleasure of storing up the memory of it. She was far beyond mere beauty, with that warmth in her eyes and her lips…

"Well then, it's fortunate there's no need to take such a risk." She set aside the trousers she was mending, rose and stepped over to the commode stand and opened the top drawer. "Will these serve?" She turned and held out a shaving cup, brush and straightedge razor. "Hattie said they were all you would need."

His mouth gaped open. "You bought me shaving equipment?"

She stiffened. Something he didn't recognize swept the warmth from her eyes. Uncertainty? Defensiveness?

"I realize it is a somewhat personal purchase. But I noticed you were clean-shaven, and thought perhaps you would want these when you were sufficiently recovered. I felt, under the circumstances, it was proper and acceptable behavior."

Yes, defensiveness. The coolness was back in her voice. Thomas stared at her. Her bearing, her face, every ounce of her formed a protective posture. "It is far more than acceptable, Viola. It is kind and generous and thoughtful. And very appreciated."

She gave a stiff little nod. "Do you need anything more?"

"Only hot water and a towel. And forgiveness." He caught her gaze, held it. "I did not mean to offend you, Viola. I was surprised by your gift, not offended. And I certainly did not mean to imply there was anything improper or untoward in it. I would never suggest such a thing to a lady like you. Please forgive me."

Her gaze jerked from his, settled on her hands. "Of course. Now, let me go get your water and towel." She set the cup and razor on the stand and hurried from the room.

Thomas stared after her, stunned by the flash of hurt he had seen in her eyes. What had he said to cause such a reaction? He frowned, looked out the window and thought back over his words.

"You should've seen what Goldie did, Vi—"

"I'm sorry, I haven't time to talk, Hattie. I have to get a towel and hot water. Thomas wants to shave." Viola turned from the startled look on Hattie's face and hurried toward the kitchen, her conscience pricking her. Because she was upset was no reason to cut Hattie short like that. She never had before.

I would never suggest such a thing to a lady like you.

Her face drew taut. A lady. If Thomas knew the truth about her, he would never call her a lady. She fought back the hurt of a past that would never let her be the sort of woman Thomas assumed her to be and stepped into the small washing and bathing room to get a clean towel. A warm drop of moisture splattered on the back of her hand.

She looked down at it, lifted her hand to her cheek then straightened and stared at her reflection in the mirror over the washstand. She'd had tears in her eyes many times, but she had not cried since Richard Dengler and his customers had shown her what men...

She stiffened, swiped the tears from her cheeks, picked up the washbowl and went into the kitchen to fill it with hot water from the reservoir on the side of the stove. What was wrong with her? She was playing the fool, allowing guilt and sympathy for Thomas Stone's condition to blind her to the truth. But no more. She knew what men really were.

She hung the dipper back in place, draped the towel over her arm, picked up the filled washbowl and headed for the bedroom, her armor firmly in place again.

The invisible barrier was so real, it seemed, if he stretched out his hand he could touch it. Thomas slid his jaw to the right, drew the blade down his tightened cheek, swished it through the washbowl on his lap to clear off the soap and stubble and repeated the process. It was just as well the wall was there, considering the way his feelings for Viola were deepening. But it was still perplexing. He had gone over and over his words, and could not imagine how they could have hurt her. But they had.

"Turn the mirror a little to the left, please." He drew the blade down his cheek a couple more times and eyed his face. Not bad. Only two nicks so far, and he was all done but for the part around his mouth. He stretched his upper lip down tight and positioned the blade below his nose, wishing Viola would say something. The silence weighed heavily.

"Watchin' him shave, it's easy to see why men grow beards on the trail, right, Viola?"

He glanced toward the door, winced. Nick number three—compliments of Hattie.

"Yes. It does seem shaving would be a difficult task while living in a tent."

He looked up at Viola, eager to keep the conversation going. "Not after four years of practice. The hard part is not breaking the mirror while you're packing up and down the trail." He leaned a bit to the side, so he could see in the tilted mirror, and finished in quick strokes. "It's pretty hard shaving when you can only see a couple inches of your face at a time." He swished the blade through the water, wiped it off on the towel draped over his knees, then dipped his head and splashed water on his face to wash off the blood and the residue of soap. The cuts smarted as the soapy water ran into them, a small price to pay for getting rid of the itching. And for looking his best in front of her.

Hattie laughed. "I imagine it would be. You'd probably cut yourself up worse than now. Even havin' two good hands to use."

He blotted his face with the towel, looked up at the elderly woman and grinned. "Are you saying I've made a poor job of shaving myself one-handed?"

Hattie snorted. "I've seen better. Look at them cuts. If you'd done this the day after you come here, you'd have bled to death for sure." She turned to Viola. "Just come in to tell you supper's ready when you two are." She turned to the door, looked back at him. "Better give that nick by your mouth another dab with the towel."

Thomas stared after her. Had she *winked?*

Viola placed the mirror she was holding on the commode stand and reached for the washbowl. "Let me move these things out of the way and I'll help you back into bed. Then I'll carry them to the washroom and bring back your supper."

Thomas laid his hand on hers to halt her. An urge to lace his fingers through hers surged, his fingers twitched. "Forgive me." He drew his hand back, knew a sense of loss at the broken contact. "I merely wanted to say I'm not going back to bed now. I'm going to the table to eat my supper."

"But you can't—"

"Yes. I can. If I can sit in a chair here in this bedroom, I can sit in a chair at the table. There's no reason for you to have to feed me any longer. At the table I will be able to manage one-handed."

"That's not wise, Thomas." Her gaze slipped away from his. She moved the washbowl to the stand and folded the towel beside it. "It's not a great distance to the kitchen. But Doctor Calloway said—"

"Jacob has no say in this. With your help, I will make it to the kitchen just fine." Her gaze returned to meet his. His heart thudded. There was concern for him in her eyes. It firmed his resolve to leave her home as soon as possible. "Now, if you are ready, I need you to steady me while I get out of this chair."

She shook her head, picked up the washbowl and towel. "I'm sorry, but I will not help you disobey the doctor. I do not want you bleeding to death…in my home. I will be right back with your supper."

Thomas watched her walk away, a frown creasing his forehead. Why did her leaving feel like she was making an escape? What had he done that she had taken refuge in that polite coolness? He looked down at the bulge of bandage beneath his shirt at his chest and shoulder, the sleeve hanging empty at his left side. He lifted his hand and ran his fingers through his hair, shifted his gaze to the window and stared at the mountainside. He was doing his best to resist his feelings for Viola. But his best was falling far short.

Goldie's baby chatter fell on his ears, landed square in his heart. He set his jaw against the guilt and pain and lifted his gaze to the sky. "Please heal me, Lord. Please heal me quickly. I need to get out of here."

Chapter Nine

Viola's heart lurched. She bolted upright in bed, listening for a repeat of the thudding sound that woke her. *Was someone trying to break in?* She cast a quick glance at Goldie sleeping in her cradle, grabbed her robe and shoved her arms into the sleeves.

"Let go of my arm!" A thump echoed through the bedrooms' dividing wall.

Thomas. Someone was hurting Thomas. His shoulder! She sprang from her bed, clutched the poker by the fireplace in a death grip and peeked out the door. Hattie was asleep on the settle. No one else was in sight. *Lord, help me!* She inched out the door, tiptoed along the wall to the other bedroom and peeked in. Thomas was in bed struggling with an imagined foe. She hurried to the bed, her knees wobbly with relief. "Thomas, wake up."

"Got to help them…"

"No, Thomas, stop!" She dropped the poker and grabbed for his hand as he tugged at the bandage that held his other arm bound to his side. The poker clanged against the fireplace stone, clattered to the floor.

Goldie squalled.

"I'm coming, Susie baby!" His fingers tore at the bandage.

"Viola, what's wrong?" There was a hurried patter of stocking-clad feet behind her.

Goldie squalled louder.

"Stop, Thomas! You'll hurt yourself!" She took a firmer grip on his wrist and looked over her shoulder. "He's dreaming again, Hattie. You'll have to tend to Goldie." She turned back as Hattie hurried away, gave up her useless effort to pit her strength against Thomas's and slid her hand beneath his clutching fingers to protect the bandage.

"I said, let go!"

He gripped her fingers, wrenched his hand around. Her wrist twisted and she fell forward on top of him. She rolled to her side and tugged at his hand. "Thomas, *stop!* You're hurting me!"

"Louise?"

"I'm not, Louise. I'm Viola." She gave his hand a quick, hard slap.

He blinked, stared down at her sprawled across his waist. "Viola? What—"

"Let go of my wrist, Thomas. You're hurting me."

His gaze shifted. His hand jerked open.

She pushed up off him, winced and rubbed her wrist. Tremors chased through her. She leaned against the bed, afraid her legs would give way if she moved.

He gave a quick shake of his head, scrubbed the nape of his neck. "What was—" Awareness came into his eyes. A scowl darkened his face. "I was dreaming again, wasn't I?"

"Yes."

"And this time I've hurt you." Anger chased the remaining confusion from his eyes.

"Not on purpose." She leaned down and lifted the tangled, dangling blankets back onto the bed out of her way, spread them over his legs. "I need to check your bandage." She pulled the low-burning lamp close and turned up the wick.

"Let me see your wrist." He caught hold of her arm, slowly turned it until her wrist and palm were facing up. "Push up your sleeve."

She drew breath to protest, glanced at the set of his jaw and obeyed.

"It's swelling." The muscle along that strong, square jaw twitched. He slid his hand down to hers. "Why would I do such a thing?"

She stared down at his hand cradling hers, the gentleness of his touch bringing a lump to her throat. "You said you had to help someone, and you thought the bandage was a person holding you back. You kept pulling at it and saying 'let go of my arm.' I tried to stop you." She took a breath to control her trembling. *She was trembling. And it wasn't fear.* "You didn't know what you were doing."

"Maybe not. But it's not going to happen again. I am leaving this house tomorrow."

A sick feeling hit the pit of her stomach. "That's ridiculous!" She jerked her hand from his grasp. "Your wound is not healed. You cannot manage on your own." Fear for him pushed unguarded words out in a torrent. "What happened was my own fault. I knew you dreamed about your wife and baby, and if I had stayed here in the rocker I could have—"

"You know about Louise and Susan?"

She froze, which was foolish, why should she feel guilty? "Yes." She untied the bandage at his waist that held his arm immobile, and straightened out the part he had wrinkled. "You speak about them when you dream. I—I think perhaps Goldie upsets you."

His gaze caught hers, held it. "Why do you say that? What did I say?"

"Nothing really. It's only—when she cried, you called out, 'I'm coming, Susie baby!' and fought me to get free and go to her. It was the same before. You were trying to reach your wife and child." She retied the bandage, tucked in the ends. "I know your wife and child died, Thomas. And I'm so sorry for your loss. It must be very painful for you to be around Goldie."

His face drew taut. "I'd like to deny that, but it's true. Goldie makes me remember. And then my guilt rears up, and…I guess that's what's making me dream." He stared off into the distance. "If I'd only known… But I had no idea how primitive my living conditions would be as a missionary, or what a toll they would take on Louise's health. And then, when she and the baby caught pneumonia…" He sucked in air, ran his hand through his hair. "There was no doctor. And the hut was so cold and damp from the storms…. I built the fire as high as I dared. Did all I knew to doctor them, but it was no use."

Tears stung her eyes. Her heart hurt for him. She knew what it was to carry guilt. She looked into his eyes, searched for something to say to comfort him. "You did your best for them, Thomas. You bear no fault for their deaths. The other day, Hattie told me the Bible says there is both good and evil in this world, and because of that bad things happen to us. That we're not always to blame. You're a missionary. Surely you must believe that." She looked away, unwilling to let him see her doubt.

"Yes, I do. I just—I guess it's different when it's myself."

She nodded, looked back at him. "I can understand that. But doesn't the Bible say God is no respecter of persons?"

His gaze locked on her, the clouded look of pain in his eyes giving way to one of contemplation. "Yes…it does."

She straightened out the still-rumpled blankets, gladdened that she had perhaps helped him a little. "Your pillows are dislodged. Let me help you sit up and I'll fix them."

He shook his head. "I'll do it. I don't want you hurting your wrist more."

"But—"

"If all that thrashing about didn't bust my wound open, pushing myself up and shoving around a few pillows won't hurt." He rolled to his right side, pushed up onto his elbow and then his hand.

She reached behind him and snatched the pillows before he could turn toward them, began to fluff and replace them, ignoring the growing ache in her wrist. She'd had much worse.

"Viola—"

"I told you I was as stubborn as you." She had the strongest urge to smooth the frown from his forehead. She pummeled the last pillow instead. "There. All done. You can lie back now."

He lowered himself against the pillows and rolled onto his back.

He no longer needed her help. Her throat tightened. She brushed her palms against her robe, forced a smile. "If there is nothing more…" She reached to turn down the wick in the lamp, stared at her shaking hands that manifested the trembling in her body. *Just wait until you go all weak-kneed and trembly when you're around your special man. Just wait until you fall in love!* Her breath caught. It couldn't be…

"There *is* one thing."

"Yes?"

"If you don't mind telling me. When you were talking with Hattie the other day…what were you blaming yourself for?"

His voice was as soft as the dimmed light. She shrugged away the warmth that touched her heart. Fought her way back to her senses. "For Goldie being kidnapped and you being shot."

Surprise swept over his face. "How could that possibly be your fault?"

"I took a nap." The guilt washed over her again. "If I had stayed awake, perhaps the kidnapper would never have tried to take Goldie. Perhaps he would only have tried to claim her, as the others have."

"And perhaps you would have been hurt—or worse." His voice was tight, gruff. "You're not to blame for Goldie being kidnapped or my being shot, that kidnapper is…was."

"That's what Hattie said."

His gaze slid over her face, he gave a small nod, as if he saw something written there. "What else did Hattie say?"

"That God turns the bad to good for His children.

And she thought God had made things turn out for the best."

"And what was your reply to that?"

There was something probing, questioning in his eyes. She let out her breath and squared her shoulders. He might as well know about her lack of faith. "I told her I didn't understand how she could say that when you were lying wounded and helpless in this bed."

Something flickered deep in those green depths. "Did she answer that?"

"Yes. She said, 'it isn't over yet'."

Thomas's thoughts tumbled through his head the way he'd seen stones tumble willy-nilly down the Chilkoot Trail. The difference was, a tumbling stone had no direction—he knew *his* destination. The turmoil was because his heart had become divided between his calling to minister to the Tlingit Indians and his growing feelings for Viola. His spirit and his flesh were warring. And the image of Viola standing beside his bed, clad in her blue robe, with her dark red curls tumbling across her shoulders, looking at him with such warmth and concern in her violet-blue eyes, was not helping matters. It undermined his determination to do what he knew he must. It was definitely time to leave.

It isn't over yet. Hattie's words brought him up short. Sent his thoughts roiling again. He scowled into the darkness. It *had* to be over. Nothing good could come of his staying here. He had a vow to keep. And a ministry to uphold.

And we know that all things work together for good to them that love God, to them who are the called, according to His purpose. He stirred, slipped his hand beneath his head and stared up at the ceiling. He was sure that was the scripture verse Hattie had been referring to when she spoke with Viola. Why wouldn't it leave his mind? No matter which direction his jumbled thoughts traveled, when they reached their limit it was there waiting, clinging to his consciousness like a burr to a dog's coat. Why? He already knew his calling and purpose.

It isn't over yet. He muttered Hattie's pronouncement into the silence, felt again the shock of the words, followed by a hushed stillness, as if something inside him was waiting. Was he supposed to stay here? Was he supposed to learn something from this torment of temptation? Grow stronger in his faith perhaps? Was that the good that was to come out of his being shot? Or was there something he was to do for Viola? Or Hattie? Or… He gave a growl of frustration. "What do You want of me, Lord? Should I go? Or should I stay? Have You placed me here for a purpose? Or am I here only as the result of an evil circumstance? Show me what to do."

He turned onto his side, pushed to a sitting position and slid his legs over the side of the bed, then gripped the bedpost and stood to his feet. A frisson of satisfaction ran through him. He snatched his shirt off the back of the chair, spread it out on the bed, then lifted the back hem and ducked his head inside. It took some maneuvering, but he got the shirt on and the button fastened.

The next test was his pants. He snatched them off the hook, leaned against the bed and pulled them on over his long drawers. After a few fumbled attempts he got his belt buckled. His boots, however, defeated him. He would have to wear them untied. Still, he could do it! He wouldn't want to wrestle a bear, but most of his strength had returned. And he could manage one-handed. Even so...

His elation died. Until his wound healed, he would not be able to return to his hut and his work with the Tlingits. Where would he live? Mavis Goodge. He would take the next empty room at her boardinghouse. *God grant that it be tomorrow.*

He took a couple of turns about the small room, exalting in the returned strength in his legs, stopped by the chair, gripped the back and lowered himself to the seat, then stood again and faced his last challenge, getting back into bed. He took off his clothes, gripped the bedpost and sat on the edge of the mattress, pushed back as far as he was able, lifted his legs and rolled onto his back on the pillows. The resulting pain in his shoulder was no match for the satisfaction that filled him. He pulled the covers over him, turned his head and stared at the lamp Viola had turned down before she left the room. How small the flame was against the surrounding darkness. But how bright its glow.

Thy word is a lamp unto my feet, and a light unto my path. How apt was the scripture. "Thank You, Lord, for Your word. And for showing me the way I should go." He smiled, closed his eyes and settled himself comfortably under the covers.

Viola strained to hear any sound, was rewarded by nothing but silence. The faint sounds from Thomas's room had stopped. What had he been doing? Was he really going to leave tomorrow? The sick feeling worsened. She took a deep breath and pressed her hand against her stomach. Perhaps a cup of tea would make her feel better and help her sleep.

She glided by Goldie's cradle, slipped out of her bedroom and tiptoed across the living room, past Hattie, snoring on the settle, and into the kitchen. The slight warmth from the stove felt good. She fitted the coil-handled lifter into the slot and raised the front cook plate. Red coals winked up at her through the round hole. She added a couple of small chunks of wood from the woodbox, replaced the cook plate and adjusted the draft. A quick peek showed the iron teakettle was dry. She filled it from the reservoir, placed it on the stove and walked to the window. Light rimmed the clouds, glazed the mountains with gold and cast spidery shadows of tree limbs on her sun-kissed yard. She was accustomed to the unending daylight now, but she missed the black nights of Seattle, the starry skies when it was not raining. But that was all she missed.

She shuddered, turned her thoughts from the past, though the present was as disturbing—in a different way.

She didn't want him to go.

She wrapped her arms about herself and faced that truth. It was so foreign to all she had known. Bewildering. Why was she no longer frightened of Thomas? When had her fear of him turned into concern for him? Or was it more than concern? *Just wait until you go all weak-kneed and trembly when you're around your special man. Just wait until you fall in love.*

How could that be? She knew what men were beneath their social facades. But he was so different, so thoughtful and caring, he made her feel…safe.

The word whispered through her like the soft, warm sighing of the water heating on the stove. Tears flooded her eyes, overflowed down her cheeks. She clasped her hands over her mouth and leaned against the wall, shaking with the sobs she wouldn't release. It had been so long. So very long since she had felt safe.

Chapter Ten

Viola brushed her hair back from her face, secured the mass of curls into a bun, tied the snood in place over them and stared at her reflection. Shadows clouded the eyes looking back at her. And her mouth looked... *pinched*. Well, she couldn't help it. How could Dr. Calloway have agreed to Thomas moving into Mavis Goodge's boardinghouse? Was she the only one that cared about Thomas's wound being reinjured? She hadn't nursed him this far along, only to have him rip his shoulder open again.

The sick feeling in her stomach intensified. What if he started dreaming and she wasn't there to stop him from pulling at his bandage? Tears shimmered in the shadowed eyes, her lower lip quivered. Oh, what was wrong with her? She was being foolish. Thomas Stone was a strong man, well able to care for himself. And with him gone, she could get back to mending and sewing for her customers full time. Making the drapes and curtains for the new hotel had been put off by all that had happened, and the place would be opening soon—construction was almost finished. Thomas's departure was for the best.

Still, she had to get out of this house, get hold of herself. Thankfully, measuring the hotel windows had given her a perfect reason to offer Hattie for her escape.

She spun away from the mirror, slipped on the fitted, worsted jacket that matched her long, blue skirt over her white, cotton shirtwaist and buttoned it as she walked into the living room. "I'm ready to go, Hattie. All I need is my sewing tape." She glanced toward the other bedroom. "Is Thomas—"

"He's gone. Said he'd been inside so long, he wanted to see was the mountains still there."

She nodded, stepped into Thomas's—*Hattie's*—bedroom, snatched her measure out of her sewing basket and hurried out again. She would move the rocker and her sewing things out of the bedroom when she returned.

"You all right, Viola? You look a mite…pinched."

"I'm fine. A little tired perhaps." She turned away from Hattie's sharp gaze.

"Guess it'll be a blessin' havin' Thomas move down to Mavis's place. You won't have the care of him wearin' on you no more."

Oh, Hattie, please don't. She nodded, dropped the measure in her purse, drew the drawstrings tight and looked down at Goldie. The baby was swaying to and fro on her hands and knees and chattering to herself. "One of these days she is going to crawl."

"And surprise herself in the doin' of it." Hattie chuckled, then looked up at her and frowned. "Whyn't you take that snood off and let them pretty, eye-catchin' red curls of yours show?"

"You know I like to keep my hair neat and controlled." *And hidden.* She tugged the hem of her jacket down into place. "Are you sure you will be all right here, alone with Goldie? I don't want to overburden you—"

"Fiddlesticks! Goldie's no trouble."

"All right, then. Well…" She kissed the baby, then turned and walked to the door while she still had the courage to leave. "Come lock the door behind me, Hattie. And should someone come, don't unlock the door unless you know who it is. Any new customers can return later."

Hattie put down her knitting and rose. "We'll be safe, Viola. Don't you worry none. Frankie did a good job puttin' those locks in. And they're good and strong."

"Yes." Viola leaned down and planted a kiss on Hattie's wrinkled cheek. "I won't be long." She turned and made herself step outside. But she couldn't walk away until she heard the *snick* of the small metal bar on the door frame dropping into the socket on the door and knew the lock was in place. She took a deep breath and turned toward the road. *"Thomas!"*

"Finding it hard to leave Goldie and Hattie home alone?"

There it was—that caring tone in his voice, that *look* in his eyes that was her undoing. She swallowed hard, nodded, placed her hand in his proffered one and stepped down off the stoop, marveling at how safe and right her hand felt in his. How had she gone from fearing his hands to loving his touch?

"I checked the locks before I left. They're strong."

"Yes." She looked down at the small cloth bag she'd given him to carry his shaving equipment. The top was stuffed into his belt, leaving his hand free. Her own felt naked, now that he had released it.

"I couldn't leave without thanking you, again, for all

you have done. For sheltering me and caring for me. I am very grateful."

Tears threatened. She ducked back under her shield of cool politeness. "It was little enough, since I am the one responsible for your being shot." She squared her shoulders and started down the road to town. He fell into step beside her.

"I thought we settled on the fact that it was the kidnapper at fault, not you."

Don't think of that night. "I'm the one who took the nap."

He nodded, looked off toward the mountains. "It's hard to let go of guilt, isn't it? Even if it's self-inflicted and undeserved."

His wife and child. She stopped, looked up. Their gazes locked in perfect understanding.

"Guilt is a heavy load to bear, Viola." He lifted his hand and touched her arm. "Please don't carry that burden on my account."

The gentleness in his voice and his touch swelled her heart and her throat. She couldn't speak. Didn't dare try. The golden flecks in his eyes darkened. His fingers twitched, tightened. His gaze dropped to her mouth. Her breath fused to her lungs, refused to release. He sucked in air, jerked his hand from her arm and stepped back.

"Shall we continue on?"

Her breath expelled. She nodded, drew on her experience and arranged her features in her old mask of detachment. But this time it was not to hide her fear or pain. This time it was to hide her heart. It seemed to crack a little more with every step they took.

They turned right at the corner and walked toward the harbor, no longer alone but moving through an ever thickening throng of townspeople and stampeders. *Whyn't you take that snood off and let them pretty, eye-catchin' red curls of yours show?* She reached up and touched her hair to make sure the snood was in place. The last thing she wanted was to draw attention. If any of her old customers at Dengler's decided to try their luck at finding gold, and recognized her while passing through Treasure Creek to reach the Chilkoot Trail… She cringed at the thought of meeting one of them while in Thomas's company.

A lady like you. Thomas's good opinion of her would quickly change if he knew the truth. As would the opinions of those in Treasure Creek who had befriended her in spite of her standoffish attitude. Tears clogged her throat. She wanted so much to draw close to them all, to be a true friend to them, but friendship meant questions and confidences that she dare not invite.

Guilt, sorrow and regret formed a heavy weight in her chest, pressed down on her already aching heart. She did not truly belong with these good people. Certainly not with a man of faith and integrity like Thomas. She could only live on the fringe of their friendship, returning what help and service to them she could in exchange. She blinked the film of moisture from her eyes and stole a sidelong look at Thomas from beneath her lowered lashes. Perhaps she could help him with his missionary work in some way. Perhaps that would help atone for her past.

They passed in front of the newly built school and the sound of hammering from the other side of the street grabbed her attention, pulled her from her burdensome thoughts. She looked over at the church, no longer the small, log building it had been when she arrived, but beautiful now, with the new large sanctuary and white clapboard siding and new stained glass windows.

A deep, rumbling chuckle broke from Thomas. She glanced at him.

"Look on the roof."

She looked up, gasped. On the roof of the original church building, now the entrance to the new, large sanctuary, stood Ed Parker, astraddle the peak, his huge hands clamped on the side rails of a ladder leaning against the steeple tower under construction. On the rung just above the level of his hands was a pair of small, booted feet, the hems of a divided, kersey wool skirt tucked into their tops. *Frankie!* She jerked her gaze up over the leather belt jammed with various tools, skimmed it over the blue cotton shirt that enhanced instead of hid Frankie's shapely form and stared at the freckled face beneath the mass of short, windblown black curls. There was no unhappiness there today.

"Hey, Viola. Preacher Stone."

"Don't wave, Frankie!" Viola closed her eyes, pressed her hand against her abdomen, fought down a surge of nausea.

"She's safe, Viola."

She nodded, kept her gaze glued to the ground and hurried down the road.

"Whoa! Wait a minute." Thomas's hand gripped her elbow, gently pulled her to a stop. "You're trembling. What's wrong?"

"Nothing. I just…if she fell…" She shuddered, tried to close out the image of Sally's broken body after a drunken customer had thrown her out of a third-story window. So many horrible, horrible memories.

"Viola…"

She looked up, found him studying her.

"Something is wrong. If I can help…"

The warmth, the caring was back in his voice and eyes. She reached down beyond the dark place inside her and dredged up a smile. "I'm fine. I just can't bear to see people…hurt." She took a breath, continued walking. The low stone wall that enclosed the hotel grounds appeared on the right. He would be leaving her here and going on to the boardinghouse. Her heart cracked a little more. "Before you go, Thomas, I wanted to ask you…" She stopped by one of the stone pillars that anchored the wall and guarded the hotel entrance. "I don't have many skills beyond my sewing. I do read well. And I have a little nursing ability." She tried to smile, felt her lips start to tremble and let it die. "What I am trying to say is, if there is any way I could be of service, I would be honored to help you in your work with the Tlingits. You have only to ask."

She forced her lips into a polite smile. "Goodbye, Thomas. Thank you again for saving Goldie. Be sure and take care of your shoulder." She spun about and hurried up the stone walk to the hotel, focusing her thoughts on the job she had to do to keep herself from weeping.

Thomas stepped out onto the porch, frowned and stuffed the end of the free-hanging sleeve of the jacket he'd bought at Tanner's into the pocket. The flopping was an annoying reminder of his impairment.

Stampeders swarmed the waterfront, their voices melding into a constant hum. He scanned the area, shook his head over the endless piles of boxes and crates, the stacks of different size burlap bags, the loaded barrows and tents and bedding rolls. He was used to the peace and quiet of his hut beside the Chilkoot Trail, and of Viola's cabin nestled close to the mountains at the far edge of town. He missed... No. He would not travel down that road. He had done the right thing by leaving. And this...*dissatisfaction* would pass once he was home.

He stepped off the porch and walked around behind the boardinghouse to cut across lots to the school. He wanted to walk, to feel the stretch and pull of his leg muscles, the strength flowing back into his body, but not on the waterfront street where the jostling of the crowds could hurt his wounded shoulder. That's what he told himself.

He skirted the stone wall around the hotel property and walked through the schoolyard to the dirt road. His long strides ate up the distance to the corner. He glanced down the intersecting road on his left toward Viola's cabin, frowned, and forced himself to keep walking straight ahead, beyond the final cluster of cabins, past the Dunkle farm and on toward the trees at the base of the mountains. Frustration gnawed at him. What caused those flashes of fear and that vulnerability Viola hid behind a wall of cool politeness? It was obvious she was troubled, fearful of something. Or someone? A man? Is that why she had been so nervous and jumpy around him at first? He was a pastor. Why wouldn't she confide in him? Let him help her? He'd tried to breach that wall, but she evaded his efforts to draw her out.

He huffed out a breath, shoved his fingers through his hair. Something was very wrong. But unless she chose to tell him, it was none of his business. His concern was ridding himself of this sense of connection, this deepening love he felt for her. His work with the Tlingits had to be enough.

A cool breeze flowed down off the mountains, carried the fresh scent of water, the musky odor of forest soil and the astringent smell of firs. He filled his lungs, thought about his hut on the Chilkoot Trail and frowned. What he had viewed as solitude now seemed like loneliness.

I would be honored to help you in your work with the Tlingits.

He let out a sound that was half moan, half growl, pivoted and headed back toward town. He could stay away from Viola on his own part, but how could he refuse her help for the people he was called to serve? He needed an answer. He quickened his pace, held his gaze straight ahead as he came to the intersecting road, strode across the street to the church and climbed the newly laid stone steps. The door opened. He stopped dead in his tracks.

"Hello, Thomas." Mack Tanner smiled, stepped outside and pulled the door closed behind him. "Were you looking for me?" The smile turned hopeful. "You weren't by chance coming to tell me you have decided to take me up on my offer and become the first official ordained pastor of Treasure Creek Church, were you?"

"You know my answer to that, Mack. I'm called to minister to the Tlingits and the stampeders climbing the Chilkoot, not to townspeople." Thomas returned his smile, started back down the steps. "I was out stretching my legs and decided to take a look around. I hear you've made a lot of changes since I was last in the church. But I'll see them at services tomorrow."

Mack frowned, shot him a speculative look. "I was just praying over tomorrow's message. The townspeople need to be fed, and I'm running out of food to give them. This church needs a real pastor, Thomas. I don't suppose the fact that the organ I ordered from Seattle has come would induce you to change your mind?"

"Afraid not. I have to be true to my calling."

"Well, the offer stands open, should you change your mind. Good night, Thomas. It's good to see you out and around."

"Thanks. I'll see you tomorrow morning." Thomas watched until Mack reached his home and went inside, then turned and climbed the steps. He moved through the log entrance into the new, white-plastered sanctuary, walked down the center aisle between the new pews and knelt before the altar. "Almighty God, your Word says, 'If any of you lack wisdom, let him ask of God'.... I have a problem, Lord, and I come to You, humbly asking for Your wisdom and guidance. You know of my affection for Viola, and You also know I'm trying my best to conquer it. But she has offered to help me minister to the Tlingits. How can I refuse help for those You have called me to serve? But how can I be with her and not grow to feel more for her? Please give me wisdom and let me know Your will. Amen."

He stayed on his knees, waiting. No answer came. There was only silence—and the beat of his heart. He put his hand on the floor and pushed to his feet, turned and walked back up the aisle. It was at the doorway to the entrance that he heard the soft whispering in his spirit. *It isn't over yet.*

Hattie's words. Not God's. He shrugged them off, left the church and headed for the boardinghouse.

Chapter Eleven

"Ladies, your attention please."

Viola pulled the empty spools she had strung on a short cord from her purse, handed them to Goldie and focused her attention on Lana Tanner.

"I asked you all to meet me here because this room is not a fit entrance to our lovely new sanctuary. I talked to Mack about fixing it up, but he said buying the organ was enough for the church to do right now, and he doesn't want to ask for more donations. You all know he's ordered the bell, and I thought it would be lovely if the church is all finished when it comes. Mack is willing to help, if it is necessary, but he thinks fixing this room would be a good project for our ladies' group to undertake. And we all know how much money is in our coffers." She pulled a face, bringing general laughter. "Anyway, I'm hoping some of you lovely, talented ladies will volunteer your time and skills to turn this sow's ear into a silk purse. Though that may be more appropriate for a barn. But you all know what I mean."

A small frown creased the forehead of Mack Tanner's pretty, petite blond wife. "The first thing we need to change are the walls. These logs are so dark and rough. I thought perhaps…"

Viola followed her gaze toward the Tucker sisters. Frankie murmured to her married sisters, nodded and looked back to Lana.

"Seems like Margie and Lucy and me could help out with that. What'd you have in mind?"

"I'd like them plastered to match."

All three sisters shook their heads. Frankie planted her hands on her hips. "Can't do it, the logs are too rough and uneven. Best thing would be to shim them out, nail on vertical boards and paint them white to match the plaster." A smile curved her lips, broke into a grin as she nudged her sisters. "Might be you could get the owner of the sawmill to donate the boards."

Lana Tanner joined in the general laughter, batted her eyelashes. "I'm sure Mack would be delighted to do so. And that takes care of the walls. Now, about the windows… They look so plain.…"

Viola shook the spools to distract Goldie, who was beginning to fuss, and smiled as every eye turned in her direction. "If you would like, I could sew something to dress them up, Lana." She glanced at the small windows set deep in the log walls. "As you said, this room is already dark, and though white paint on the new board walls will brighten it considerably, I think regular curtains or drapes would close out too much light." There was a murmur of agreement.

"What would you suggest, Viola?"

She narrowed her eyes, imagined various window treatments, thankful to think of something besides her problems. "Well…a narrow swag in a white silk that would reflect the light would be quite elegant and appropriate."

"I had thought about a swag. But the white silk…" Lana glanced at the windows, nodded. "You're right. It would add elegance and shine to the room."

"I could add a long, silk fringe on the ends."

"Oh, that sounds beautiful!" Lana beamed at her. "I knew I could count on you to come up with a wonderful idea. And remember how we decided to make seat cushions for the chairs in the schoolhouse?"

She smiled and jiggled Goldie, who was rubbing her eyes and whimpering. "Would you like me to make a nice pad in velvet for the bench? In one of the colors in the stained glass windows…a dark crimson perhaps? And a runner—in white silk, with fringe on the ends that would match the window swags—for the collections table?"

"That would be perfect, Viola! And also pads for the pews. If we have the funds to buy the materials."

"If you would wish it…"

Everyone stopped talking and looked toward Teena Crow.

"My father once dived beneath the ice to save a white child. The child's father's heart was grateful. He gave my father a bowl of glass the color of violets in the sun. I could bring it and put it on the collections table to hold the money gifts, if you would like?"

"That would be lovely, Teena. Gracious, this meeting is turning out much better than I'd hoped. This room is going to be so lovely and welcoming." Lana favored them all with a happy smile, then looked down and frowned. "Has anyone any suggestions as to what we can do about the floor? I asked Mack about buying a carpet, but he said this is our project, so the rug is up to us, ladies. Has anyone an idea?"

"What about a rag rug?" Hattie rose from the rough wood bench along the wall and Viola moved to give her space to stand beside her. "Might be it's not elegant like a carpet, but it's serviceable, and we could make it our own selves. Wouldn't take long neither. Most everyone has old worn-out blankets or clothes and such they can give us. They can bring them to church, and when there's enough we'll get together, cut them into strips and braid them up, then sew them into a rug. If there ain't enough strips to do a big rug, we can make a long skinny one that'll stretch from the door to the sanctuary."

Goldie stuck her thumb in her mouth. Viola shoved the spools back in her purse. She could wait no longer, though she hated the thought of going outside and walking home alone. She cuddled the baby close and leaned down until her mouth was by Hattie's ear.

"I'm taking Goldie home." She picked Goldie's blanket up off the bench, tucked it around her and edged toward the door.

"A rag rug is a wonderful idea, Hattie. Everyone in the church can share in making it. Even the single men can donate their old blankets or clothes. I shall tell the congregation."

Viola stepped out into the sunshine and closed the door. "Poor, tired little baby. It's time to give you a bottle and put you down for your nap. Would you like that?" She kissed Goldie's cheek, searched the area for any men lurking about, crossed the road to the school and walked to the corner. She would come back to the church and measure the windows after Hattie came home. It would be good to have another project to work on, not that she didn't have enough sewing and mending from her customers to keep her busy. But the fabric had come quickly, and the hotel drapes would be finished in another week. And then she would have more time to think. And worry.

The dry leaves, fallen from the trees that lined her road, rustled at the brush of her long skirts, crunched beneath her feet. She looked up at the sky, blue and clear, forced her mind to pleasant wonderings. How long before snow started falling? It was odd not to know what to expect from the weather. But everyone said it got cold. She would have to make Goldie a winter coat and warm dresses. Thomas's wife and baby had died of pneumonia. Her heart stalled on the thought. Would Thomas be warm enough in his hut?

She frowned, stared down at the leaf-strewn dirt road. No matter how she tried, thoughts of Thomas still crept in. It had been a week since his departure, and it felt like only yesterday. It was as if there were a large hole… She turned onto her path, froze at sight of the strange man standing by her stoop.

"You the lady that lives here?"

His gaze dropped to Goldie, lifted back to her face. The look in his eyes made her heart lurch, start beating again. He was not from Dengler. He was another gold seeker. Perhaps the kidnapper's partner? She tightened her grip on Goldie, kept a pleasant tone in her voice. "Yes." *If only she could get by him into the house and lock the door.* "If you have mending you want done, you will have to come back tomorrow."

"I ain't got no mending. I come for my baby and my gold." He started toward her.

"Stay back!" She stepped backward onto the road.

The man stopped, scowled. "What's wrong with you, lady? All I want is what's mine." He looked at Goldie and mimed a look of sadness. "I been missin' my baby somethin' awful."

She didn't believe him for a second. Still… "Yes, it's been a while since you left her. How long ago was it?"

The scowl reappeared. "I misremember."

She nodded, shifted Goldie and inched backward under cover of the movement. "I have wondered ever since you left her with me, what is her name?"

Anger darkened his face. "I ain't here to answer questions, I'm here t' get my kid an' the gold." He took a step toward her. "If you know what's good for you, you'll give 'em to me."

She heard footsteps, the rustle of leaves behind her on the road. A friend, or his cohort? She dared not turn and look. She lifted her chin and shook her head. "Not unless you tell me her name, and describe her cradle."

"Is this man giving you trouble, Miss Goddard?"

Robert Harris!

She turned and nodded to her neighbors from across the way. "He is trying to claim Goldie is his but will not answer my questions about her."

"Gracious, another scapegrace after that baby's gold!" Evelyn Harris poked her husband's arm. "Do something, Robert!"

"He's running for the woods, Pa!" Matthew Harris pointed.

Viola whirled, saw a flash of blue disappear among the trees.

"You want me to chase after him, Pa? I bet I could run him down."

Robert Harris shook his head, placed his hand on his son's shoulder. "Not in your Sunday clothes, Matt." He glanced at her. "Do you want me to send Matt after the sheriff, Miss Goddard? I doubt it will do much good. Judging from the direction he ran, I'm sure the sluggard intends to lose himself in the horde of stampeders climbing the Chilkoot."

"No doubt. I'm sure he will be gone up the trail before Sheriff Parker could find him." Viola took a deep breath to control her trembling and gave them a grateful smile. "Thank you for stopping to help me. I was… concerned."

"You're welcome, though it's only the right thing to do. That fellow was pretty bold, but I doubt he'll return. You're safe now. Come along, son." Robert Harris took hold of his wife's elbow and started across the road.

Viola took another breath, hurried into her cabin and threw the lock on the door. Hattie would just have to knock to be let in. She crossed to the rocker and collapsed onto the seat, shaking and sobbing and holding Goldie as tight as she dared.

Thomas stared down at the wound just below his left shoulder. "So what do you think, Jacob?"

"It's healing well, Thomas. I'm going to remove these stitches today. But you must continue to be careful and limit the use of your arm. It wouldn't take much to tear this wound open again, at least on the surface. And that could present complications."

"I'll be careful." He watched the doctor swab the stitches, snip one and pull it out.

"I guess you'll be glad to get home to your hut?"

"Yes." He concentrated on the snip and pull of another stitch to block out the thought of leaving and not seeing Viola about town.

Teena Crow looked at him and smiled. "My people's hearts will be happy when you return, Thomas."

"At least a few of them." He grinned, watched her applying some sort of herbal mixture to a stampeder's burned arm. She looked back up at him, her dark eyes solemn.

"My people who come to hear about your God at Treasure Creek Church come because of the way you have led them. It is true they are few. But they are like the seeds of a plant that scatter on the wind. So they will be among my people. New plants will grow where the seeds land. You will gather those plants and tend them, that they also may grow to know your God." She went back to treating her patient.

Thomas stared at her bent head with the long, black braids hanging over her shoulders. Her words made him sound more like a pastor than a missionary.

"We whites could use a few of those seeds scattered among us, too. Right, Thomas? No matter how God-centered Mack Tanner and the rest of us try to keep Treasure Creek, men like the one who tried to claim Goldie and her gold yesterday crop up. If—"

"Someone tried to claim Goldie?" Thomas's heart slammed against his ribs. He stared at the scissors, felt as if they had pierced his heart. "Is…everyone…all right?"

"Don't tense up like that. Yes, everyone is fine." Jacob shot him a look, went back to work on the stitches. "The way I heard it, the man was waiting at her cabin when Viola went home after church. Good thing Robert Harris happened along. He chased the fellow off. Seems like

Viola could use some protection. You can't count on co-incidence saving her every time one of those thugs come around.

"There, I'm finished. You can put your shirt on now."

"What? Oh, right. Thanks, Jacob." *Thank You, Lord, for protecting Viola.* He slipped his arms into the dangling sleeves of his shirt, pulled the fabric up over his shoulders and buttoned it, his hands shaking at the thought of what could have happened. Was it the kidnapper's partner? His stomach knotted.

"Do I have to come back?"

"Not unless there's some change to the wound. But if it gets red or swollen or painful, come to see me immediately."

He nodded, stepped aside so the next man in line could take his place, dropped his payment in the bowl on the table by the scales and left the clinic.

The clamor of the waterfront rose above the murmur of voices from the throng of people crowding the board walkway. He frowned, stared out at the boat disgorging men in a steady stream. How many of them would learn about the baby and her gold and become a danger to Viola? Every fiber of his being ached to go see her, to see with his own eyes that she was safe. But it was none of his business.

He scowled, wove his way through the press of people and crossed the road to Tanner's store. A few supplies and he would be on his way home. But he couldn't muster up much enthusiasm for the idea. He glanced again at the harbor, looked up at the darkening sky. A storm was brewing. And late summer storms in this area usually rolled in fast. Most likely, he wouldn't make it to his hut before it hit. He would wait and go tomorrow. He picked up his pace, strode by Tanner's General Store and headed for the sheriff's office. Ed would know if she were in danger.

"Bye-bye, Goldie. We're going to keep you nice and safe." Frankie tickled Goldie under the chin and walked to the door. "I know the exact right pistol for you, Viola. I'll have Mack order you one. Might be they'll have one over in Skaguay. If not, it'll be some time before it gets here. I'll let you know when. And then we'll start shooting lessons. Once word gets around about it, it ought to put a stop to them potwallopers coming around trying to claim Goldie." She opened the door, stopped it with her booted foot when the wind caught it. "Looks like a storm's breaking. I'm going to have to run for it."

"You can stay." Viola braced the door against another gust of wind, peeked out to see Frankie sprinting down the road toward her cabin, leaned against the door and locked it. White light flickered through the room. Thunder rumbled.

Hattie walked over to look out the window. "Peers like this might be a nasty one. It's comin' on dark, right quick. I'll light the lamps."

Lightning sizzled through the air with a loud snap. Thunder crashed. Goldie let out a squall. "Shh, baby girl, there's nothing to be afraid of. I'll keep you safe. I promise." *I'll keep us both safe, once I have that gun.* "Shh, shh…" Viola kissed Goldie's silky, dark hair and cuddled her close, humming to soothe her. She walked to the rocker, back in its customary place in the living room, and settled herself, pushed against the floor with her feet. The rockers creaked against the wide puncheons, the chair whispered forward and back in an ageless motion of comfort. Goldie stuck her thumb in her mouth, her eyelids drifted closed. Rain tapped against the windows, drummed on the roof.

Hattie came into the room shielding a burning spill with her cupped hand, raised the chimney on the oil lamp on the mantle, lit and adjusted the wick, then turned and lit the lamp on the stand beside the settle. "You nervous 'bout learnin' how to shoot a gun?"

"A little." Viola rested her hand over Goldie's ear to deaden the sound of the storm.

"You figure a gun is gonna keep you and Goldie safe?"

She looked up at Hattie. She knew her well enough by now to know she was heading somewhere with her questions. "It will certainly help to do so, once I learn how to shoot it." *Please God, let it be soon.*

"Mmm."

"You sound doubtful."

"Some. Air's coolin' down, gonna get dampish. You want me to light the fire?"

She nodded, watched Hattie touch the burning end of the spill to the tinder beneath the logs piled on the hearth. Flames flickered, grew, set greedy tongues licking at the wood. "Won't you feel safer once I know how to use a pistol?"

Hattie shook her head, the gray wisps of hair sticking out from the bun on the back of her head fluttering. "I figure there's nothin' makes a woman as safe as a good, strong man takin' care of her."

So that was it. Thomas. Viola took a breath and lifted her chin. It was time to stop this nonsense once and for all. "That may be, Hattie. But there is no 'good, strong man' to take care of us in *this* household. Nor will there ever be. A pistol will have do."

Hattie nodded slowly, plunked down in her favorite chair and picked up her knitting. "Mayhap you're right, Viola. Then again, you could be wrong. None of us knows what the good Lord has in store for us." She looked over at her, firelight deepening the wrinkles of her aged face, a look of knowing brightening her faded blue eyes. "It ain't over yet."

Chapter Twelve

Viola stepped onto the wide stoop at Tanner's General Store and gave a polite nod to the man who lunged in front of another to open the door for her.

The dim interior buzzed with voices. Customers roamed in front of the shelves that climbed the walls, crowded past one another in the spaces between crates and barrels and tables laden with wares, formed a line at the counter to pay for their purchases. The store always put her in mind of an anthill. From morning to night it teemed with activity. She cast a sympathetic look at Danny Whitehorse and Clem Whitmore patiently answering questions while tallying orders, and stepped to the side to clear the way for those entering behind her.

A man, standing at a nearby table holding wool mittens, lined buck mitts, moccasins and heavy, woolen sweaters, looked up. His eyes widened. He gave a low whistle of appreciation, nudged the man beside him and nodded his head in her direction. She turned her back to them, edged by a group of men examining the shovels and picks leaning against the wall, and headed for the shelves that held fabrics and sewing materials. There had been no suitable cording for the hotel drapes the last time she was in, but a supply boat from Skaguay had arrived this morning and—

Her skirt snagged. She leaned down, tugged it free of the jagged sliver on a crate and straightened.

Dolph!

Her heart lurched. She stared at the back of the hefty, heavy-shouldered man ahead, who was talking with some stampeders, dropped her gaze to his broad, scarred hands. Her stomach churned. She'd know those hands anywhere. She cast a wild glance around the store, didn't see Karl or any other men who worked for Dengler, looked back at Dolph. *Had he come for her?* How had he found her? Her pulse throbbed, roared in her ears. If he turned—

She forced her frozen body to move, hid herself behind two men looking at a stack of granite buckets, and turned toward the door.

"Better get two of 'em." The taller man grabbed the bails of the two top buckets and yanked. The stack toppled over with a resounding clang. Heads swivelled their way. The men bent to pick up the buckets.

Viola jerked her face from Dolph's direction, stepped over a rolling bucket and walked to the door, feeling as if a target were pinned to her. Had he seen her? Recognized her? She didn't dare look to see if he was coming after her.

The door was pulled open. She nodded to the man holding it for her and stepped out onto the stoop, forcing herself to walk when everything in her was screaming *run!*

For the first time since coming to Treasure Creek, she was grateful for the mob of stampeders that crowded the waterfront and swarmed in and out of the businesses along the boardwalk.

She stepped into the middle of the milling throng waiting to enter Tanner's, wove her way through them to the corner, then slipped in with those walking up the dirt road. Every step was agony. Had Dolph seen her? Was Karl or Dengler somewhere hidden in the crowd, following? When she reached the hotel, she mingled with those going up the stone walk, felt a rush of relief when the door closed behind them. She would stay until she was sure—Goldie! And Hattie. If Dengler's men learned where she lived…

Bile burned in her stomach, pushed upward to her throat. She rushed down the hallway and out the back door, fear driving her. She ran to the back of the school-house, heard Matthew Powers reciting multiplication tables as she ducked beneath the window. So ordinary a thing. And her life was falling apart—or would soon end.

Don't try to run away again, Viola. The next time it won't be a beating.

She shuddered, pressed back against the building and peeked around the corner toward the road, spotted neither Dolph nor Karl. She snatched up her hems and raced across the open schoolyard to the copse of trees that spilled off the mountain to tower over the clustered cabins. Heedless of broken branches and the prickly needles of the firs, she ran a weaving path through the massive trunks and low-hanging limbs, then broke cover and darted to her cabin.

Her strength gave out when she reached the wood-pile by her back door. Her quaking legs folded. She collapsed in a heap on the ground, the tightness clamped around her chest and throat, squeezing the air from her. She tugged at the high collar of her shirtwaist, tried to breathe, felt the darkness coming and was helpless to stop it. The sunlight faded…

She opened her eyes, blinked, stared at bark, wood chips and soil. What— Memory flooded back. She shuddered, pushed herself off the ground and leaned against the woodpile. How long had she been unconscious? She looked down at the dirt and bits of dried leaves clinging to her clothes, the bloody scratch on the back of her hand. What was she going to tell Hattie? How could she explain— *Goldie.* What if Dengler and Dolph and Karl had come while she was unconscious?

She surged to her feet, braced herself against the stacked wood and took a slow breath. She had to be prepared…. Memories streamed. She closed her eyes. *Let them be all right, Lord. Please let Goldie and Hattie be all right! But if— Help me face what I must.* She tried the door. It was locked. A good sign? She fisted her hand and knocked. *Please, Lord.* She knocked again, louder. Snagged her lower lip with her teeth to hold back a sob when slow footsteps approached.

"You got business in this house, you can come to the front door and show yerself!"

They were all right! *Thank You, Lord.* Tears stung her eyes. "Hattie, it's me!"

"Viola?" The metal bar snicked free of the socket. The door opened. She pushed inside, sagged against the wall.

"Viola, what— *Gracious!*" Hattie gaped up at her. "What happened to you?"

"I felt ill, so I cut through the back lots to come home. I—I fell." All true. As far as it went.

"Well, don't stand there, go and sit before you fall down." Hattie stepped back, squinted up at her. "You look awful! Where's your snood?"

She lifted her hand, felt the curls dangling free. "It must have caught on a branch. Lock the door!"

Hattie nodded, flipped the small bar into place. "Must be a branch got your hand, too. You're bleedin'. Set down and I'll clean—"

"No. I'll do it, later. I want to see Goldie." She started for the living room.

"She's nappin'." Hattie's gaze sharpened. "Remember, you put her down before you left for Tanners. It ain't been that long."

It seemed like forever. Another shudder shook her, she couldn't seem to control them. "Is the front door locked?"

"Just like when you left. What's wrong, Viola? And don't say nothin', cause I—"

"No questions, Hattie! I—I have a headache." She rubbed her throbbing temples, felt the grit clinging to her skin. "I'm going to wash, then lie down with a cold cloth." She grabbed the quilted pad she'd made, lifted the iron teakettle off the stove and started for the small bathing room. "Don't let anyone in, Hattie." She turned back, looked at her. "No customers, not *anyone!* Do you understand?"

Hattie stared up at her, shook her head. "Not a whit, Viola. But I'll do like you say. Any fool can see there's somethin' serious wrong."

Thomas lowered his Bible and looked around the room that formed his home. No matter how much he prayed and asked God's help, he couldn't seem to concentrate since he'd come back. The cramped quarters of his hut seemed to close in on him. There was no comfort. No warmth or beauty. No comparison to Viola's cabin. He scowled and pushed the memory aside. It might be true, but it wasn't the reason for his dissatisfaction. It was the unrelenting sense of something left undone that stole his peace.

It isn't over yet.

He thrust his fingers through his hair as if he could pull the words out of his head. They *haunted* him. No matter how many times he asked God to erase them, there they were, burrowed in like a tic on a dog and sucking off his strength and energy, his enthusiasm for any other task.

He placed his Bible on the pallet where he slept and shoved out of his chair, the only one he owned, bumped his head on the bark ceiling. He couldn't even stand up straight, except right in the center of the room. He checked the fire in the small steel stove, grabbed his jacket out of the crate that held his clothes and ducked through the canvas door.

The weather didn't help his mood. His choices were limited to cramped and stuffy, or wet and windy. At least outside he could move without bumping into something. He pulled his collar up to protect his neck from the cold, misty rain, strode across the small rocky ledge, into the surrounding trees and followed his path to the Chilkoot. He could see fires, small as fireflies, flickering in the distance both above and below him in the areas where stampeders normally camped. This section of the trail, except for his small ledge and another larger but unstable ledge clinging to the mountain farther down on the other side, was too steep for camping.

He'd chosen the site for that reason. It both protected him from thieves and gave him the privacy he craved. But not tonight. Tonight he wanted company other than his own. The sound of something more than the rustle of the needles on the wind-tossed branches of the firs.

He hunched his shoulders against the wind and stepped out of the protection of the trees, onto the trail, and started the descent to the stampeders camping below. Maybe one of them needed to hear about the Lord. Maybe— He paused as he rounded the sharp curve, listened to the voices carried on the wind, faint but… Someone was in trouble! He crowded the side of the mountain where the trail was less trod and his boots had more grip, and broke into a trot.

"Halt"—the wind stole words—"break"—another gust blew more words away—"neck!"

Ed Parker. Thomas skidded on some loose stone, caught hold of a boulder to gain his balance and ran on. Two figures stood at the outer edge of the trail, heads bent down. Ed and Mack. He slowed, trotted over to them. "Is there a problem? Can I be of help?"

Ed Parker threw him a sour look. "Not unless you know some way to get sense into a drunken thief bent on getting himself killed. Fool thinks he's a mountain goat."

Thomas moved closer, spotted the man slipping and sliding down the mountainside from boulder to boulder. "You there! Stop! Stay where you are! That ledge below you is unsafe!"

The man shouted something the wind snatched away, kept jumping and sliding from one boulder to another, slid onto the ledge.

Thomas turned back toward the trail. "I'll go get a

rope. We're going to need one. Don't try to go onto that ledge to get him, Ed. It's nothing but a clump of soil hanging there, held together by roots."

Mack cupped his hands around his mouth, leaned forward. "Get back from the edge! Get back! It's not safe!"

"You—"

A scream split the night air. The wind whipped it away, left only silence.

Lord, have mercy. Thomas pivoted back, looked over the edge. The outer rim of the ledge had fallen away, become only a dark smudge of soil scattered among the rocks and boulders beneath it. There was no sign of the man...or of his body.

"Another one. How many lives will this lust for gold claim?" Mack Tanner shoved his hands in his pockets, hunched his shoulders and turned away. "What a waste. And this one died for gold that isn't even there. Why won't they *believe* me that I have no gold buried?" He looked back over the rim of the hill. "The poor fool gave his life for a treasure that no longer exists. I used my gold to buy land. Now there is only the deed to that land and the note I wrote in the box. Even so, it's led to more harm than it could ever do good. I wish I'd never buried that treasure in the first place!"

"Don't go taking on blame for that fellow's death, Mack." Ed Parker frowned, stepped back from the edge of the cliff. "It was his thieving ways that killed him. If he wasn't trying to dig up your treasure, it would have been something else."

"Even so..."

"Ed's right, Mack." Thomas laid a hand on Mack's shoulder. "You can't take on the blame for something you can't control. And as for that deed you've buried, some day someone will need that land and the blessing of the note, and with your faith and prayers behind it, I'm sure the Lord will have the right person find it."

Viola stared into the darkness of her bedroom, listening to the normal night sounds. With every creak of a tree branch, every crackle and snap of the fire in the living room, her heart jolted. Sleep was impossible.

She slipped out of bed, shrugged into her robe and pulled on her slippers. Goldie made a soft baby sound, stuck her thumb in her mouth and sucked. She bent down and tucked the blanket more securely around small baby shoulders.

Please take care of her... I know I can trust you.

The knots in her stomach twisted tighter. Whoever Goldie's father was…whatever his reason for writing those words in the note he had left with her, he was wrong. Leaving his baby in her care had placed her in danger. If Dengler…

She swallowed hard, walked into the living room, crossed to the windows and slipped the curtains out of their ties to cover the windows. She wanted no one peering into her home from the dusky August night. She shivered, moved to the fireplace and added wood to the low-burning fire. Flames licked at the new fuel. Firelight flickered through the darkened room.

She rose, wrapped her arms about herself and glanced at the empty settle, listened to Hattie snoring in her bedroom—felt hollow and frightened and sick and alone. She wanted Thomas. Everything in her was crying out for him. She wanted to look into his eyes and see the caring, hear him chuckle, feel the strength of his hand holding hers, the comfort of his presence. She wanted *him*. But it could never be. Never. She could bear anything but that Thomas learn what she was.

Or that Hattie and Goldie should be harmed because of her.

She sank to her knees on the hearth, hunched her shoulders and buried her face in her hands.

Chapter Thirteen

Viola hurried up the stone steps to the wide stoop and reached for the doorknob, paused at the sound of hammering from within. Her lungs emptied in a long sigh. Frankie and her sisters were hard at work. She would not be alone in the church. *Thank You, Lord.* She glanced around, saw no one following her, arranged her features in a mask that hid her fear and opened the door.

"Watch you don't trip over that pile of lumber on the floor." The end of the board Frankie Tucker was sawing fell off with a thud. She leaned the saw against the sawhorse leg and looked up. A smile warmed her face. "Hey, Viola. Come to pretty up the windows?"

"I'm going to make a start at it. As soon as I can see." She blinked her eyes to adjust to the dimmer light after the sunshine of outdoors. "I'm here to measure the windows." She glanced at Lucy and Margie, busy pounding nails into a board that stretched from the floor to the ceiling. "Will I be in your way?"

Frankie grinned, shook her head. "Nah, if we get close before you're done, we'll either work around you or board you up into the wall." Her sisters laughed. Frankie lifted the board off the sawhorse, swung it around and leaned it against the wall next to where they were working. "Here's your next board."

Viola stared at the three sisters, trying hard not to envy them. They laughed and teased each other—and everyone else—with such raucous abandon. They were so carefree while she... The knots that had become a permanent part of her stomach twisted tighter. She stepped around the pile of lumber and headed for the nearest window, took her measurements, then looked around. "I have to measure the bench and the collections table, too. Where are they?"

"We carried them into the sanctuary, out of our way." Frankie lifted a board from the pile to the sawhorses, measured and marked it. "They're bigger than the windows. You need my measure?"

"No, my sewing tape will work fine." She took a breath, forced a casual tone into her voice. "Have you heard anything about my pistol, Frankie?"

"Danny Whitehorse ordered it from Seattle." The saw bit into the wood, slid down, chattered back and slid forward again. "Says it should be here in a few days." Frankie halted her work and looked up, her eyes agleam with interest. "Is someone giving you trouble, Viola?"

"No." She shook her head, smiled. "I was simply wondering when my shooting lessons would start."

"Quick as the pistol comes in to Tanner's, I'll bring it over and we'll get started."

She nodded, looked away. Frankie's law enforcement yearnings were showing in the suspicious look she was giving her. "I'd best get back to work, I want to be home before Goldie wakes from her nap." She stepped into the sanctuary, measured the bench and turned to the table.

"Hey, Mack… Preacher. Come to look over our work?"

Frankie's words stilled her hands. Preacher?

"I've come to admire it, that steeple tower is a work of art."

Thomas. She pressed back against the wall, closed her eyes. There was no way to avoid seeing him; and somehow he always knew when she was upset or…

"It is indeed. But the best part is that it stands high above every other building, so it is the first thing seen by those coming in on the boats from Skaguay. It announces to all arrivals, lawless or Christian, that Treasure Creek is a God-centered town." Triumph rang in Mack Tanner's voice. "Once this room is finished and the bell I've ordered arrives and is hung, this church will be complete. Except for an ordained pastor in its pulpit. But I'm working on that."

She opened her eyes, peered around the doorway and saw Mack Tanner smile and clap Thomas on the back. Thomas smiled, lifted both hands, palms out, in a "not me" gesture and glanced her way.

She instinctively ducked back, but there was no hiding now. She grabbed up her tape, wound it around two fingers as she walked back into the entrance. "My work here is done. It's time I get home to Goldie." She stopped, smiled. "Hello, Mr. Tanner." She met Thomas's gaze and gave a polite nod. "Hello, Thomas." She looked down at his left arm, covered by his shirt sleeve, and forced a smile. "I see you are able to use your arm now."

"Yes. In a very limited way. Jacob still cautions about

the danger of injuring it again." His gaze caught hers, held it. "How have you been, Viola?"

"I'm…busy." She included everyone in a sweeping glance. "If you will all excuse me…." She moved to the door, couldn't stop herself from stealing one more look at him. "Hattie will be pleased to hear you are continuing to heal well, Thomas." She turned and hurried outside, rushed to the corner and turned down the road toward her cabin, tears flooding her eyes, blurring her vision.

"Hello, there, Miss Goddard."

She jolted, looked up. Zeke Jefferson was coming out of her door, a package under his arm. She took a deep breath, squared her shoulders.

"Hattie gave me my mending. I left my payment on the table."

"That's fine, Mr. Jefferson." She glanced at the trees crowding the end of her cabin, at the darkness beneath them where a man could easily hide. Two steps and—

"I'm leaving for Dawson City tomorrow. I've heard of some new fields opening up, and I'm going to try and find some of that gold everyone is talking about." He gave her a warm smile. "Wish me luck, Miss Goddard."

A faint whimpering floated out of the partially open door behind him, then nothing. Hattie must be soothing Goldie back to sleep. She would have to speak with her again about keeping the door locked.

"If I find gold, when I get back I'll buy you one of the fancy brooches they have in the store at Skaguay." Zeke Jefferson's voice had lowered, turned husky. "Or a necklace or bracelet. Or whatever—"

She stiffened at the look in his eyes, gave him a cold

look. "You can keep your gold and your jewelry, Mr. Jefferson. And from now on you can take your mending needs elsewhere."

He flushed. "I meant no insult, Miss Goddard. I only—" He pressed his lips closed, gave a polite nod and stepped off the stoop.

She turned, watched him stalk off up the road, then stepped up onto the stoop, pushed open the door and stepped inside. Home. She released her tension in a long sigh, placed her purse on the table and turned to close and lock the door and…looked into the face of her fear.

"Hello, Viola."

Dengler. Cold washed over her. Everything went black. She blinked, took a breath, came to herself and shoved the door. It didn't move.

"Now is that any way to treat your boss?" Richard Dengler moved his foot.

The door shoved open.

She staggered back as it hit her, bit back a cry. Dolph followed Dengler inside, wearing the smile that meant he was anticipating the pleasure of inflicting pain on someone.

Bile swirled in her stomach, pushed at her throat. She clenched her hands, dug her fingernails into her palms to fend off the fear, stiffened her quivering legs and squared her shoulders. "You are no longer my boss. Get out of my house."

Dengler's hand flashed forward. The crack as it met her cheek sounded like a gunshot. Her head snapped back and to the side. Lights exploded in front of her eyes. She reeled back, planted her feet to stay erect.

"I'm your boss until you're of no further use to me

or my customers, Viola. Now let's talk about the money you stole from me."

That cold, soft voice. He never raised his voice. Not even when— *Don't think about it. Don't show fear!* She lifted her chin. "I only took the wages you promised and never paid me. I wouldn't take a penny of your money. I want nothing from you."

Dolph fisted his hands, stepped close.

Her heart thudded so hard it shook her, but she refused to cower. It was what he wanted. What he loved.

Dengler raised his hand. "Not yet, Dolph. She has some questions to answer first." His eyes narrowed. "I want that money, Viola. Where is it?"

She looked into his cold face and knew he wasn't after the money. He had come to punish and kill her, just as he said he would if she ran away again. *Lord, let Hattie be quiet, and Goldie stay asleep. Keep them safe!* She braced herself to face the inevitable. If she made him angry, perhaps it would be over with quickly. "I don't have the money. And I wouldn't give it to you if I did. I earned every bit of that money. It was mine, not yours."

His hand flashed again. She rocked back, tasted the blood that spurted from a split on the inside of her cheek. Her knees sagged, she locked them, staved off the blackness. So it was to be a beating first.

"The baby's gold will do, Viola. Where is it?"

He knew about Goldie! Bile surged. She swallowed it back, raised her hand to her stinging, swelling cheek to gain time. *Think! Get them out of here, away from—*

"Get the baby, Dolph."

"No!" She whirled, ran to bar her bedroom door. "Leave the baby alone! I'll give you the gold. But it's

not here. It's—" Dolph's hands clamped on her arms, squeezed as he lifted her and tossed her aside. She slammed against the wall, shook her head, fought for breath and the strength to stand.

"The kid's not here. The cradle's empty."

Where was Goldie? Oh, God, keep her safe! She snagged her lower lip to hold back the sobs.

"Check the other rooms."

She turned her head, blinked to clear her vision. Hattie's room was empty. *The kitchen.* She pressed her palms against the wall and inched toward the kitchen doorway. If she could reach a knife… Dolph caught her by the shoulder, shoved her aside and walked into the kitchen, came out and shook his head.

"No one there."

The coarse, gruff words brought joy surging through her. *Hattie must have heard and taken Goldie away! Thank—*

"Well, it seems you will just have to come back to work for me, Viola." Dengler stepped close to her and smiled. "It won't take you long to earn the money to pay me back. You were always a favorite among my customers. And there are so many men clamoring for satisfaction in Skaguay, I haven't girls enough to answer their nee—"

"She's not going anywhere with you."

Thomas! Her heart jolted. She whirled.

Dengler grabbed her arm, looked at Dolph and jerked his thumb toward the partially open front door. "Take care of him."

Dolph nodded, stepped forward.

"No!" She clutched hold of Dolph's jacket. *"Run, Thom—"* The slap slammed her head back against

the wall. Bursts of light rushed toward her. Her knees buckled.

"Viola!"

Thomas's cry scattered the encroaching darkness. She forced her eyes open, pushed against the wall, saw Dolph grab for Thomas. Her heart seized. Her body froze. Thomas dodged, shoved the door into Dolph, sent him reeling back and leaped toward him. The henchman let out a snarl, lowered his head and charged.

Her limbs twitched back to life. She shoved off the wall.

Dengler grabbed her hair, jerked her back. Tears smarted her eyes. She blinked them away to see Thomas smashed up against the wall, Dolph's fisted hand driving toward him. Thomas ducked, drove a fist into Dolph's stomach. Dolph doubled over and Thomas drove his knee up under his chin. Dolph slumped forward, slid into a sprawl on the floor. Thomas flopped him onto his back, yanked the gun from his belt.

Dengler's arm clamped around her neck, pulled her back against him. "Drop the gun and get out, or I'll kill you!" He lifted the gun in his other hand into her line of sight. "Tell him, Viola." His arm pressed tighter against her throat, then loosened a bit.

"Do it, Thomas! Please!" She croaked out the words, gasped for air. "Please go. He means it! He'll kill yo—" Dengler's arm jerked, shut off her air.

Thomas straightened, looked beyond her to Dengler. "I'm not going anywhere. And neither are you, Viola."

His voice was quiet, calm, his hand holding the gun steady. *She had to do something! Make him leave.* She clawed at Dengler's arm, fought to breathe, to think.

His arm tightened. Her ears buzzed, her sight faded. Darkness hovered.

"Would you rather see *her* dead?"

The words echoed through the fuzziness in her head. *Dead…*soon… The darkness came closer. Cold washed over her.

Thunk!

Dengler jolted, slumped against her. She collapsed beneath his weight, crashed to the floor.

"Looks like I got here just in time." Frankie Tucker dropped a long, thick piece of branch to the floor, stepped over Dengler's legs, grabbed hold of his suit coat and rolled him off her. "You all right, Viola?"

She nodded, sucked in air. The darkness receded.

Frankie rolled Dengler over onto his stomach, scooped up the gun beneath him.

Viola pushed to her hands and knees, grabbed hold of the end of the settle and hauled herself to the seat. Her head reeled. Her body shook. She took a slow, deep breath, fought to hold back the churning bile.

"Looks like things are under control here."

She lifted her head, turned. The sheriff stood in the front doorway, his gun held ready in his huge hand.

"Sorry it took me so long to get here, Viola. Hattie had to hunt me down." He looked down at Dengler sprawled on the floor at her feet. "Guess it's a good thing she found Frankie first." He looked down at Dolph. "You, too, Thomas."

"She didn't find me. I came on my own."

The tone of his voice said clearer than words he had come because he had been concerned and wanted to be sure she was all right. *But no more.* Her control shattered. She hung her head, caught her breath, held it to hold back the sobs.

Dolph groaned. She saw him twitch, flinched back against the settle. Ed Parker placed a knee on Dolph's back, shoved his gun back into its holster and pulled two long, leather thongs from his pocket. "You hogtie that one, Frankie." He tossed her one of the thongs, grabbed Dolph's hands and wound the other thong around his crossed wrists. "These varmints after Goldie's gold?"

She braced herself, drew breath to answer.

"I heard it mentioned."

Thomas's words were terse, his tone strained. Shame flooded her. He knew what she was.

"Viola's a prostitu—"

Frankie's knee banged down onto the back of Dengler's neck, shoved his face to the floor. "You'd best shut your lying mouth, lest you want me to knock you on the head again!"

Viola closed her eyes, gathered every ounce of courage she possessed. This had gone far enough. She raised a trembling hand, wiped away the blood pooling at the corner of her mouth. "Let him speak, Frankie. The sheriff has to know the truth." The words came thick and slurred from her split and swollen lips, sounded as dead as her hopes and dreams.

"Viola's in no condition to answer questions, Ed. Can't this wait until tomorrow?"

The caring in Thomas's voice brought tears surging to her eyes, clogging her throat.

"Don't see any reason why not. I'll just take these thugs off to jail for tonight and—"

"Must be Viola's been plying her trade, boss." Dolph sneered up at Ed as he hauled him to his feet. "No one cares about a piece of trash prostitute, except one of her customers."

"A pros—a lady of the evening!" Evelyn Harris gasped, gaped at her from the doorway. "And to think I heard the commotion and came to see if I could help!" She lifted her nose into the air and shifted her gaze to Ed Parker. "I expect you will do your job, Sheriff. Treasure Creek is a God-centered town with no place for the likes of her!" She whirled and hurried outside.

Viola rose, stared after her neighbor, her head reeling. Frankie's hand touched her arm. She looked into her friend's angry blue eyes.

"Don't pay her no mind, Viola." A scowl knit the freckles on Frankie's nose together. "I've a good mind to wallop Evelyn upside her head, too. Might knock some sense into her."

"Not a good idea, Frankie." Ed Parker, growled the words, looked in their direction, skimmed over her and focused on Frankie. "I'd have to arrest you for that. And I need your help to get these two to jail." He nodded toward Dengler, still prone on the floor. "Can you manage that one?"

Frankie's face lit like a candle. "Watch me!" She straddled Dengler, leaned down and grabbed hold of the back of his collar and yanked him up onto his knees, stepped back and tugged his gun from where she'd shoved it in her belt. "Now get on your feet and get moving, you no good piece of garbage woman beater!"

Dengler struggled to his feet, looked her way and started to speak. Frankie raised the gun. He clamped his mouth shut and staggered toward the door, Frankie prodding him along. Ed Parker shoved Dolph into line behind them as they left the cabin.

Silence. So thick it pressed against her shivering body, hurt her throbbing temples. How long had it been since Dengler came? A matter of minutes only, yet it felt like forever. She tried not to, but she couldn't stop herself. She had to look at Thomas, store up one more memory against a lonely forever. She turned, caught her breath at the sight of blood staining his shirt. "Your *shoulder.*" She forced her shaking legs to carry her to him. "Let me—"

He caught her hand, set it away from him. "I'm no longer needed here. I'll go to the clinic. Jacob or Teena will tend it." He pivoted, laid Dolph's gun on the table and walked out the door.

Chapter Fourteen

Thomas sat on the edge of the table and concentrated on the knot in the floorboard beneath his dangling feet. If he looked at the dark shape right, it looked like a dog's head. And it kept him from thinking. *Viola a prostitute.* He clenched his hands until the knuckles turned white. Sucked in to replace the air fury squeezed from his lungs.

"Hold still." Jacob Calloway wiped at the blood on his shoulder and scowled. "I told you to be careful. How did this happen?"

Thomas glanced at his gaping wound and shrugged, winced at the pain that shot through his shoulder and down his arm from the movement. "An altercation."

Jacob's scowl deepened. "Don't you know missionaries aren't supposed to get into fistfights?"

Viola's cut and swollen face flashed before him. "Sometimes they're unavoidable." He clenched his hands on the edge of the table in spite of the pain it caused, wished it were Dengler's neck. Great thought for a preacher.

Jacob uncorked a bottle, splashed liquid over gauze

pads and suturing equipment in a bowl. "Did you win?"

"The fight, yes." The battle to conquer the rage in his heart, no. He'd wanted to beat Dengler and Dolph senseless. Still did.

It won't take you long to earn the money to pay me back. You were always a favorite among my customers. And there are so many men clamoring for satisfaction in Skaguay I haven't girls enough to answer their need.

He clenched his hands tighter, dug his fingernails into the underside of the wood table. He'd known Viola was hiding something, had offered to help. But he'd never thought she— *You were always a favorite among my customers.* His stomach churned, knotted. All those men…

"What's that mean?"

Thomas gave him a sour look. "It means I'm in a foul mood."

Teena carried a tray of bandaging material to the table, looked up at him. "I think it means you have pain in your heart."

Did the woman sense *everything?* He took a breath and made an effort to get his boiling emotions under control.

"Well, he's going to have pain in this shoulder for sure." Jacob held his hands over another bowl, rubbed them together as Teena poured liquid from the bottle over them. "I can't say what damage you've done yet, Thomas. But judging from your pain on moving your arm, I would say it's extensive. You're going to have to stay in town again until it's healed. And that may take quite some time. I hope whatever you were fighting over was worth it."

Thomas glanced at the people waiting for treatment and clamped his jaw to keep from spewing out the whole story. Evelyn Harris would spread the news about Viola soon enough, and the malicious gossip would start. She would be so hurt....

He shoved away the thought and stared down at the knot on the floor to erase the image of the hurt in her eyes when he'd turned away from her. Now all he needed was something that would erase her from his heart.

She couldn't stop shaking. Or thinking. Oh, if only she could stop *thinking*. She winced, sucked in a breath.

"Sorry, Viola. That cut's a deep one. But the dried blood's cleaned off now." Hattie dropped the cloth into the basin of water and picked up the jar of salve.

"Unhh—" Viola bit off the moan, clenched her hands, and sat unflinching as Hattie spread the salve on the gash at the hairline of her temple.

"Mayhap you should go to the clinic an' see Doc Calloway. This one might need stitches."

"No. I'll be fine. I've had worse." She shuddered, rubbed at the scar on the edge of her hand below her little finger. She would heal, and a jagged scar was better than exposing her swollen cheek and split, swollen lips to the stares of the crowd of people waiting to be treated at the clinic. With hundreds of stampeders passing through town daily, on their way to and from the gold fields, the place was always busy to overflowing, even in the evening.

And Thomas might be there still. He had witnessed

enough of her past life tonight to make him turn from her. She could not bear to suffer his rejection again. Tears stung her eyes. She blinked them away.

"Which one of them give you that? Dengler or Dolph?"

She looked up. Hattie nodded toward the scar she was massaging. "It was Dengler. The second time I ran away." Her throat tightened.

"Second time, huh?" Hattie squeezed water out of the cloth, dabbed at the split skin along her jaw. "I'm guessin' that ain't all he give you."

"No." She tried to hold back the shudder, failed.

"You must have been awful valuable to him, Viola. A woman beautiful as you would be a real moneymaker." Hattie dropped the cloth back in the basin and dipped her knobby, arthritic finger in the salve. "I never had that problem. First off, I worked for a 'madam'—not that she didn't slap her girls around when they got out of line. But I was always one of the last ones chosen—'cept when my regulars come in. So she pretty much left me alone."

The shock traveled in small, tingling spurts all the way to her toes. Sore as it was, her mouth gaped open. "You were a prostitute?"

"Yep. Twenty-some years. Hold still." Hattie applied more salve, frowned. "Can't do nothin' 'bout them splits in your lips. Best thing will be to hold somethin' cold on them. It'll help the swellin' some, too. Good thing the good Lord gives us ice year round up here." She put the cover on the salve, snapped the bale in place and padded across the room, her moccasins whispering against the puncheon floor.

Viola turned on her chair, watched Hattie kneel down

in front of the hutch that held their dishes and flatware and lift out the two short, wide, floorboards covering the hole where they cached their perishable foods. Hattie…a *lady of the evening*. No wonder she had taken Goldie and slipped out the back door to get help when Dengler pushed his way into the house. She understood about men like Dengler and Dolph. Who ever would have guessed? Hattie was a wonderful Christian woman. One of the staunchest she'd ever met.

Hattie's chubby, flannel-covered arm jerked up and down. She listened to the *thwack…thwack…thwack* of the hatchet biting into the ice that was always beneath the cabin and tried to comprehend what seemed, to her, impossible. She now understood why Hattie was so… accepting and nonjudgmental in the face of all that had happened. But what had happened to Hattie? How had she changed her life?

She turned back to the table as Hattie covered the hole and returned carrying a few, small chunks of ice— fought the desire to ask questions. Hattie's past was none of her business. But the questions were quivering on her tongue, the need to know what had happened to change Hattie burning in her heart. And Hattie must have brought it up for a purpose. Hattie always had a purpose. She sighed and gave in. She was too battered and exhausted to fight her need to know. "Did you run away, too?"

"Me? No." Hattie squeezed the water from the cloth, smoothed it out on the table then folded the ice chunks in it. "Here hold this on your mouth. The left side's worst."

She lifted the cloth to her face, winced as it touched her swollen cheek and mouth. "What happened? How did you leave?" The words were thick and slurred. It was hard to form them correctly with her lips so distended and painful.

"Charley." Hattie picked up the washbowl, padded across the room and dumped the bloody water into the bucket beneath the dry sink. She swished clean water around in the bowl, dumped it out and carried the bucket to the back door.

Viola's breath caught. "Don't open the door!" Her stomach roiled. She braced against the chair, ready to leap to her feet.

"Not going to." Hattie shot her a sympathetic look. "I'm just settin' the bucket here 'til mornin'."

"Oh. I—I should have realized." She moved the pad of ice a little higher to ease the throbbing in her temples. "I'm sorry for yelling, Hattie. I'm…nervous." Should she tell her about Karl? No, she would not burden her with that knowledge. She'd been through enough tonight.

"You got a right to be. A good hot cup of tea might soothe you some." The iron teakettle clanked against the stove. "Like I said, I never was real pretty, and I was gettin' older and bigger." Hattie patted her round hips and plunked down into the chair opposite her. "More and more of the customers were passin' me over. Truth is, I was gettin' a mite worried 'bout what I would do when I couldn't ply my trade. And then Charley came in."

There was a smile in Hattie's voice. She searched the elderly woman's face. Yes, she definitely had a purpose.

"He looked over all them pretty young girls, doffed his hat, walked up to me and smiled. On our third time together he asked me would I marry him." Hattie fixed a sober gaze on her. "I wasn't never sorry I said yes. We said our vows in a church and then kept goin' back. Charley turned into a good Christian man, and he never once threw up my past to me."

A good Christian man. Thomas. Thomas was Hattie's purpose. But that could never be. Thomas was a man of God, called to lead others to the Lord. She had never hoped for a future with him. Not even after—after she knew she cared for him. Her past would destroy his ministry. But she had so wanted to have his…regard. The ache that crushed her heart was worse than all the pain in her body. She swallowed back a rush of tears and moved the cloth higher on her throbbing temple.

Sewing was impossible. So was sleep. And prayer. Prayer? What was the use?

Viola wrapped her sore arms around her aching ribs, turned from the window and resumed her pacing. Obviously, she did not know how to recognize God's answers to prayer. She stopped, stared at the sampler she had worked: "With men it is impossible, but not with God, for with God all things are possible." She had been so certain—and so wrong. If God had wanted her to come to Treasure Creek and start a new life, why would He have let Dengler find her? Why would He let everything she had so carefully built be destroyed? And it would be.

She turned from the sampler, looked around the living room, walked to her bedroom door. This small log cabin was her home. She had bought it with money she had earned working in Dengler's "house." And now she would lose it because she had been a harlot. *I expect you will do your job, Sheriff. Treasure Creek is a God-centered town with no place for the likes of her!*

She put her hand on her stomach, took a deep breath to ease the nausea. Evelyn Harris was a terrible gossip. By tomorrow night every member of the church, every citizen of Treasure Creek, would know about her past. Over and over again, on the face of every person she knew, she would see the disgust, the judgment that found her guilty and the cold distance it created. And she would have to face the hurt and rejection she had seen in Thomas's eyes.

Tears welled, overflowed and slipped down her cheeks, stung the cuts on her face. She could not blame Evelyn Harris for wanting the sheriff to throw her out of town. It was clear she did not belong in a God-centered town like Treasure Creek. But what of Goldie? What if her father returned and found his baby gone? And what of Hattie? Where would Hattie live? Who would feed and shelter her?

The tears flowed faster, sobs built to a pressure in her chest she could not contain. She sank down onto the side of her bed, snatched a pillow and, heedless of the pain, pressed it to her face to cover the sounds of her breaking heart. She had tried so hard to be good. Tried so hard to live a godly life since leaving Seattle. She wanted so much to be clean, to be free of the horrible stigma of her past. "Oh, God, I am so sorry. So sorry for what I have been…for what I have done. Please, *please* forgive me. And please show me what to do. Help me. I don't know what to do."

Thomas moved slowly through the darkness under the trees, brushing aside branches with his good arm, turning sideways and inching forward in tight spots to protect his injured shoulder. Exhaustion from the day's events and the loss of blood dragged at him. But there was no question of sleep for him tonight. Not when there was a possibility Dengler may have more than one man like Dolph with him. They wouldn't answer when Ed questioned them about that. Dengler and Dolph had only smiled.

His hands flexed at the memory. He'd wanted to rip the smirks right off their faces! Satisfied that there was no one lurking in the woods, he stepped into a small clear area and glanced at Viola's cabin. No good. He needed to find a spot where he would have an unobstructed view of both the front and back doors. He moved on through the copse, feeling his way through the gloomy light, his mood at one with the darkness that surrounded him.

He bumped into a low-hanging branch of a fir tree, ducked to go under it and found the perfect place. The fir made a triangle with the two doors, and the feathery branches would hide him from the sight of anyone approaching the cabin. He shivered, pulled the collar of his jacket up around his neck, and sat, leaning his back against the trunk of the tree in as comfortable a position as the pain in his shoulder would allow. The weight of the pistol in his right pocket skewed the bottom of his jacket sideways. He tugged the jacket into place and pulled his knees up, letting the pistol rest in the V his body formed.

His shoulder throbbed, his arm ached. He stared through the branches at the cabin. The windows were dark. Was Viola able to sleep? Or was she in too much pain? His muscles twitched with the desire to go to her, to hold her and comfort her. His heart hurt with the desire to have her safe in his arms. But that was never to be. Love had never been a possibility between them because of his commitment to the Tlingits. And it was out of the question now. But he would still watch over her. No matter what she was, she didn't deserve to be beaten.

You're going to have to stay in town again until it's healed. And that may take quite some time.

He sucked in air, expelled it. Did it again. What did it all mean? Everything that had happened—his finding that injured miner and bringing him to the clinic the day Goldie was kidnapped; Viola running into him when she was looking for Mack Tanner; his being wounded and forced to stay in her cabin and accept her care; the uneasiness that had sent him to her cabin tonight and now this new injury to his wound that would keep him in town again. Was it all coincidence? Was it all so that he was here tonight to protect her? What did it mean?

He scrubbed his hand through his hair, glanced up through the branches to the purple and gold midnight sky, then again fastened his gaze on Viola's cabin. Every time he went back to his work with the Indians and the miners, something brought him back to Treasure Creek. Was God leading him onto a new path? Or was it all for Viola's sake? What if he hadn't been here tonight?

He took a breath, shoved his hand in his pocket and clasped the grip of the pistol.

Viola a prostitute.

The acrid churning in his gut started all over again.

Chapter Fifteen

"**I** did not steal any money from Richard Dengler, Sheriff." Viola formed her words as best she could. Her lips had become more swollen, her bruised facial muscles stiffer overnight. She ignored the pain in her ribs, kept her back straight and refused to look away, lest Ed Parker think her reluctance to meet his steady gaze was caused by guilt, not shame. "He never paid me the… wages…he promised me. Not in five years." She took a breath, kept her head high despite the roiling sourness in her stomach. "I took the money owed me when I left. Not a penny more. I want nothing from that man."

Ed Parker nodded, frowned. "Did he ask about Goldie's gold?"

"Yes. When I told him I did not have the money he accused me of stealing, he said he would take Goldie's gold in place of it."

"Did he threaten Goldie?"

She clenched her hands, massaged the scar and waited for the tautness in her throat to ease. "He told Dolph to get her. I tried to bar his way. I told him to leave Goldie alone, that I would give him the gold, but it wasn't here."

"That when he did that to you?" He fastened his eyes on her face, dipped his head.

"Dolph? Yes. He…threw me against the wall." The bands around her chest and throat tightened. The old feeling of suffocating made her heart pound. She tried to breathe normally. "Dengler had already…hit me. They both hit me again…later."

"When you tried to warn Thomas to run?"

She nodded, blinked to hide the tears stinging her eyes. "Yes. And when I…tried to stop Dolph from… going into the kitchen."

"You thought Hattie and Goldie were hiding in there?"

She nodded again, tugged at the collar of her dress, managed a shallow breath, then another.

"Well, that all fits with what Hattie, Thomas and Frankie told me. And that's enough for me to have those plug-uglies locked up over to Skaguay for quite a while. And when their time's done there, I'll personally see to it they're put on a ship back to Seattle. And the mayor and I will let the ferry and supply boat captains know they're never to give them passage to Treasure Creek again— lest they want their boats barred from our harbor. We don't need Dengler's kind hanging around our town." He hesitated, turned his hat in his hands, then looked down at her. "I got one more question. Has Dengler got any more men like Dolph working for him, or is he the only one?"

The sourness swirled upward, pushed at her throat. She shuddered, rubbed her palms on her skirt. "Karl. Karl and Dolph usually…work together."

"What's this Karl look like? He as big as Dolph?"

"No." She closed her eyes, fought to control the shivers shaking her. "He's a small, wiry man with dark hair and a scar on the back of his left hand. He…he likes to use a knife."

The sheriff rose, his giant frame towering over her. "You're a brave woman, Viola, trying to protect Hattie and the baby and Thomas like that. Special when you knew what it would cost you. You've got my word you won't ever have to worry about them two coming around again. And I'll be looking around for Karl. He won't be any too pleased if I find him skulking around our town."

She looked up at him and nodded. Perhaps he would find Karl and she wouldn't have to be so afraid.

He slapped his hat on and walked out the door.

She rose, hurried over to throw the lock in place then headed for the kitchen, froze. He had called her brave. And not once—not *once*—had he condemned her for what she had been.

"Send whoever it is away, Hattie." Viola winced, raised her hand to cup her jaw. She was in no condition to face anyone. Not that she would be able to hide from their censure for long. But she hoped to avoid any confrontation until her face was back to normal and she could speak properly.

"Who's there?" Hattie dipped her head, listened, then threw back the lock and opened the door.

"Hattie!" Viola jumped to her feet and hurried to the kitchen to hide. Footsteps, too quick and light to be Hattie's, sounded behind her. She stiffened her spine, turned.

Teena stepped into the doorway and stopped. Sunlight

from the window gleamed on her long black braids, the strings of colored beads dangling from her ears. "I heard."

Thomas. Her stomach sank. Viola rubbed her palms against her long skirt, feeling betrayed. Not that she had any right to. "Thomas told you?"

Teena's long braids swung side to side. "No. Though when Jacob was tending him I knew his heart wanted to speak." Her dark eyes warmed with compassion. "Many are talking. Some with cruel words and mean spirits, others with kind words and good hearts." She moved forward, set the basket she carried on the table. "I have come to help. There are plants and leaves that will take away the swelling and heal the cuts so they will not leave a mark."

Viola swallowed back the tears that were choking her throat. She had expected judgment, not this kindness. She drew a breath to steady her voice. "If you could…" She looked toward the living room, waited until she got control. "Goldie is afraid of me."

"Her heart is too young to understand." Teena looked down and began unloading her basket. "I will need hot water."

She nodded, pulled the teapot forward over the coals in the stove and turned to the table. Teena had set her empty basket aside and was taking herbs out of small leather bags and placing them in a bowl.

She reached out and touched one of the bags. "These are the same as the miners use to hold their gold."

"Yes." Teena took some larger leaves from one of the bags and held them in her palm. "This is my gold." The leaves went into a tall, narrow crock. "Gold sometimes makes men do cruel, hurtful things to others. But my gold is only for healing. You will see." She crushed the herb mixture with her fingers. A pungent aroma filled the kitchen. "These will take away the soreness and swelling and help the cuts to heal. This will make them hold on." She uncorked a bottle, poured in a bit of thick liquid and stirred the mixture with her finger. "You will please sit down and look up at me."

Teena's touch was quick and gentle. Even so, pain pulsed in the swollen flesh and cuts on her face. She tried to concentrate on what Teena was doing, but the question that had sprung to her lips when Teena arrived would not be denied. "I was wondering about Thomas. Is he all right? His shoulder, I mean."

Teena glanced at her, then picked up a pair of scissors and snipped a small piece of gauze bandaging material off a roll. "The muscle in his shoulder was injured again. But it will mend when time passes." The bandage was gently placed over the herbal paste covering the deep gash at her temple. Teena lifted the steaming teapot, poured the hot water onto the leaves in the tall, narrow crock, then cut another piece of bandage and applied it over the herb-plastered cut on her jaw. "It is Thomas's heart that bears the deepest pain. I think your heart carries the pain, also."

She caught her breath, looked up and met Teena's soft, compassionate gaze.

"I do not know of any herbs for that pain." Teena touched her swollen, split lips with the herbal paste. "Your cuts I can heal. Thomas's shoulder, Jacob can heal. But I think it is only God who can heal your wounded hearts."

Thomas stepped off the porch and strode around behind the boardinghouse to cut across lots to the school. He had to get away from the crowded waterfront before he forgot he was a missionary. Evelyn Harris had done her work well. Rumors about Viola had been flying around town all day. And they were spreading among the host of stampeders swarming about the waterfront with the speed of news of a rich strike in the gold fields. There was no way he could stop the gossip, but every lascivious comment he overheard made him wish his shoulder was in good shape and he had an occupation instead of a calling.

He skirted the stone wall around the hotel property, remembered the way Viola had looked when he left her there the day he had moved to the boardinghouse. He clenched his jaw, shoved his hands into his jacket pockets and stepped off the wood walkway into the dirt road His long strides took him past the school and the church and a small, newly built house on the corner. He turned right and strode down the intersecting road, beyond the clustered cabins and on into the trees at the base of the mountain.

Silence greeted him. His boots crushed dried leaves and pungent fir needles, pressed the musky odor from the forest floor. It should have calmed him. It always did. But not now.

He'd never felt this way. Never in his whole life. It was as it his insides were boiling like a volcano, spewing out a dark, hungry rage. He wanted to pummel someone Dengler. He wanted to rip Dengler apart with his bare hands for what he had done to Viola.

How could she?

It stopped him. Stopped him cold—his movement and his thoughts. He stood there in the quiet of the forest and suddenly knew that was the truth he must face if he was ever to have peace. Not Dengler. Not Dolph. Viola. She had worked as a harlot. Sold herself to men for money. That knowledge was the pain he wanted to tear from his own heart. He lifted his head, looked up at the light filtering down through the branches and took a long, deep breath. "How could she, Lord? How could she?"

The sense of betrayal brought a fury so strong it shook him. But it was of his own doing. He had put her on a pedestal. In his heart, she was equal to the virtuous woman in the Psalm. And her fall from that elevated place was tearing him apart. Viola had not changed. It was his image of her that had splintered. It was clear from what he had overheard Dengler say that she had left her past behind. It was he that must now let it go.

He sank to his knees on the soft earth, faced his own sin and ran to the One who could cleanse him, who could make him whole again. "God, I have judged without knowledge, and blamed without cause. I have sinned against Viola and against You, Lord. I have broken Your word by standing in judgment on another. Forgive me and cleanse me, I pray. And help me, Lord, to accept… and to forgive."

The rockers whispered against the floor, the sound soothing to her strained nerves. Viola glanced at Goldie, sucking on her thumb, sleeping so soundly. She rose from the rocker and went to her knees beside the cradle, touched Goldie's silky, brown hair, her tiny, fisted hand. Who was Goldie's father? Why had he left Goldie in her care?

Please take care of her until I can—if I can—make it back home. Use this gold to care for her. I know I can trust you. The note he had left with Goldie proved he did not know her. The acrid taste of bitterness formed on her tongue. He never would have left his baby in her care if he had known what she was. But he would not be sorry. She had given the gold nuggets to Mack Tanner for safe-keeping against Goldie's future. Cold knots twisted in her stomach. Thank goodness the gold was not here for Dengler to find. That it was safe for Goldie's care if— tears blurred her vision—if she must leave her. *Oh, God, help me to know what is best for Goldie. Should I go or should I stay?*

The knock on the door sent her heart slamming against her ribs. She pushed to her feet, hurried to the bedroom doorway and watched as Hattie came out of the kitchen, wiping her hands on the apron that spanned her thick body. She pressed her hand to the base of her throat and bit back words of admonition. Hattie knew not to open the door to—

Another sharp rap made her jump.

"Hattie! Viola! It's me, Frankie."

The muffled words made her knees go weak. She smoothed back the curls that had escaped the ribbon that imprisoned her long hair at the nape of her neck and stepped out into the living room. She didn't want to wake Goldie.

"Hey, Viola." Frankie dropped a blanket-wrapped bundle on the floor and crossed the room to gaze at her. A smile curled the corners of her mouth. "Looks like Teena's been here."

She nodded.

Frankie chuckled. "Sort of hard to talk with that stuff stuck on your lips, huh?"

The hard knots in her stomach loosened. Trust Frankie to make her feel better. "Yes."

"Well, if Teena got up that concoction, it for sure ought to work."

She nodded. "The cuts hurt less already."

"Swellin's gone down, too." Hattie turned, headed back for the kitchen, looked over her plump shoulder. "Supper's late tonight, what with one thing and another. We're havin' soup. You're welcome to stay, Frankie."

"That all right with you, Viola?"

It was very all right. She felt safer with Frankie around. "Please do."

Frankie nodded, cleared her throat. "I come for a purpose, Viola. I thought maybe I could sleep here on your settle for a couple of nights. I'd feel better, seeing as how your pistol hasn't come in yet. That be all right with you?"

She stared at her, shocked beyond comprehension. "You want to stay here? With *me?*"

Frankie's chin jutted out. "That's what friends do, help out when there's a problem. Ain't it?"

Friends. Her throat tightened. Tears welled. She swallowed hard, nodded.

"Good. I brought my gear in case you said yes." Frankie walked over, picked up the bundle she had dropped and carried it to the settle.

Viola used the time to get her frayed emotions back under control.

"I got news."

Her heart lurched, then settled back to its normal rhythm. Frankie sounded happy. "What is it?" She braced herself just in case.

"First off, Teena and Doc Calloway went to Skaguay and got married this afternoon."

"Truly!" She winced, pressed her fingertips to her lips. "I knew they were planning to marry, but—"

"About time if you ask me." Hattie appeared in the kitchen doorway, shot her a look. "Any fool could see those two loved each other. Where they gonna live?"

"In Doc's room at the clinic. Teena moved her stuff in before they took the ferry. Guess they want to be there in case there's an emergency or something."

Her thoughts winged off to Thomas alone in his hut. A jolt of envy shamed her.

"You said, 'first off'—" Hattie glanced into the kitchen, looked back. "I've a pot about to boil over. What's the other news?"

Frankie's face turned into one huge grin. "I'm a deputy!"

She stared, reached up and held her lips again when she started to smile. "I'm so happy for you, Frankie!"

"About time for that, too, I'd say." Hattie went back to the kitchen.

"What happened? How did this come about?"

Frankie's grin died. "Ed said I handled myself real good last night, sneaking in the back and knocking Dengler cold with that tree branch."

She looked at the kitchen doorway and shuddered. "I haven't had a chance to thank you, Frankie—"

"No thanks needed, Viola." A blush crept into Frankie's cheeks. Her freckles looked larger and darker. She looked down at the settle, fussed with her bundle.

She had never seen Frankie look so uncomfortable. She motioned her friend to follow her, stepped into her bedroom and turned to face her. "What is it, Frankie? What's wrong?"

"Nothing's wrong. Everything's special right." Frankie looked back toward the kitchen, then faced her, happiness glowing in her blue eyes. "I been doing like you told me, Viola. You know, dressing more girly and asking Ed for help and all. And he's been coming around some. Then, last night, after we got those owl-hoots jailed, Ed said he was peacock proud of me, and, well…I been wanting that so long I got these silly tears in my eyes." She gave an awkward little wave, looked down. "Ed put his arms around me—to comfort me like—and then, well, one thing sorta led to another." A deep blush swept across Frankie's freckled cheeks. "Next thing I knew, Ed asked me to be his bride. I said, yes. Me! Frankie Tucker. I'm getting married, Viola."

"Frankie!" Tears swam into her eyes. "Oh, Frankie, I'm so happy for you!" And she was. Truly. The ache in her heart didn't detract from that.

Her friend looked up, a plea in her blue eyes. "Will you make me a special dress for my wedding, Viola? One that'll make me look all…all girly and pretty?"

The knots in her stomach uncurled. She stared at Frankie, thankful, so very thankful, for an opportunity to think about something normal and safe and fun. "Oh, Frankie. Of course I will."

Chapter Sixteen

"Well I *never!*"

Viola's heart sank. She put down her mending and rose, stared at Lana Tanner's angry face, then shot a look at Hattie.

The older woman shrugged, then closed and locked the door.

Viola squared her shoulders, looked back at the mayor's wife. "Hello, Lana. What happened to so upset you?" Judging from the parade of stampeders Hattie had been shooing from her door all morning, she feared she already knew the answer.

"I was just…*accosted* by a miner outside your door. He thought…" Lana pressed her lips together, tossed her head. "Well, never mind what he thought. The man is obviously lacking in mental capacity!"

"Oh, Lana! I'm so sorry—"

"It's not your fault, Viola." The petite blonde broke into giggles. "Besides, some good may come of it. After the tongue-lashing I gave him, I'm quite certain the man will change his immoral ways." Lana hitched her son higher on her hip and came to stand beside her. "Those beasts! Look at what they've done to you."

"Ouch."

She looked down at Lana's two-year-old who was pointing at her face and nodded. "Yes, I have 'ouches.' But they're getting better." She lifted her hand and pointed to her mouth, gave the best smile she could manage. "See, the herbs take the hurt away."

Georgie looked up, put his little hands on his mother's cheeks. "'Erbs?"

"Gracious, Viola! Don't get him started asking questions." Lana looked down at her son and laughed. "There aren't enough hours in the day once he starts that."

"Why don't I take Georgie out to the kitchen?" Hattie smiled at the toddler. "I have some cookies out there you can chew on whilst I finish feedin' Goldie her lunch. How about that?"

The toddler nodded and held out his arms. Hattie scooped him off Lana's hip and headed for the kitchen. "I can tell you all about herbs and such. There's these great *big* herbs, you see. Grow bi-i-ig as a house. And little boys can play under a leaf."

"Are you all right, Viola?" Lana made a face of disgust. "That's a foolish thing to ask. But you know what I mean." Her blue eyes warmed. "Is there anything I can do to help?"

"Your coming is enough, Lana." *Truly.* She cleared the lump from her throat. "Teena's herbs are helping with the soreness, and the rest will just…take time."

A sharp rap echoed through the room.

She blanched, jerked toward the door.

"Let me." Lana whirled and marched to the door.

"Lana, no!"

Lana waved her hand in dismissal of the admonition, threw back the lock and opened the door. "Yes?"

The man whipped off his hat. Balding, with graying hair. *Not Karl.* Viola took a deep breath, gripped the back of the settle for support.

"Er…are you Viola Goddard?"

"I am not."

The man frowned, glanced inside. She flinched back. "Is this her…house?"

The man's voice was low-pitched, with that underlying tone she knew so well. Her stomach curdled. She took a breath and started forward. She had to help Lana.

"It is her *home.* May I help you?"

She stopped, stared at the man's frown. He was obviously perplexed by Lana's cold tone.

"Depends." He smiled, stepped closer to Lana. "I've come to give her my…business. Less you're—"

"Where's your mending?"

"Mending? Wha—"

Lana's hand shot out, her index finger pointing toward the sign in the window on her right.

"Seamstress?" The man scowled. "Look here, lady! I don't care what that sign says. I heard different, an' I'm here for—" He glanced at Lana, set his jaw. "I'm here to spend some *personal* time with Viola."

"Oh, my gracious! Silly me. You've come *courting.*" Lana fluttered her hand through the air. "I shall tell Viola you called. And I'm sure she would be accepting of your company in church. Service—"

"Church?" The man's mouth gaped.

A low mumbling of men's voices rose.

"Why, yes. Viola attends every service faithfully. Would you care to leave your name—"

"Never mind. Looks like I've made a mistake." The man slapped his hat on.

"You have indeed. As have those men behind you. Tell them all, if they want to see Viola, church services start at eight o'clock Sunday morning!" Lana closed the door, flipped the lock into place then looked at her and burst into laughter. "Did you see his *face,* Viola? Oh, my! And you should have seen the others scatter when I mentioned church. They looked for all the world like ants when you step on their hill."

The tension across her shoulders released, her stomach stopped churning. "I don't know how to thank you, Lana. I—"

"Poof! There's no need for thanks. The truth is, I rather enjoyed that. Though I don't think it's going to increase our congregation." Lana smiled and linked her arm with hers. "Shall we join Hattie in the kitchen for a cup of tea? I think we need to talk about how best to handle this situation. And I have an idea."

Thomas stepped out onto the porch, wishing he hadn't eaten. There was nothing wrong with the food. Mavis Goodge set a good table for her boardinghouse patrons. It was the conversation at the table that had turned his stomach sour. Or more accurately, the lack of it. There had been no unsavory comments about Viola's past, his presence had taken care of that. But the unnatural silence and the surreptitious, leering looks cast his way had left no doubt as to what the other diners were thinking.

He jammed his hands into his jacket pockets and

looked out toward the harbor. The last ferry of the day from Skaguay was disgorging another slew of hopeful gold seekers and their supplies. Where they would find a place to put down their tents and packs and other possessions was more than he could figure. The waterfront was already so packed with people and wares it was all but impossible to wend your way through them to reach the long, wood piers that stretched out to the deeper water.

And the noise…

He shook his head, looked at the men and women streaming off the pier in front of the boardinghouse. What did they think when they first saw the swarms of stampeders camped out on the muddy quagmire while they prepared for their trek up the Chilkoot Trail? He had learned early on it did no good to warn the newcomers of the horrendous, dangerous climb. Or of the incredible backbreaking work of carrying, then caching, their supplies daily on the first leg of their journey to the gold fields. They wanted to hear nothing but tales of gold waiting to be picked up for the taking.

He stepped forward, leaned his good shoulder against the porch post. The hundreds that had come at the beginning of the gold rush had turned into thousands, all of them with their heads full of dreams and their hearts full of the lust for gold. The sad part was, most would find nothing but disappointment and heartbreak. He ministered to the disillusioned and broken every day. It left him little time for the Tlingits, who were his original purpose for coming north.

He frowned, scanned the nameless faces. How many dead had he prayed over? How many injured had he helped rescue and bring to Treasure Creek for treatment and care? How many angry, bitter men, defeated by the weather and the hardships of climbing the Chilkoot before they ever neared the gold fields, had he tried to convince of God's love for them?

How many of these would he find injured, or life-less and beyond his succor, along the trail? He was only one man and the distance was great, the climb slow and dangerous. How could he hope to reach the thousands of miners before they lost everything in their search for riches?

"Lord God Almighty, may You have mercy on them all."

He moved down the steps, halted as he spotted Ed Parker standing by a stack of crates and watching the people coming off the pier. Something in his posture said it was not casual observation. He left the porch and wound his way through the stampeders to the sheriff.

"Expecting someone, Ed?"

The big man shot him a look, shook his head. "Nope. But I'm gonna be here to welcome him, should he come. Where you been all day?"

"Up the trail. Jacob says I have to stay in town on account of busting open my wound again. I hired Jimmy Crow to pack some clothes and such down to Goodge's for me. Spent the day getting things together." He stepped closer to the stack of crates as a man pushed a barrow loaded with supplies toward them through the press of people. "Were you looking for me?"

"Yeah. I need your help looking for a man. I'm watching for him now, but it's possible he's already here. I been looking around all day and haven't spotted him, but with all these stampeders everywhere…" Ed's massive shoulders lifted in a shrug. "Keep watch for a small, wiry man with dark hair and a scar on the back of his left hand. Name's Karl. He's likely dressed in city clothes."

"What's he done?"

"Nothing…yet."

The timbre of Ed's voice had changed. Thomas moved around to get a better view of his face. "What's that mean?"

Ed glanced at him, then went back to watching the pier. "It means he's Dengler's man and he might be after Viola. Dengler and Dolph won't say if he's in town or not."

It hit him in his gut. The muscles in his legs tensed, ready to run to her cabin and make sure she was all right. "How'd you find out about him?"

"Viola. I talked with her this morning. Asked her if Dengler had any other men like Dolph working for him. She said this Karl and Dolph usually work together."

The nerve along his jaw jumped. Thomas clenched his hand around the pistol in his pocket, turned.

"Where you headed, Thomas?"

He stopped, looked back at Ed. "To watch Viola's cabin."

"You got a pistol?"

"Yes."

The sheriff nodded. "I'm making you my deputy. Frankie's staying nights with Viola, but if this thug shows up, we need to stop him before he can get anywhere near them. I'm gonna keep searching here amongst the stampeders. If he gets by me, and you get him cornered, don't let him get close. He likes to use a knife, and you'd be no match for him with that bum shoulder. You keep him covered and have Frankie hogtie him, then come for me."

His blood turned gelid at the thought of a man with a knife near Viola. He nodded, turned to go.

"One more thing, Thomas."

He looked back.

"I don't know if he's a thrower. But if it looks like he's fixing to toss a knife at you, shoot him."

A special dress. One that would make her look all girly and pretty.

Viola added a few chunks of wood from the fire-box to the coals in the stove, to chase away the chill of the night air, took her seat at the table and pulled the oil lamp closer to the paper. Frankie—raucous carpenter, pistol-shooting avowed spinster and deputy, Frankie Tucker—was in love.

All girly and pretty. That request was so far from Frankie's normal boots, split skirt and leather belt hanging with tools. But love made you want to be beautiful for the man who held your heart.

Tears filmed her eyes, blurred the profile outline of a woman's body she'd drawn on the paper. For her that was impossible. She would forever be tarnished, *defiled* in Thomas's eyes. But Frankie would have her girly dress. And she would see the love and admiration in Ed Parker's eyes. And she would know she was beautiful to him.

Viola blinked her vision clear, picked up the pencil and sketched in short, dark curls on the figure's head. First…a collar that would stand up in the back—so Frankie's curls would touch it—then curve around and end in a modest V above her breasts, with a rose at the joining. Next, a fitted bodice with small mother-of-pearl buttons, dipping to a V at the front waist that mimicked the line of the collar. And long sleeves that ended in a lace-trimmed V on the back of Frankie's hands. She drew the lines, studied them, nodded. She would gather fabric along the bottom edges of the V, and then bias-cut it so it fell back in a graceful swoop to become a modest train.

She sketched in a full underskirt, ended it in a scalloped hem trimmed with roses at ankle height, then added a deep, gathered flounce that would brush the floor. What else? Something to make it special. She looked at the drawing, noted the way the bodice ended in a V at the front but was plain in the back. She added a small, lace-trimmed semicircle of fabric that draped over the back of the overskirt, reminiscent of a bustle, drew a large bow where it joined the bodice in the back, and smiled.

She winced, touched her fingers to her sore lips. The dress was special, feminine and beautiful. She would make it in a lovely, cream-colored silk. But one thing more was needed. She added a wide band of fabric, clustered with roses, among the dark curls. Now it was perfect. Frankie would have her wish.

Tears flooded her eyes. She tried not to, fought with all her strength to keep from imagining herself in such a gown, standing before an altar, being wed to Thomas. But the image was there before her. And then she looked into his eyes. The image dissolved in another spate of tears. All she could see was the hurt and disillusionment that had been there when he had turned away from her. She could not bear to do that to him again. Not ever again. A marriage between an ex-harlot and a man of God was impossible.

She tucked the hopeless dream deep into her heart, turned down the wick to extinguish the light and walked from the room.

Chapter Seventeen

"You look done in, Thomas." Ed Parker lifted the blackened pot in his hand toward him. "Coffee?"

Thomas shook his head, winced. "I had some before I came."

The sheriff set the coffeepot back on the potbelly stove and took a swig of the hot, dark brew in his cup. "Looks like you need sleep more than coffee. You get any?"

"Some. I spotted Jimmy Crow on his way into town this morning, and got him to watch while I caught a short nap. He's there now." Thomas rubbed the stiff muscles at the back of his neck. Leaning against that tree all night was playing havoc with his injured shoulder. "I came to see if you had any luck spotting Karl." Saying the name brought that chill of fear for Viola, followed by the heat of fury. He took the anger out on his stiff neck muscles. The massage loosened them.

Ed Parker shook his head. "Nope. But it'd be easy enough for him to hide in amongst the stampeders. I spread the word to the businesses. Everyone will be watching for him. If he goes into a store they'll let me know. Trouble is, I've got to get Dengler and Dolph over to Skaguay and get them in a proper jail." A frown darkened his face. "I don't like leaving town while Karl might be roaming around, but I don't wanna trust those two to a deputy."

"I gave this some thought last night, Ed." As if anything else could find space in his head. "It seems to me, if Karl is in town, it's either to meet up with Dengler, or finish the job Dengler and Dolph started." The words almost choked him. "And if he's been here, he's heard about Dengler and Dolph being arrested. That and gold are all anyone's talking about. He could have decided to leave. And there's one other possibility." He took a breath, stared at that black coffeepot. "I was thinking back over the other night and I remembered a detail I'd forgotten. Dengler mentioned having a 'house' in Skaguay. It could be Karl is there, waiting for Dengler to return." *Please, God.*

"That makes sense." Ed nodded, took another swallow of coffee. "That'd explain why Dengler and Dolph aren't talking about him." He smiled, drained his cup and hung it back on a hook on the wall. "That trip to Skaguay is looking more inviting. I'll make a call at Dengler's place, once I get him and Dolph settled comfortable in a cell. If Karl's there, I'll see if I can't arrange something, so I can take him to jail to join them."

Thomas nodded, held his hope in check. "Meanwhile, if Karl is here he'll show up at Viola's cabin sooner or later. I'll be hidden in the woods, waiting." He turned, reached for the door, jumped back as it was shoved open from outside.

"Sheriff Parker, I've come to lodge a complaint!"

Evelyn Harris burst into the small room, her face tight with anger.

"What's that Mrs. Harris?"

"I want you to do your *job* and throw Viola Goddard out of town! There is a—*parade* of stampeders on our road, coming and going from her place! Why, I could hardly make my way through them to get here."

The sickness slammed into his gut again. Thomas clenched his hands, held back the recriminations that sprang to his tongue. "Is there a law that holds a person responsible for people on their road, Ed?"

"Not any I know of." A frown touched the sheriff's broad face. "I'm afraid I can't help you, Mrs. Harris. I can't go arresting someone 'cause there's people on their road. That being the case, I'd have to arrest you, too, seeing as how you live there."

"That is ridiculous! *I* am not—"

"Not what, Mrs. Harris?" Thomas met her furious gaze.

"You know very well *what,* Mr. Stone! You were at Viola Goddard's cabin that night. You heard what was said. And you know, as well as I, why those men are swarming to her cabin."

"Yes, I do. It's because someone started a vicious rumor about Miss Goddard. The stampeders are responding to that rumor."

Evelyn Harris gasped, whirled. "I want that woman thrown out of town, Sheriff. There is no place in Treasure Creek for her kind. If you need *proof* of what she is, I suggest you go ask those stampeders." She jerked open the door, looked back. "If you do not do your job, I shall speak with the mayor about getting a new sheriff! Good day!" She stepped outside and slammed the door shut.

Ed Parker, shook his head. "Guess that woman's mama never scrubbed her tongue with soap for telling lies."

"I'd like to do it now." Thomas took a breath, blew it out slow. "A parade of stampeders." What had that woman and her vicious tongue done? Images ran through his head of Viola holding Goldie and humming…sitting in the rocker, her head bowed over her sewing…feeding him when he was helpless…talking and laughing with Hattie…her home, so comfortable, so peaceful and serene. And now, thanks to Evelyn Harris, that comfort and peace had been destroyed. *A parade of stampeders?* He'd soon put an end to that! He tugged his hat low over his eyes and slammed out the door.

Viola lifted the huge pan of dough out of the hole, put another down in its place and replaced the boards.

"Where's that dough, Viola?"

"Coming!" She hurried to the table and dumped the dough out on the floured surface. "Are you all right, Hattie? If you're getting tired—"

"I'm fine, Viola. I ain't had so much fun in ages." Hattie rolled out the dough, picked up the tin glass she was using and started cutting out circles. "You'd best give that wash pan to Mavis and get to the shakin'. We're gettin' behind."

Viola glanced at the board that stretched from the stove to the table. It was covered with fried doughnuts. She handed the empty pan to Mavis, who was busy mixing up the next batch of dough, grabbed the muslin bag off the corner of the table, dumped in some sugar and cinnamon, added a dozen of the doughnuts and shook them. When they were coated with the sugar mixture, she shifted them to a basket, grabbed another dozen doughnuts and repeated the process.

"We're running out of doughnuts!"

Margie's bellow was clear, even over the hubbub in the kitchen. "Gracious, already?" Viola added another dozen doughnuts to the basket, picked it up and hurried to the front window. A line of stampeders stretched in front of Frankie, Margie and Lucy as far as she could see.

"Here you are." Frankie handed half a dozen doughnuts to the man in front of her. "Just drop your donation in the bowl there." She nodded toward the end of the table, grabbed up her empty basket.

"Here are more doughnuts." Viola dumped the doughnuts in the empty basket Lucy brought to her and hurried back to the kitchen. "Lana, you're a *genius*. The stampeders just keep coming and coming. I couldn't see the end of the line from the window."

Lana laughed, brushed a lock of hair off her forehead with her forearm and went back to tending the frying doughnuts. "At this rate, we'll not only have money enough to pay for the materials to make the window swags and pads for all the pews, but we'll be able to buy a carpet for the entrance hall as well. Did you hear any…comments?"

Viola's stomach turned. She'd been so busy, had been enjoying the women's company so much, she'd almost forgotten. She shook her head. "No. By the time the miners reach the stoop, they seem to have forgotten about…everything…but doughnuts."

"Or Frankie's fierce look changes their mind." Lana

giggled. "I do think Frankie's volunteering to do the selling was smart. That pistol she has tucked in her belt discourages more than someone being light-fingered with the donations we're collecting."

"Yes." She blinked her eyes, cleared her throat. "Frankie is a true blessing."

"And so are you, Viola. To many of us, in many ways." Lana smiled, started lifting fried doughnuts out onto the draining board. "Now let's get back to work. We've money to make today."

Thomas stepped away from the pile of plump burlap bags, tried to decide from the look on Ed Parker's face if the news from Skaguay was good or bad.

The sheriff squinted, pulled his hat brim down against the lowering sun. "What're you doin' here? I figured you'd still be hiding in the woods."

"I don't need to until later."

"What's that mean?"

"It means Viola is safe until tonight. Some of the women from the church are at her cabin baking and selling doughnuts."

"Doughnuts?"

"All day." Thomas fell into step with the sheriff as he headed for his office. "Evelyn Harris was right, Ed. You can hardly walk down the road for the stampeders beating a track to Viola's cabin." He frowned, felt that clutch in his stomach. "It doesn't start out that way, but by the time they get to her road, it's doughnuts they're after. And guess who's standing on the front stoop selling them?" He glanced up at his friend. "Margie, Lucy and Frankie. Pistol and all."

Ed Parker threw his massive head back and let out

a belly laugh that drew gazes from the crowd around them. "No man would buck a crowd of women, especially if one is wearing a pistol like she knows how to use it." He shook his head, grinned. "Trust women to come up with a way to protect one of their own."

"For today." Thomas followed the big man into his office. "But there's still tonight. And tomorrow… What did you find out in Skaguay?"

"Good news. For Viola, not Karl." Ed Parker tossed his hat onto a hook on the wall, stomped over and flopped down into his desk chair. "You'll be able to sleep in that room you're paying for at Mavis's tonight."

Thomas sat in the other chair, held on to his patience as the sheriff leaned back, lifted his legs and plopped his booted feet on his desk.

"I went to Dengler's 'house' in Skaguay. And you were right. Dengler left Karl to keep an eye on things while he and Dolph came to Treasure Creek. But Karl got greedy and tried to rob a miner of his winnings from a card game. Turns out the miner was better with a knife than Karl. Slit his gullet. And that's not all the good news." He crossed his huge arms over his massive chest and grinned. "Seems Dengler left Seattle in a hurry after one of his girls turned up dead. He come up to Skaguay and opened a place to get his share of the stampeders money. But one of the stampeders in Skaguay knew about the girl. He wrote his brother about Dengler's new place, and a sheriff's deputy come up north to arrest Dengler and Dolph and Karl for murder. He was looking for them when I brought them in. They're going back to Seattle on the next ship. And they won't be coming back."

Thank You, Lord. Thank You for protecting Viola.
"That *is* good news, Ed. Very good news." He rose to
his feet.

"Where you going?"

"To the boardinghouse. To get some sleep."

"I thought maybe you'd like to come along while I tell
Viola she doesn't have to be afraid of Dengler or Dolph
or Karl ever showing up at her place again."

He wasn't ready for that. He had a ways to go before
he could talk with her about her past. The way his heart
felt, maybe he'd never be ready to do that. But there
was one thing he knew for sure. All that had happened
proved he was head over heels in love with Viola Goddard. He shook his head, reached for the door. "I think
she'd prefer you went alone."

"Oh, Hattie, it's over. I can hardly believe it." Viola
sank down onto the settle and buried her face in her
hands. "Five years…five years of…" She shuddered,
lifted her head. "It doesn't matter. Not any more. It's
over. I'll never have to live in fear again."

Hattie nodded, knit another stitch on the mittens she
was making for Goldie. "Seems like the good Lord is
givin' you a new beginnin' all right. Mayhap now you'll
stop hidin' them eye-catchin' red curls 'neath them ugly
snoods."

"You knew?"

Hattie glanced up, shook her head. "Not 'til Dengler
showed up. But once I learned 'bout everythin', it wasn't
hard to figure out why you kept tryin' to make yourself plain as possible. A woman beautiful as you would
of had a lot of customers. Ain't unlikely some of them

would come passin' through Treasure Creek, headin' for the gold fields."

"Yes." The relief vanished like the smoke drifting up the chimney to disappear in the sky. What had she been thinking? She touched the healing cuts on her lips, massaged the scar on her hand. It wasn't over. It would never be over. She would always have the scars. And the shame.

She looked up at the sampler she'd worked on in such faith. How foolish she'd been to believe it was possible for her to leave her past behind.

Tears filmed her eyes, blurred the words into shapeless forms without meaning. Thomas hadn't come with the sheriff to tell her. And he would have. She knew he would have...before.

Chapter Eighteen

Thomas gritted his teeth, clenched his hands on the edge of the table at Jacob's probing. "I was planning on using that shoulder again."

"Not for anything strenuous. Not for some time." Jacob frowned, put padding over the wound and covered it with a clean dressing. "This is not healing as fast as I would like, Thomas. That second tearing did more damage than I first thought."

"Are you saying—"

"You have to stay in town, baby this shoulder and arm. No chasing around on the trail, no trips to Indian villages until I give permission. One slip…one *wrench* of that shoulder and you might lose the full use of your arm."

"That's not what I wanted to hear." Thomas slipped off the table, donned his shirt and tucked it into his pants. "I was hoping to go home today."

Jacob shook his head. "Not a chance. I know how rough conditions are at that hut you live in. And at Goodge's you won't be chopping wood or hauling water.

Or carrying injured stampeders off the trail and bringing them to me, for that matter. You stay in town."

He nodded, frowned. He'd known something was not quite right with his arm, but…Jacob's hand clamped on his good shoulder. He looked up.

"I'm serious, Thomas. The use of your arm is at stake here. It needs rest and time to heal. Do as I say." Jacob released his grip. "Come back and see me in a week—unless there's some change. Or you do something stupid."

"Me? Never." He tugged on his jacket, dropped payment in the bowl and went out the back door. *Now what?* He glanced toward the mountains that encompassed the town, stepped out from behind the clinic. Rising wind, from the direction of the harbor, chilled his face. He sniffed the air, frowned. The storm the sky had promised when he woke was getting close. A walk in the woods was out of the question. He started left across the intervening lots, toward the back of the boardinghouse, but the agitation in his gut told him it was impossible to go and sit in his room. And he sure didn't feel like talking to anyone.

He retraced his steps, bucked the flow of people heading to and from the clinic and the new hotel a short distance behind it, crossed the road and cut through the lot between Mack Tanner's house and store. People clustered at the corner of the road, milled around the store. He turned away from the hubbub of the waterfront, skirted Lana Tanner's fenced backyard garden, put his right hand on top of a picket in the fence that separated the Tanners' yard from the church property and hopped over.

The hum of conversation from the crowded waterfront

muted, then faded away as he strode across the wide, deep lot behind the church. He paused beneath a tree with bare branches and scowled up at the sky. It was as gloomy as the grim prognostication for his shoulder and arm, as stormy as his thoughts.

The faint sound of chatter from the cabins that lined the road running along the other side of the churchyard floated to him through the quiet. He leaned against the tree trunk and rubbed his gritty eyes with the heels of his hands. He'd spent a restless night going over every single thing that had happened since Viola ran into him on the walkway outside Tanner's General Store the day of Goldie's kidnapping. It was impossible that it was all simple coincidence. And the logical conclusion for it all…the only answer that made sense…was that God had wanted him to stay in town to protect Viola. But Dengler, Dolph and Karl were no longer a danger to her. So why had things worked out so he could not go home and return to his ministry of the Tlingits and the stampeders on the trail? He'd figured everything was over. Except the way he felt.

He picked a piece of loose bark off the trunk, absently sliced his thumbnail along its length, shredding it. Viola's need for his protection was gone. And his love for her, his desire to be with her forever would fade…in time. Not that he would act on it, even though he now accepted that Louise's and Susie's deaths were not his fault. As Hattie had told Viola, there was both evil and good in the world, and bad things happened because of it. He'd just forgotten that for a while. Allowed the truth to be pushed out by his emotions. But God turned the bad to good for those who loved Him, who were called according to His purpose.…

He brushed the clinging bits of bark from his hands, folded his arms across his chest and stared down at the ground, examining a new thought. What if God had a *twofold* purpose in all that had happened? Perhaps God had purposed to set him free of the burden of guilt he had carried for the past three years *and* to protect Viola. Falling in love with her was his own doing. But things had changed.

Only your knowledge of her past.

The words flashed into his head, settled in his spirit. Conviction came, swift and unrelenting, leaving his heart stripped bare. He had come to a place of understanding that night in the woods. But the hurt and anger were still lodged in his heart. He was still sitting in unfair judgment of Viola. Blaming her for not trusting him enough to tell him of her past. And for a betrayal that existed only in his own heart.

Thunder rumbled. Dark clouds tumbled across the sky. But the light had never shone brighter. He pushed away from the tree and strode toward the church, heedless of the rain that was starting to fall. A hinge squeaked quietly as he opened the door and entered the building. Frankie, Margie and Lucy had wasted no time. The pile of lumber and the sawhorses were gone. A smell of paint hung in the air. He swept a glance over the new, vertical-sided walls and stepped into the sanctuary.

A hush enveloped him, broken only by the rain tapping softly against the stained glass windows. He walked down the center aisle between the pews, knelt in front of the altar and bowed his head.

Teena's herbs had worked wonders. Viola peered at her image in the mirror, turned her face this way and that to better see in the tenebrous light from the window. The cuts were healed. Only the redness of the scar at her temple remained, and it was fading. A few more days and the redness would be gone. There would be nothing left to remind her of Dengler's last, terrifying attack. Except the stain on her soul.

Lightning flickered, the white brilliance dancing across the mirror. Thunder grumbled. She pulled her hair back into a cluster of riotous red curls at the crown of her head and reached for the blue snood that matched her skirt. No. She lifted her gaze, looked straight into the violet-blue eyes in the mirror. "You will not cower and hide in shadows. You will *not* live in fear any longer."

Goldie gurgled and waved her arms in the air. Rain spattered against the window.

Viola leaned down, caught and kissed the chubby little hands. "I wasn't talking to you, little Miss Goldie. But thank you for offering your opinion. I guess, since you're smiling, it's a favorable one." She straightened, looked in the mirror at the dark red curls at her temples and on her forehead, lifted her hand and touched the ones that nestled against the nape of her neck. She would not hide her "eye-catchin' curls" any more. A smile touched her lips. Hattie would be so pleased.

Lightning slashed a yellow streak through the murky gray outside the window. Thunder crashed. Goldie let out a squall. "No, no, little one. There's no reason to be afraid. I'm right here." She scooped her up, cuddled her close and carried her to the kitchen.

"'Bout time you two got here. This gruel's fixin' to boil away to—" Hattie stopped and stared. The pan in her hand dipped dangerously.

"Hattie, the oatmeal!"

"Now see what you made me go and do." Hattie clucked like a hen and set the pan back on the stove, padded across to the dry sink, grabbed a damp cloth and came back to wipe up the spill. "I knew you was beautiful, Viola, but...*my!*" She straightened, shook her head. "I ain't never seen such gorgeous hair. It's shameful the way you been hidin' it."

"Well, no more, Hattie." Rain tapped on the chimney cover, echoed down the pipe. She propped Goldie on her hip, used her free hand to spoon a little of the oatmeal into a small bowl and carried it to the table. "I've decided my hair is to be my symbol of freedom from... from everything." She added a sprinkle of sugar, poured milk on the cereal and stirred it smooth. "Here you are, sweetie." She spooned some of the oatmeal into Goldie's welcoming mouth.

"More like a banner of victory, if you want my thinkin' on it. The Good Book says a woman's hair is her glory. An' my, *my,* but the good Lord saw fit to glorify you." Hattie dished up her oatmeal and plunked down in her chair. "The glory's plumb faded out of my hair, but I got my memories." She chuckled, poured milk in her bowl and added a heaping spoonful of sugar. "Charley said he picked me that first time 'cause my hair looked like spun gold." She frowned, scooped up a spoonful of the hot cereal. "He had a weakness for gold. The old fool!"

"Well, judging from the thousands of stampeders passing though town and braving the Chilkoot Trail, Charley was not alone in his weakness for gold."

Lightning glinted against the wet window panes. Thunder growled. Viola fed Goldie another spoonful of oatmeal and tried not to wonder if Thomas was safe in his hut, or caught in the storm somewhere on that dangerous trail, climbing the mountain.

Thomas lifted his head. The rain had stopped. The storm was over. He rose to his feet, glanced at the splotches of shimmering colors thrown on the floor by the sun coming through the wet, stained glass of the windows. A smile tilted his lips. He turned, started up the aisle and stopped, staring at Mack Tanner who was staring right back at him.

"Hello, Thomas. I didn't expect anyone to be here." Mack strode down the aisle toward him. "Why the smile?"

"I was remembering the look on your face the day I gave you the gold nuggets to buy the stained glass windows."

"Nuggets *I* had buried, in the hope men would get sidetracked into looking for them and stop looking for my real buried treasure." Mack shook his head, laughed. "I sure didn't expect you to be the one that found my decoy treasure."

"That was obvious from the look on your face when I gave them to you."

"I guess."

Thomas frowned. "I hadn't thought of it before, but…I think that may have been the beginning."

"The beginning of what?"

"All that has happened since."

"You mean with Viola?"

"Yes." Thomas looked up at the windows. "If it weren't for finding those nuggets, I could not have afforded to stay in town like I have. And I wasn't even looking for them…. God always pays for what He ordains."

Mack stared at him. "Now see, it's nuggets of truth like that…" He shook his head. "Pure gold. The true riches…" He narrowed his eyes. "Did you ever think God might have had more than one purpose in giving you the 'wherewithal' to stay in town, Thomas?"

The prickle of his flesh told him Mack was about to say something he needed to hear. "What are you talking about?"

"Treasure Creek. This thing with Viola has split this town apart. People who were best friends are no longer talking to one another because they have chosen opposite sides of the 'Viola' issue. Half of them think she should stay, half think she should be thrown out of town.

"And they both use the same argument—*Treasure Creek is a God-centered town.* I don't know what to do. I only know something has to be done, because I sure don't like the atmosphere in this town any more."

He fixed an assessing gaze on him. "I felt an 'urging' to come here, Thomas. I thought it was to pray about the situation, but now I'm not so sure. I think God may have had a different reason for drawing me here right now. Let's sit down and talk about it."

Thomas nodded and slid onto a pew. Mack joined him, leaned back and stared up at the ceiling.

"You know, Thomas, that I've thought, since that first day I heard you preaching to a group of stampeders on the Chilkoot, that you are the man God wants to fill the pulpit of this church. I feel that more strongly than ever." He turned his head and looked at him. "You have the strongest faith I have ever witnessed in a man, Thomas.

My preacher dad would have said you're a man 'on fire with the Holy Spirit'."

He straightened, fastened his gaze on him. "I know you're concerned with the Tlingits and the stampeders on the trail. So am I. But more and more of the Tlingits are coming to services every Sunday. And this split that is happening among our church members shows the people of Treasure Creek need God's truth every bit as much as the Indians and the stampeders."

So they will be among my people. New plants will grow where the seeds land. You will gather those plants and tend them that they also may grow to know your God.

The prickles chased down his spine, spread through him in waves. This was the truth he was to hear.

"If your faith ignites the people of Treasure Creek, this place will become so alive with faith, it will draw the stampeders before they ever start up the Chilkoot! And it's better to prevent a tragedy than to patch up the damage after one. Treasure Creek needs you, Thomas. The people need to hear the truth…those nuggets of God's riches…that *pure* gold that you speak without even being aware that you are teaching others. Let the stampeders and the Tlingits and the townspeople find the true riches right here, Thomas. I think God wants you to take the pulpit of Treasure Creek Church and heal this town. What do you say?"

Thomas locked his gaze on Mack and held out his hand. "I say you're right. Do I start this Sunday?"

Mack grinned, shook his proffered hand. "You sure do! I've been wanting to hand that pulpit over to you for months. And meantime you can move into your new home."

"My new home?"

Mack's grin widened. "Yeah. Haven't you noticed the new house that was just built on the corner?"

"You mean—"

"Yep. It's the Treasure Creek Church parsonage." Mack laughed, thumped him on his good shoulder. "You're not the only one with a path to God's ear, you know. Come on, I'll show you your new home while we discuss an agreeable remuneration for your services."

Thomas stood, swept his gaze around the sanctuary and felt the peace of knowing he was letting God's will fill him. "I'm already home."

Chapter Nineteen

Viola glared at her trembling hands. Willed them to stop. To no avail. Why would they? Her entire body was quivering over what she might face today.

She smoothed her long skirt, turned to the mirror and arranged the ruffles that tumbled from her high collar to meet the broad lapels of her green, fitted jacket, tweaked the restrained fullness at the top of the long, leg-of-mutton sleeves. Her outfit was modest in the extreme, but her hair…

She stared at the mass of dark red curls at her crown, itching to reach for a snood to hide them. It was one thing to declare them her symbol of freedom here at home, but quite another to have them exposed to public view.

Evelyn Harris and her friends would be there.

She drew a deep breath, blew it out and turned from the mirror. It had been ten days since Dengler's attack. Ten days that she had hidden in her cabin, waiting for all trace of the bruising to disappear. She would cower no longer. And what safer place than church to make her first appearance? Not even Evelyn Harris would dare speak out there. And she would have her friends to support her.

"My friends." How lovely those words tasted on her tongue. What warmth they brought to her heart. She would concentrate on them. And on the happily gurgling bundle of joy at her feet.

God chose you to watch over the baby.

Tears stung the backs of her eyes. There had been such caring, such…*respect* for her in Thomas's voice as he had said those words. And now… She took another breath, blinked the tears away. And now Thomas was gone. Most likely, he was back in his hut on the trail, ministering to the Tlingits and the stampeders. And her chance to help him with his work was gone with him. But that was for the best. She could not bear to see that hurt, that *disillusionment* in his eyes again. And she would not have to face him today. Her love for him was safe. Folded up and tucked away in the deepest part of her heart, along with her dream.

"Are you ready to go to church, Goldie?" She bent and lifted the baby into her arms, cuddled her close and walked into the living room. Goldie twisted around, her chubby little hand grabbing for the curls that dangled at her temple. "Oh, no, you don't. You pull hard." She laughed and sat Goldie on the rug, gave her the little wooden dog to play with and walked to the table by the door.

One last thing to do and she was ready. She counted out a tenth of the money in the bowl and dropped the coins into a small leather poke. They made a muted click as they fell on those already in the bag.

"That poke looks right hefty." Hattie drew the sides of her jacket together over her ample bosom and fastened the fancy frog loops over the buttons. "That rumor of a big strike beyond Dawson City sure brought them stampeders swarmin' round to get their mendin' done before they took off up the trail. And their minds wasn't on nothin' but the gold, either." She chuckled, tugged the peplum of her jacket down over her abundant hips. "Makes me wonder if God Hisself is the one planted them gold nuggets that started the hubbub. It sure took them stampeders attention off of you."

"*Hattie*. That's…preposterous."

"I've known of God to do harder things than that, Viola." The faded blue eyes fixed a look on her. "I've been here since the beginnin' of this gold rush and I ain't never seen the likes of this. A steady stream of gold chasers comin' off the boats and settin' out to climb the trail soon's there's space enough for them to set their boots down." She looked up from smoothing her skirt over her round stomach and smiled. "You're prettier than any gold nugget I ever saw. You ready, Viola?"

She wasn't talking about being washed and dressed. *Bless Hattie, Lord. She always understands.* "Yes." She dropped the poke in her purse, drew the strings tight and walked over to pick up Goldie and the little wooden dog.

Viola fussed with Goldie's dress, tugged the sleeve of the sweater Hattie had knit the baby down over her pudgy wrist, smoothed a lock of her baby hair back beneath her bonnet. Anything to keep from looking at the other people filing through the church door. Anything to keep her mind off the murmur of comments she could hear in the background.

"Mornin', Mavis…Rose." Hattie moved into the entrance, sniffed. "Smells like paint in here. But don't it look bright and pretty. Them Tucker girls do good work." Hattie glanced back over her shoulder at her. "Wait'll you get them curtains made, Viola. This place'll really be spiffy then."

"More like gaudy...."

"Indeed..."

"What is *she* doing here?"

The under-the-breath comments came from a small group of women on the left. She turned right, glared down at her free hand. *Don't you dare tremble!* She pulled the poke from her purse and emptied her tithe into the basket.

"Ill-gotten gain..."

"Tainted money..."

The whispers followed her into the sanctuary. Hattie started down the aisle. She put her hand on her arm and nodded toward an empty pew on the right, in front of those filled with Tlingits from the nearby village. She had no desire to sit down front and be a source of disturbance during Mack Tanner's sermon.

She followed Hattie into the pew, cuddled Goldie close and tried not to see the covert glances thrown her way, or hear snatches of whispered conversations. She lifted her chin and held her face impassive when Judith Smith and Elizabeth Dunn glanced over their shoulders at her, stood and moved with their families to the other side of the aisle.

Mavis and Harold Goodge came in, glanced around and slid into a pew in front of her. Beverly Fogel followed with her husband, James, glanced her way, stuck her nose in the air and marched forward to take a seat on the other side of the aisle behind Evelyn and Robert Harris.

Hattie's elbow dug into her ribs. "That one looks like she's been suckin' on a pickle."

She forced her lips into a smile.

Hattie nodded. "That's better."

Frankie Tucker came in with Ed Parker, scanned the congregation and spoke to Ed. He nodded and stepped back to let her precede him into the pew in front of the Goodges.

Viola caught her breath, looked over the congregation. They were choosing sides! Over her. She should not have come. Perhaps—

The organ sounded. Conversations hushed. The congregation stood. Tabitha Burger stepped to the front of the aisle, nodded to the organist and began to sing, "O Blessed Lord, our God and King."

Viola stood quietly, drew in long breaths to control the churning sourness in her stomach. It was too late to leave. She would have to stay for Mack Tanner's sermon, then leave during his closing prayer. She sank to her seat when the hymn ended, smoothed Goldie's dress down over her chubby little legs.

"Good morning, everyone."

She glanced up at Mack Tanner, looked back down and took the little wooden dog out of her purse to give Goldie. How was she to endure the waiting?

"Most of you here know that I have been hoping and praying for an ordained preacher to fill this pulpit since I built the church. This morning I am pleased to tell you that God has heard and answered that prayer. It is with pleasure and anticipation that I turn this pulpit over to the first pastor of Treasure Creek Church, Thomas Stone."

The little dog fell from her fingers. Her heart lurched. Her lungs froze. She ducked down to retrieve the dog, stayed there fighting to hold back tears. No one must see. If they should guess… Oh, if only she could leave. But it was impossible now. She would have to stay and—

"…speak to you about judgment."

The word sent bile surging to her throat. She jerked upright, praying she had heard Thomas wrong, knowing she had not.

"For my scriptural basis I will use the woman caught in the act of adultery that the scribes and pharisees brought to Jesus."

Heads turned, sent cruel glances her way.

Pain, swift and sharp, pierced her heart. She had trusted him. Trusted in his caring and kindness. What a fool she was!

"…were waiting to see what Jesus would say and do. The punishment for such an act in those days was death by stoning. And there was no doubt about the woman's guilt. She had been caught in the very act they accused her of."

His deep, rich voice drove the pain deeper with every word. She caught her lower lip in her teeth, bit down to keep the sobs building in her chest from escaping.

"Do you remember what Jesus said to those gathered there awaiting His sentence of the woman?"

His gaze swept over the congregation, found her.

"He said, 'He that is without sin among you, let him first cast a stone at her.'" His gaze held hers, then, again, swept over the congregation. "'He that is *without sin* among you'…"

A thick, heavy silence fell. And then his voice came again, quiet and deep.

"Thou shalt have no other gods before me….

"Thou shalt not make unto thee any graven image…."

There was a stirring, a clearing of throats.

"Honor thy father and thy mother…."

A soft sobbing came forth.

"Thou shalt not kill….

"Thou shalt not commit adultery…."

A moan.

"Thou shalt not steal…."

She couldn't listen to any more. She knew now what she had to do. She kissed Goldie's cheek, hugged her tight for a moment, then handed her to Hattie, rose and slipped from the pew.

"Thou shalt not bear false witness against thy neighbor…."

Crying.

"Thou shalt not covet thy neighbor's house…."

The words followed her through the entrance. She stepped outside and closed the door, her heart sick and heavy. He had used her as an example. No matter that he had said he was talking about the adulterous woman in the Bible. Everyone knew…. A sob burst from her throat. She caught up her skirt hems and ran down the road, shoved open her door and dashed to her bedroom.

The cradle first. She grabbed hold of the footboard and backed toward the door, tugging the cradle after her into the living room. Now Goldie's clothes and toys. She ran back into the bedroom, swiped the tears from her cheeks and pulled Goldie's clothes and booties, blankets, diapers and hats from the chest, carried them out and piled them into the cradle. Her toy rattle, the string of spools, the little bag of buttons she'd made her that she liked to shake. She dropped the toys into the cradle and ran to the kitchen for the banana bottles, snatched up the little spoon she'd bought her and ran back to put them in the cradle.

Pressure built in her chest, pulsed against her throat in broken sobs. *Stop it!* There is no time for your self-ishness. Lana and Mack Tanner will be wonderful parents for Goldie. And she will have Georgie to play with when she's older, if her father doesn't come back. And Mack Tanner already had custody of Goldie's gold nuggets.

She spun about and ran back to the bedroom, dragged her mother's old carpetbag from beneath the bed. Her breath came in labored gulps. She hauled her necessaries, nightgown and robe from her dresser, thrust them into the bag, then added her brown merino and blue tweed outfits, two white shirtwaists and her slippers. Her toilet articles! She ran through the living room and kitchen to the washing and bathing room, grabbed her toothbrush and powder, brush and comb, snatched up the small hand mirror and hurried back to her bedroom.

If only her head would stop pounding so she could think! What else? What else…?

Chapter Twenty

Goldie's things were all ready. The sight of the cradle with Goldie's clothes and bottles and toys packed into it tore at her. She turned away before she lost all strength, walked back into her bedroom and picked up her mother's old carpetbag. Everything else, her cabin and her savings, she would leave for Hattie. That would be enough to keep her. *She* would go the way she had come. Only this time, there would be no hope in her heart for a clean life, a "normal" life. She knew now that the stain of her past would always be with her. And that the stain would spread to infect anyone she drew close to. Anyone she loved. Just as it had those who had befriended her here in Treasure Creek.

The rent in her heart split wider. The pain seized her lungs, stole her breath. The beloved faces flowed before her on a river of sorrow and regret. Hattie and Frankie… Teena and Lana…Mavis… She should never have allowed them to come close to her. She should never have taken them into her heart. The stain that was there had smeared them all with its darkness. She had brought hurt and division to the church and to the town. She had set friend against friend.

She blinked her eyes, caught her lower lip between her teeth to hold back the sobs. The way they had chosen sides in church…lined up for or against her.

She forced air into her lungs, carried the carpetbag out into the living room, opened the sewing cupboard and took out her pincushion, measuring tape and scissors. She would need them to make her living. She put them in the carpetbag and closed it, then tore a clean sheet of paper out of her account book and picked up her pen.

To Mayor Tanner and any others it may concern,
I leave my cabin, its furnishings and all of my savings to Hattie Marsh.
Viola Rose Goddard

She folded the note and tucked it into her purse, then tore out another sheet of paper, the tearing sound echoing the one in her heart.

Dearest Hattie,
For all the reasons you know and understand so well, I must leave Treasure Creek. Precious Goldie I will leave in the Tanners' care. I pray her father comes back for her one day, but if not, the Tanners will be wonderful parents to her.

To you, my beloved friend, I leave my cabin, its furnishings and all of my savings. I will leave a note stating that with Mack Tanner, but keep this one in case anyone should question your right to what was mine.

Thank you, Hattie dearest, for being my friend.
My fondest love always,
Viola

She pushed away the agony inside and squared her shoulders. There was no time for self-pity, church would soon be over and she could not bear to be here when Hattie brought Goldie home.

Home.

No more.

She ran to the table by the door, tucked the note for Hattie under the bowl, grabbed enough coins to pay for her passage back to Seattle and yanked open the door.

Her carpetbag.

She ran back and picked it up, whirled and froze. *Thomas.* The carpetbag thudded to the floor at her feet.

He'd frightened her. "I'm sorry, Viola. I should have thought about— The door was open." Thomas stared at Viola's pale face, cursed himself for a clumsy fool, startling her that way. "May I come in?"

She shook her head, made a helpless little pushing motion with her hand. "Please leave."

He dropped his gaze to the carpetbag at her feet, felt his heart drop to its level. "You're leaving?"

"I feel under the circumstances it is best for everyone if I do. I'm sure you agree." Her shoulders inched back, her chin lifted, but the tiny tremble of her lips gave her away.

"No. I don't." He took a breath, turned and closed the door to keep from taking her into his arms and begging her to stay. *Please, Lord, don't let it be too late. Give me the right words.*

"I asked you to leave. I have a ferry to catch."

Her voice was cool, controlled. The way it was when he'd first met her. Except that hint of a quiver hadn't been there then. He grabbed hold of it as a good omen, shook his head. "I asked Hattie to give us some time, Viola. And I am not going anywhere…and neither are you…until we talk."

She stiffened. "Very well, though I don't see what there is left to say."

"How about…I'm sorry." He jammed his hands into his suit coat pockets to keep from reaching for her, and stepped forward. "That night when Dangler was here…I was hurt that you hadn't trusted me or my position enough to tell me about your past. I knew there was something frightening you, and—"

"It was my *past*. And I was foolish enough to think that it had no bearing on who I *am*. That I could be free of it and live a clean, 'normal' life." Her voice caught, she jerked her head up a notch. "That's why I told no one. But I've learned that my sinful past will always be with me, and that the stain that covers me will spread to those I allow close and do harm to anyone I love."

"Viola—"

"No, Thomas." She blinked her eyes, swallowed hard. "There's nothing more to be said. You cannot deny the damage I have done to the people and town of Treasure Creek. I saw the way they chose sides for and against me at church. Friends against best friends, Thomas! And *I* did that! Simply by being who I am—"

"*Was*."

She stopped, stared at him, sucked in a deep breath and shook her head.

"You walked out of church before you heard the end of my message, Viola."

"The one about the adulterous woman?"

The hurt in her voice lanced his heart. "Yes."

"I don't care to hear more." She wrapped her arms about herself, turned her back.

He reached for her, drew his arms back and jammed his hands back into his pockets. Her hurt was too great, the pain too deep for him to declare his love. She would never believe him. He would have to be patient, let the Lord heal her heart before he asked her to let him in. *Lord, help me to be patient. Give me the words, Lord!*

He fastened his gaze on her ramrod-straight back. "Under the law, the punishment for adultery was death by stoning." A shudder made her shoulders shake. He hurried on.

"That is what the pharisees, scribes and those in the crowd around them expected. A harsh rendering of judgment and a swift execution of the sentence. You see, they didn't know the One to Whom they had brought the woman. They knew the law. But Jesus knew their hearts. He stooped down and wrote something on the ground with His finger. There is no way of knowing what He wrote. But I believe it was the Ten Commandments. And when they asked Him about the woman, and He again wrote something on the ground, I believe it was the words, 'Judge not, lest ye be judged.'

"When they pressed Him for His judgment on the woman He straightened and said, 'He that is without sin among you, let him first cast a stone at her.'" Conviction rang in the words. "He knew there was no one there without sin. Except Him. The pharisees, in the darkness of their ignorance, had brought the woman to the One True Judge."

He clenched his hands to keep from grabbing her and forcing her to face him. "Every person standing there in judgment of that adulterous woman had to examine their own hearts. And one by one they walked away, convicted of their own sin. Until there was only the woman and the sinless one." *God, let her hear.* "He asked her, 'Woman, where are those thine accusers? Hath no man condemned thee?' And when she replied, 'No man, Lord.' Jesus said, 'Neither do I condemn thee. Go, and sin no more.' He acknowledged her sin and forgave her. The Lord, merciful and mighty, made her clean and set her free. And He has done the same for you. You were right, Viola. Your past is over and forgotten. It has no bearing on who you are. You *are* clean, Viola."

He looked at her bowed head, her trembling hands covering her face, her shaking shoulders, and hated himself for contributing to her hurt. "That is the message I preached this morning, Viola. A message to remind every person in church this morning, including myself, that we have all sinned before God. That we all stand in need of God's mercy, forgiveness and love. A message every person in the church needed to hear. A message *I* needed to hear. I allowed my hurt and my pride to overrule mercy and love and sat in judgment on you without knowledge—"

"Then you shall know now."

She wiped the tears from her face and turned. The look in her eyes silenced his protest. He did not need to hear the story. But she needed to tell him.

"I was fourteen when my parents moved to Seattle.

My father had purchased a business and a home for us. Three weeks later, my parents were killed in a carriage accident. And three days later, on my fifteenth birthday, the banker foreclosed on the house. I was set out onto the streets of Seattle with what necessities I could carry in my mother's carpetbag."

He followed her glance down to the worn carpetbag, knew it was again packed with her necessities. His heart clutched.

"I knew no one in Seattle. I was alone and afraid." She shivered, wrapped her arms about herself. "Dengler found me crying on a park bench. He said I reminded him of his dead daughter and told me it would please him if I would stay in her room and let him provide for me until I could find a means of earning my own way. It was all a lie, of course. But I believed him."

I believed him. Three small words that said so much. Thomas clenched his hands, fought the outrage that gripped him for the innocent, young girl Viola was then.

"A month later he presented me with a bill for my room and board. I had no way to pay it. He said he was sorry, but I would have to leave, as he could not go on providing for me without recompense. And then he offered to 'let' me earn the money to pay my bill and for my keep by working in his 'house.' I had no one to turn to for help. No place to go. And he knew it. I… accepted." A shudder shook her. "I had no idea…"

She straightened, ran her hand along the top of the settle. "I ran away. Twice." Her hand lifted, massaged the scar on her other hand. "The second beating was so bad I didn't try again. Until one Sunday about four months ago, when another carriage accident happened."

She glanced at him, turned away again. "Some of the other girls and I went for a stroll every Sunday, and that accident forced us to alter our usual path. We went by a church and heard those inside singing a hymn. It stirred something in me. When I got back to my room I dug my mother's carpetbag out of the back of a closet and took out my mother's Bible. It fell open. There was an underlined verse on the page. This verse...."

She stopped before the sampler on the wall, touched the last words, "With God, all things are possible."

"My desire to leave my life of degradation and shame rose again, stronger than ever. But I had no money to pay for my escape. And no way to earn a living other than... what I had learned. I asked God to help me. And the thought came—I could become a seamstress. I did all the mending and made new gowns for the other...girls. But where could I go and be safe from Dengler's reach? And then the customers started talking about the gold fields and laughing about a God-centered town named Treasure Creek that allowed no gambling or bawdy houses. A town they swore they would never visit."

He thought of Dengler and Dolph, of the scar on her hand. How brave she was to try to escape a third time. "How did you get away?"

She smiled. A wonderful, beautiful smile that made his throat tighten and his pulse pound.

"I asked for permission to go to church." The smile died. She dropped her gaze to her hands. "Dengler agreed, as long as Dolph or Karl escorted me there, then returned after the service and walked me back to the house. He knew the church members would have no part of me. He was right.

"I sewed myself a modest waist and skirt, of the sort

other women wore, and hid it under the skirt of the frilly gown I wore to church, and then waited. I still needed money. One Sunday there was a disturbance in the… selection room. While Dengler and Dolph were subduing the drunken customer, I took enough money to cover the promised back wages I had never received. Dolph walked me to church. I waited in the small lady's room until the service started and he went away. Then I changed into my new outfit, hid my frilly dress behind a bench, covered my hair with a snood and walked to the docks and bought passage to Treasure Creek."

Thank You, Lord, for keeping her. And for bringing her safely here.

"Viola—"

She turned and looked at him. He cleared the huskiness from his voice and moved close to her. "I'm so sorry for hurting you, Viola. For not living up to the example Jesus set us all. Please forgive me. And please— unpack that carpetbag and give me and Treasure Creek a second chan—"

The door opened, banged against his foot. Hattie stepped inside, jiggled Goldie on her hip and smiled. "You better go put water on for tea, Viola. You got company."

"I don't need tea, Hattie. I only want a few minutes of Viola's time. If she will grant me permission to come in."

Evelyn? Viola stared, tried hard not to allow her astonishment to show as her neighbor stepped into the doorway.

"I wouldn't blame you if you refused to see me, Viola. But I hope you will allow me—"

"Of course I will see you, Evelyn. Please come in."

She shook off her shock at Evelyn's contrite tone and teary eyes and stepped forward. Her toe caught against her packed carpetbag.

Thomas shot out his hand and caught her arm, kept her from falling.

She looked up, met his gaze. Warmth crept into her heart. The icy cold that had seized her began to melt away. His fingers flexed, tightened, released their hold. But not his gaze. His gaze held her prisoner.

"Please think about what I said, Viola. And please stay. Now, I will leave you ladies to your conversation." He turned, made a polite bow to Hattie and Evelyn and walked out the door.

She wiped her palms on her skirt, got a tight hold on her emotions and looked toward her neighbor. The older woman was staring at the packed cradle and carpet bag, her face pale.

"May God forgive me for my wicked tongue." Evelyn Harris looked up, tears flowing down her cheeks. "And you, Viola. Please forgive me. I was *wrong* to sit in judgment on you. And to spread those vicious rumors. Pastor Stone's sermon showed me that. And then, afterward—" her voice caught on a sob "—when I was through at the altar… Hattie told me your story. Oh, Viola, I am so sorry." She rushed forward her hands extended in entreaty. "Please don't leave Treasure Creek. We need women with your integrity and courage. Please stay."

Chapter Twenty-One

Her heart seemed light. Almost as if it would fly right out of her chest. Viola fastened her nightgown, looked down at Goldie asleep in the cradle that had been carried back into her bedroom where it belonged and whirled around for sheer happiness. She was staying in Treasure Creek!

She still couldn't believe it. Thomas's sermon had brought about a wondrous change in the church members. Not all of them, of course. But a good many had mended old rifts. And Evelyn Harris, Beverly Fogel and Elizabeth Dunn had come that very Sunday to apologize and ask forgiveness for gossiping about her. And when they had seen Goldie's packed cradle and the carpetbag, they had asked her to stay in Treasure Creek. They knew about her past, and they wanted her to stay.

It was so hard for her to believe. She did not have to hold herself aloof for fear of questions about her past. She no longer had to live in fear of one of her old customers spotting her and revealing her past. She had been accepted as she was. She was free! *Free,* just as Thomas had said.

Thomas… The elation drained away. The one stumbling block to her staying in Treasure Creek was the one who had made it possible for her to stay. There had been something in Thomas's eyes when he had asked her to stay. Something warm and personal and wonderful. She was accustomed to seeing admiration in men's eyes. But this had been different. He had made her feel— No. She would not think about her feelings in these moments. Would not see more in them than was there. He had been speaking to her as her pastor. He had asked her to stay and give him a second chance as her pastor. And as a good pastor, he cared about her as one of his flock. To make it more than that was foolishness.

She walked to the living room, added a log to the coals to keep a chill from settling in overnight. Hattie suffered greater discomfort in her joints when it was damp or cold. She glanced up at the sampler, shook her head and walked back to her bedroom to finish preparing for bed.

She knew her dream would not come true. Nor should it. Love, marriage and a family were hopes inappropriate for an ex-prostitute. Especially marriage to a pastor. She gathered her thick, silky curls into a mass at the nape of her neck and reached for a ribbon. Some things were impossible, even for God. And that a fine, upstanding pastor like Thomas could ever love a woman like her, was one of them. And truly, she did not wish it.

She slid the ribbon beneath her other hand and looped it over the mass of hair she clutched. In spite of the kindness being exhibited toward her by the present church members, marriage to her would hurt Thomas's ministry. And she could not bear that. She would be content with Goldie and Hattie as her family. She formed a bow, tugged it tight. All the same, there had been a moment—before Hattie and the other women had interrupted—a moment when Thomas was looking down into her eyes.…

She stepped out of her slippers, climbed into bed and pulled up the covers, looking out the door to watch the flames licking at the log. His look had meant nothing. It was only Thomas's caring as a man of God. She knew it was only her traitorous heart wanting the foolish, selfish dream that had been born within her, the night she designed Frankie's wedding dress, to come true. But it gave her something to dream about. And everyone needed a dream.

She turned onto her side, cuddled into her pillow and sighed. "God, thank You for showing me what I should do. And for allowing me to stay in Treasure Creek."

Thomas splashed off the soap, ran a hand over his face and neck to check for any missed whiskers, then grabbed a towel and dried off. The sun streaming in the open window beside him glinted on the mirror. He leaned over the washstand to better see his reflection, looked into the green eyes peering back at him. Yep. There was a definite scheming look about them. He grinned, swished his razor clean, dried it and laid it on the stand.

Would she like the washbowl and pitcher? Maybe plain white had been a bad choice. He probably should have bought one with flowers, or a vine or something. He frowned, picked up the washbowl and tossed the soapy water out the window. Every furnishing he'd bought so far had been with an eye to the day when he brought Viola Goddard to the parsonage as his bride.

But she sure wasn't cooperating with his plan. She was a little cool the few times they had run into each other around town. And now that the Lord had set him free from his guilt over Louise's and Susie's deaths and provided this home for him, he was having a hard time maintaining his patience. He was as eager as a kid with a first crush to tell her he loved her.

He shook his head, walked into the bedroom and snatched his shirt off the bed. He couldn't believe how much he loved her. His wanting her for his wife went clear to his toes and then some. He shrugged into the shirt, buttoned it and tucked it into his pants, eyeing the other folded shirt on the bed. His lips twitched. It had sure been hard to make the sleeve catch on that nail— the one he'd deliberately left sticking out of the fence he was putting around the garden area he'd spaded up in the backyard. If any of his neighbors had been watching, they must have thought he was crazy, leaning against the fence and jerking away a half-dozen times or more while he dug in the same spot.

He chuckled, put on his jacket and picked up the shirt. It would have been easier to just rip the sleeve, but this way he had a true story to tell if Viola asked how the tear happened. He would confess that he had made it happen after they were married.

Married. To Viola. That sounded good!

He stepped out into the short hallway formed by the stairs that climbed to the loft on his left, and the small office on his right. An office. He shook his head, glanced in the door at the desk and chair that crowded the area. The only other piece of furniture was the chest that held his books he had Jimmy Crow bring down from his hut. He grinned. Mack had apologized because the room was so small, but it was larger than the whole of his hut. And a site warmer and drier.

Three strides brought him to the living room. He stopped, looked around. The size of the house was still a shock. Other than those few days he'd spent at Viola's, recuperating, and then in his room at the boardinghouse, it had been so long, he'd forgotten what it was like to live in a house you could actually walk around in. One with sturdy walls and a solid roof that didn't drip water on you every time it rained. "Thank You, Lord, for Your provision. May this home always be filled with those who love You and are called according to Your purpose."

He stepped outside onto the porch, looked down the road and smiled. Her cabin was there, at the end of the road. Close, but not close enough. Nothing would be close enough until he had her in his arms. But he had to earn her trust and her love before that could happen. And a few accidental meetings around town weren't enough to accomplish that. He had to see her, spend time with her, woo her. And he intended to do that no matter how many shirts he had to tear. He tucked the blue cotton excuse for his visit under his arm and started down the road with determination in his every stride.

"Yes, of course I will make you a dress, Evelyn." Viola looked down at Goldie, who was whimpering, and jiggled her knees to soothe her.

"Do you need to put her down for a morning nap, Viola? I can wait."

"No. She's not tired. I think she's getting another tooth." She lifted Goldie, cuddled her against her shoulder and smiled at her neighbor. "Did you have anything specific in mind?"

"Well…" A flush crept up Evelyn Harris's neck to her face. "I've always admired your green tweed outfit. If you could make me one like it in red… Only not quite so plain." The flush deepened. "Nothing fancy, of course."

"Hmm…" She swayed side to side, rubbed Goldie's back. "I could edge the jacket with a darker red braid… perhaps with a touch of black. And loop more of the braid around the hem of the skirt. Would that suit you? Or—"

"That would be lovely, Viola. You have excellent taste."

Was that another olive branch? "You're very kind. Thank you, Evelyn."

"Not at all. It's the truth." The older woman smiled. "Could you have the dress finished in time for Frankie's wedding?"

Thought of all she had to do for her friend's wedding day popped into her head. But Evelyn Harris was making a gesture of friendship, and a few late nights of sewing was a small price to pay for a friend. She smiled and nodded. "I can have it finished by then if you come for a fitting soon. Perhaps tomorrow afternoon? Hattie will be here to help with Goldie then."

"I'll be here. Now, I'll just go home and let you tend to the baby." Evelyn stood, smoothed her long skirt and started for the door. "I remember how fussy my babies were when they were teething. Matthew screamed something awful."

She rose to see her guest out. "Teena made me an herbal medicine to rub on her gums the last time Goldie was teething. It worked really well. I'm going to the clinic to get some more when Hattie returns and I put Goldie down for her nap this afternoon."

The older woman nodded. "Teena's skill with herbs is a blessing to this town. I'm so glad she and Dr. Callo- way married. They seem very happy." The streak of sun- light streaming in the partially open door highlighted her smile. "Thank you, Viola. I shall look forward to my new dress." Her neighbor turned, pulled the door wide. "Oh! Good morning, Pastor Stone."

Thomas. Her stomach fluttered.

"Good morning, Mrs. Harris."

His deep voice made the fluttering soar and dip. She swallowed, put her foot back to turn, then stopped. It was too late to hide. Too late to call back Evelyn Harris, who was hurrying across the road to her cabin. She dragged up her old, aloof mask and lifted her chin.

"Good morning, Viola."

"Good morning, Pastor Stone." Something flickered in the depths of his eyes. Disappointment? Her heart squeezed. She didn't want to disappoint him. Not ever.

"*Thomas* will do. I'm not here as your pastor, I'm here as a customer." He smiled, pulled a shirt from under his arm. "May I come in?"

No. A thousand times no. "Yes. Of course. I'll get my account book." Goldie started to whimper again. *Of all the times for Hattie to be gone…* She jiggled Goldie, opened the door of her sewing cupboard and reached for the gray-backed volume, realized too late the folly of her excuse to turn away from his steady gaze. She could not write—

"Would it help if I hold Goldie?"

Hold Goldie? She turned, the question in her eyes.

"You're not the only one God has set free of their past, Viola." His gaze caught hers, held it. Her pulse sped. "The Lord used my time here with you and Hattie to heal more than my shoulder. He showed me the burden of guilt I was carrying over my wife's and baby's deaths was of my own making. He turned the evil intent of that kidnapper's shot into a true blessing. Just as Hattie predicted."

He reached out and took Goldie from her, started to lift the baby to his shoulder, stopped and cradled her in the crook of his right arm instead. "Hey, little one. What's the problem?"

Goldie stopped fussing, stared up at him out of her round blue eyes. He took her chubby hand in his, smiled when she curled her fingers around his thumb. "Tiny little thing, aren't you?"

The very image of her dream come true was before her. Goldie's precious face turned into a watery blur. Viola blinked, whirled back to the cupboard, picked up her pen and wrote his name. "What is the nature of the problem?"

"A tear in the sleeve. A jagged one, if that matters."

She nodded, made a notation.

"Well look who's here."

Hattie, back early. Thank goodness. She turned, threw Hattie a grateful look and took Goldie from his arms. "That's all the information I need. I will have your shirt ready for you by Wednesday. Now, if you will excuse me, I must see to Goldie." She gave a polite nod in his general direction and hurried off toward her bedroom.

Thomas finished his lunch, wiped out the pan he'd fried the fish in, grabbed his jacket and left the house by the back door. If he remembered correctly, Viola put Goldie down for her nap just about now.

He whistled his favorite hymn, cut across lots and entered the back door of the Treasure Creek clinic, grateful for the partially open door that had allowed him to overhear Viola's plans.

"What do I owe ya, Doc?"

The stampeder sporting a large bandage on his right forearm glanced his way. Thomas gave him a polite smile.

"Fifty cents will do. Toss it in the bowl on your way out." Jacob Calloway looked up from scrubbing his hands, spotted him and frowned. "Are you having problems with your wound?"

"No. I just want to borrow a corner of your operating room for a few minutes."

Jacob's frown turned to a scowl. "What kind of nonsense is that? I'm too busy to play games, Thomas."

"It's no game, Jacob. I overheard Viola say Goldie was getting another tooth and that she was coming to get some herbs from Teena." He knew he looked sheepish, shrugged and grinned. "I thought maybe I could accidentally run into her and walk her home."

"Ahh." Jacob grinned, burst into laughter. "I guess I can help you out. But get over in that corner and stay out of my way."

"Yes, Doctor." He snapped off a salute, lounged back against the wall and turned his ear toward the door.

"Next." Jacob shot an amused glance his way, left the door open a crack, then ignored him. So did the patient.

He waited through the lancing of a carbuncle and the stitching of a gaping wound above a miner's eye before he heard her voice. He stayed in place through four thudding heartbeats, then opened the door. "Thanks, Jacob."

Teena looked up, her dark eyes wide with surprise. Viola jerked around, almost dropped the large package she was holding. He hurried to her side, sent Teena a silent "don't say anything" message with his eyes before she gave him away. "Hello, Viola. Out doing some chores?"

"I was, yes." Her voice was cool, tight. "I'm going home now." She fumbled to reach her purse around the package.

"Permit me." He withdrew the package from under her arm.

She frowned, reached in her purse for some coins.

He glanced at Teena, noted the speculative expression in her eyes, the tiny upward curve at the corners of her mouth and smiled. She gave a tiny nod, then held out the small, sealed crock to Viola and accepted her payment.

"Ready?"

Viola glanced up at him, reached for the package. "Yes. Thank you for helping."

He drew his hand back, shook his head. "I'm going your way. I'll carry this for you. Shall we?" He stepped forward, opened the door with his free hand and made a polite little bow.

She glanced at the clients who were looking at them, lifted her chin and stepped outside.

He heard a soft giggle, turned and glanced at Teena, gave her a wink and closed the door.

Chapter Twenty-Two

"I don't know how you figure out them pieces, then put them all together to make a dress, Viola." Frankie Tucker shook her head and grinned. "I'd probably have an arm coming out the neck hole."

Viola laughed, finished cutting out the second sleeve and added it to the pile of pieces beside her on the rug. Only one piece left to cut out. "And I don't know how you figure out all the pieces and put a building together, Frankie. I'd probably have the door in the roof." She leaned forward over her knees and started cutting out the collar.

"Mayhap the two of you should change places and give it a try some day." Hattie chuckled, then knit another stitch in the coverlet she was making for Frankie and Ed's wedding gift. "It'd liven up conversation for a while. Things are kinda dull, now that all the gossipin's stopped."

"Hattie." It came out as a chorus.

"Don't be lookin' so shocked, the two of you." Hattie knit the last stitch in the row, turned the piece and purled the first stitch. "I ain't talkin' about the mean-spirited, hurtful kind. I'm talkin' about the fun kind." Her gray head lifted from her work. "Don't tell me neither one of you didn't notice that the color of Rose's new dress made it look like there was a big frog sittin' in her pew Sunday mornin'."

Viola gasped. Laughter boiled up and shot out of her mouth in an unstoppable burst. Frankie slapped her knee and erupted in unrestrained hilarity.

Hattie nodded, went back to her knitting. "That's the kind I'm talkin' about, the fun kind. Ain't nobody hurt by that except maybe Viola's gettin' a stitch in her side. I already told Rose the dress put me in mind of a frog."

Frankie gulped back her laughter. "What'd she say?"

Hattie fixed her faded-blue eyes on her and grinned. "Ribbbetttt."

Frankie let out a whoop.

"Oh!" Viola pressed her right hand against her side and rocked back and forth, helpless to stop her laughter in spite of the little stabbing pain. "Gracious, Hattie. You say the most unexpected things. You've lived here for over two months now, and I still don't know what to expect when you start to speak." She made her last cut, added the collar piece to the pile and stood.

"The truth. Like…'it ain't over yet'." Hattie shot her a look and went back to her knitting.

What was that supposed to mean? Viola studied her for a moment, shrugged and turned to Frankie. "Help me carry these pieces to that table beside my sewing machine please, Frankie. I'm going to finish sewing the fringe on the swags now, then go to the church and hang them tonight, after Goldie has gone to sleep. That will free me to start sewing your gown tomorrow."

She picked up the long skirt pieces. The silk fabric flowed down over her arms and whispered softly as she carried it to the table. She put them down, glanced up at Frankie, caught her nodding in Hattie's direction. She shifted her gaze to Hattie, who was sitting, head down, knitting, and frowned. She must have imagined the nod. She looked back at Frankie. "I forgot to ask. Have you hung the hooks for the swags?"

"Not yet, I'll go hang them as soon as you take these pieces from me, they're slipping all over the place."

"Yes, silk does that." She lifted the pieces, laid them out so they would not wrinkle, and stared after Frankie, who was hurrying toward the door. That guilty look she'd had on her face must be because she forgot to hang the hooks.

Thomas laid down his pen, shoved back from the desk and hurried to open the door. "Well, hello, Frankie." He smiled at the woman standing on his porch. "Is there a problem?"

"Nope. Not if you're not planning on being in the church, praying or anything, for the next little while." She lifted the bag in her hand, patted the hammer hanging from her leather belt. "I'm fixing to hang these hooks on the windows in the entrance, and I'll be making noise." She stared straight up into his eyes. "I've got to get them done now, because Viola's coming to the church tonight, after she gets Goldie to sleep, to hang the new curtains she's made for the entrance."

"I see." He grinned, rubbed his hand over his chin. "Thank you for informing me, Frankie. I will be happy to delay any praying I was planning on doing at the church until later this evening."

She nodded. "Hattie thought you might see it that way." She lifted a hand in farewell and headed for the church.

"Tell Hattie I said thank you!"

Frankie turned, waved then kept on walking. He smiled and went back in the house. He had some praying to do right now…about later.

"Put the pad on the bench please, Matthew." Viola placed her package on the collections table, took a two cent piece from her pocket and held it out to her neighbor's son. "Thank you for helping me." The towhead nodded, grinned and scooted out the door.

"That money will be in the till at Tanner's tomorrow morning, just as soon as Matthew decides which candy he wants."

Thomas. That fluttering happened in her stomach again. She turned toward the sanctuary door, met his gaze. The fluttering spread to her heart. She looked away. "I'm sorry, Thomas. I didn't know you were here. I don't wish to disturb you. I can come back another time." She reached for the package.

"You're not disturbing me. I've finished praying." He stepped close to the table. "Please, continue with what you're doing."

No man should have a voice so deep and rich you felt…caressed by it. She nodded, tugged at the end of the string to release the bow and folded back the paper, concentrated on what she was doing. If she kept busy, perhaps he would go away.

She lifted out the top swag, spread it along the table and did the same with the second. The fabric was so rich and lustrous, it picked up the light from the small windows in a sheen that was opulent yet subdued. And the fringe… She ran her hand beneath the long, silky, twisted strands, watched them ripple like moon-silvered water over her fingers. It had been well worth the wait of placing an order for the special fabric and fringe. The swags had turned out exactly as she had hoped.

"The bench cushion looks good. I like the red color. Was that your choice?"

"Yes and no. It seemed a good idea to match one of the colors in the stained glass windows. And the crimson was the best choice for several reasons." She walked to the bench, checked the fit of the cushion, brushed off some lint, then turned back to pick up a swag. He was half sitting, half leaning against the heavy wooden table, his ankles crossed, his fingers curled over the thick edge, watching her. And that *look* was back in his eyes. He caught and held her gaze. Her heart tripped, stumbled back into a staccato beat that made her throat and wrists pulse.

He straightened. "Viola…"

She jerked her gaze away, stepped to the far end of the table and snatched up the top swag. By the time she got to the window, she had her breath back. She measured an equal distance from both ends of the swag with her eye, gathered the depth of the fabric in her hands, and raised her arms to lay it in the open hooks. They were too high. She stretched, went on tiptoe, felt him behind her.

"Allow me."

His arms came over her shoulders, stretched out along hers. His callused fingers brushed her bared wrists, the tips searing her flesh. The long, silky fringe on the swag quivered, betraying her tremble. He lifted the fabric from her hands, placed it in the hooks.

"Is that how you wanted it?"

His voice was soft, husky, close to her ear. Her nerves thrummed. She sucked in air, ducked her head and slid out from under his raised arm. "I—I have to look from back here." She stepped across the room, looked back at the window, found he'd turned to watch her and almost fell. She grabbed hold of the end of the bench, gestured toward the window with her other hand. "It's hanging a little longer on the right side. If you could take hold of it there, by the hook, and pull it a little toward the center… Yes. That's perfect. Thank you."

"That's not so hard. Shall we do the next?"

The other window. "Yes." She motioned toward the table. "You place the swag in the hooks and I'll tell you if it's right or not."

He studied her for a moment, then moved to the table, glanced down at the swag, looked back at her and shook his head. "You'll have to show me what to do."

Her mouth went dry. But not her hands. She nodded, wiped her moist palms down her long skirt and walked back to the table. He moved toward one end. She would have preferred he leave the room, but she couldn't tell him so. She eyed the swag, would have to stand at the center of the length of the table to pick it up properly. And that was much, *much* too close to him.

She swallowed, stepped into position, measured the distance from the ends of the swag with her eye and gathered the depth of the fabric into her hands. He stepped toward her. His chest almost touched her shoulder as he reached out his left hand, slid it beneath hers and cupped the fabric. His warm breath feathered across her cheek. She jerked to the side, slid along the table out of his way. He leaned forward, slipped his right hand beneath hers and took hold of the fabric, lifted it and walked to the second window.

She closed her eyes, caught her breath then hurried back over to the bench. "Both sides are longer than the other swag. Bring them in toward the center, please. Yes, that's good." *Please, Lord, let him go now.* "Thank you, Thomas, I can manage now. I've only to put the runner on the collections table and I'm through."

He nodded, stepped back to the table. "I'll just hold these out of your way." He picked up the purple glass bowl Teena had brought in and the hurricane globe candle holder, stepped a little toward one end of the table.

There was nothing to do but finish her job. She walked to the table, took the runner out of the package, folded the paper and tossed it over onto the bench. She edged to the center of the table, conscious of him standing so close she could hear him breathing, and spread the runner out, matching the amount of fabric that hung off the table at both ends.

He held the bowl out to her. She tried to take it from him without touching his hand, but somehow their fingers met. She set the bowl on the table before she dropped it, moved it to the center. "You can put the candle right there." She indicated the place she meant and hurried to the bench to pick up the paper. Finally she could leave. She turned toward the door.

"Thank you for your hard work, Viola. You've made this room much nicer. It's very welcoming, and…I guess you would call it elegant."

She nodded, forced a smile. "I enjoy doing things for the church." She reached for the door handle.

"I understand you're going to make pads, like the one on the bench, for the pews."

"Yes. I hope to have them finished in time for Frankie and Ed's wedding day." Her words brought her dream rushing into her head and heart. Her pulse throbbed.

"That promises to be quite a day." He smiled and stepped close. "Can you keep a secret?"

Her nerves drew taut. She brushed a curl back off her forehead. "Yes, of course I can."

He nodded and grinned—a crinkling of the corners of his green eyes, and a slow, crooked slanting of his mouth that made her knees go weak all over again.

"Mack Tanner checked yesterday. The carpet for this room will be here on Wednesday's supply boat. And the bell he's ordered for the church will be here in time to ring out the celebration for the bride and groom."

"Oh, Thomas, that's wonderful!" Her tension eased in her pleasure for her friend. "Frankie will be so excited. When will you tell her?"

He shook his head. "Not me. Mack's going to make the announcement on Sunday." His gaze caught and held hers. "How is Goldie doing? Has she got that tooth yet?"

That warm caring was back in his eyes and voice. She took a breath and nodded. "Two actually. She seems to like to get her teeth in pairs." She twisted the handle and pulled open the door. "Good night, Thomas."

"I'll walk you home."

She shook her head. "Thank you, but that's not necessary."

She pulled the door closed. It opened again before

she reached the bottom of the steps. "Good night, Viola. Tell Hattie I said hello."

She nodded and hurried down the road, conscious of him standing on the stoop and watching her every step of the way.

"You can't run away forever, Viola. I'll get past your fear and make you love me." Thomas whispered the vow into the soft, night air, jumped off the stoop, jammed his hands in his pants pockets and headed straight for the woods. He needed a walk. A *long* walk. To feel her trembling when his arms were around her and not pull her close and taste the sweetness of those soft, full lips had taken every bit of inner moral strength he had. And then when she had run to the other side of the room and turned and looked at him…

He shook his head. He'd misread that look. Had almost ruined it then. His love for her had caused him to see a responsive love in her, one that wasn't there… yet. When he'd started for her, her look had changed to one of fear, almost panic. Was it because of her past? Because of what—

He fisted his hands. Longed for Dengler or Dolph or Karl or those men who had abused the young, innocent Viola to pummel, to punish for every moment of hurt or fear or degradation she had suffered at their hands. Hatred, *rage* against those men who had touched her boiled up, darkened his vision. His long-legged strides drove him forward past the clustered cabins, beyond Dunkle's farm, to the woods. He shoved a branch aside, stepped onto the Tlingit path and broke into a run, a bone-jarring, lung-challenging run that would leave him exhausted and drained.

His boots thudded against the soft earth. His straining lungs dragged in oxygen, and his heart pounded. Trees flashed by, but it wasn't enough. He couldn't run hard enough or fast enough or far enough to outrun the truth.

He had to forgive those men. He *had* to forgive them. Not for their sakes. For his. If he didn't forgive, his rage would turn to bitterness and that would destroy him and any chance he had to build a life of love with Viola. If he didn't forgive them, there would be no peace for him in these woods or anywhere.

He slowed to a jog, staggered to a towering tree and drove his fists against the rough bark of the unyielding trunk until he hadn't strength enough left to lift his arms. And still, it wasn't enough. He slid down the trunk to his knees, pressed his face against his wounded, bleeding, fisted hands and sobbed out his fury, his frustration and rebellion against what he must do.

When the paroxysm had passed, he turned and leaned back against the trunk, rested his forearms on top of his bent knees and stared up at the purple sky above the branches. "All right, Lord, all right. I yield. I don't want to, but I *choose* to obey. I *choose* to forgive those men…all of them."

He felt it then, God's presence washing over him, drenching him, sluicing away the anger and bitterness, leaving him clean and at peace.

Chapter Twenty-Three

Viola added a little more milk to the batter and stirred. "Is this right?"

Hattie peered into the bowl, nodded. "Yep. Not so thick it sits in a lump, and not so thin it runs all over the griddle when you spoon it on. Now, get some water on your fingers and shake it off over the griddle."

"Why?" She dipped the tips of her fingers and shook them over the griddle. Drops of water sizzled and bounced across the hot, iron surface before disappearing.

"See that water dancin'? Means the griddle's hot enough. Spread a mite of grease on it…. Yep, that's good. Now git your batter on there."

She spooned out batter, watched it spread to a little pool and stop, repeated the process over the long griddle surface. Grease sizzled around the edges of the small mounds of batter. She smiled down at Goldie sitting on the floor chewing on the wooden dog's ear. "Are you watching me learning to cook, sweetie? I'll have some good pancakes for you to eat soon."

"Not 'less you get to flippin' them over. They're fixin' to burn."

"Already?" She dropped the spoon into the bowl and grabbed the turner.

"Slide it under, then flip them fast."

"Like this?" She did as instructed, laughed when the pancake flipped over perfectly and went on to the next. "How did you know they were ready to be turned?"

Hattie pointed a knobby finger at the one yet to be turned. "They're ready when them little bubbles 'round the edges start poppin'."

"Oh. And now?"

Hattie grinned. "Now you just know. Or else you lift them up and peek." She tilted her head, frowned. "Someone's knockin'. I'll go. You'd best push that bacon over to the side where it's not so hot."

"Hattie." Panic pounced. She grabbed one of the thick pads she had made for Hattie and pushed the sizzling bacon over to the edge of the stove. Grease popped. "Ouch!" She wiped the grease off the back of her hand onto her apron, then lifted a pancake and peeked at the underside. Perfectly browned. She grabbed a plate off the table, piled the pancakes onto it and set it on the warming shelf. A bit more grease on the griddle, more batter… A smile curved her lips. Cooking wasn't so hard once—

She froze. Was that— She stepped sideways toward the door to the living room, tipped her head and listened. It was.

Her heart jolted. Batter slid off the spoon onto the top of the stove, spit and hissed. Footsteps came close. Hattie's—and heavy male ones.

Her hair! She hadn't put it up yet. And she couldn't

get to her room without going by them. *Oh, Hattie*—
She grabbed at the curly mass with her free hand, tossed
it back over her shoulders. *The food.* She jerked back to
her place. The batter bubbles were popping. She dropped
the spoon, grabbed the turner and flipped them, scooped
up the batter that had fallen on the stove and flipped it
onto the griddle, rubbed off the bit that remained with
a corner of her apron just in time.

Hattie came through the door, all smiles. "Look who
was at the door, Viola."

She didn't have to look. Her heart had already told
her. She arranged her features in a cool, controlled mask
and glanced over at Thomas. His wavy, sandy hair was
darker than normal, slicked back by water or some sort
of pomade. There was a smile warming his green eyes,
tilting the corners of his mouth. Her pounding pulse
started dancing like the water she'd spattered on the hot
griddle.

"Good morning, Viola. I came to pick up my shirt."
He cleared his throat, looked away, then back. His brown
shirt lifted with his deep breath. "I'm sorry I'm so early.
I'm a sunrise person, and I've lived alone in that hut on
the trail so long, I forget others don't start their day as
early as I do."

"You gonna let them pancakes burn?"

"What? Oh." She looked down at the griddle, flipped
the pancakes and held the turner out. She could go
do her hair. "You finish, Hattie. I'll go get Thomas
his—"

Hattie shook her head, waved away the turner. "No
need to do that now. You got plenty of time. I asked
Thomas to share breakfast with us." She rubbed at
her shoulder. "You keep at the cookin'. My bones are

achin' some this morning. I'll just set another plate at the table, then plunk myself down in a chair and rest them a spell."

"But—"

"Smells like them pancakes is done. Bacon needs turnin', too."

She clamped her jaw, spun back around to the stove, wanting to cry or scream. She wasn't quite sure which.

"Could I help?"

She snatched the pancake platter off the warming shelf, flipped a pancake onto it and glared up at him. "If you don't want to eat burned food." *Flip.* "This is the first time I've ever cooked." *Flip.* She slammed the platter back onto the warming shelf, dropped more grease onto the griddle, spooned on batter, decided she didn't want to cry or scream. She wanted to scold Hattie. And she would. Later.

"Here's the eggs."

Eggs? A blue crockery bowl was set on the reservoir close to her hand.

"An' here's a plate so you can lift the bacon."

Hattie's knobby, arthritic hand came into view holding out a plate. Viola stared at it like it was a snake about to strike.

"Why don't I handle the bacon and eggs?"

His voice, so warm, so deep, so…unnerving. She closed her eyes, took a deep breath, back to the crying or screaming decision.

"Could you hand me that fork so I can lift this bacon, please?"

She opened her eyes, picked up the long-handled,

two-tined cooking fork and held it out. Gasped, shot her gaze to his face. "What happened to your hands?"

"I had an argument with a tree." His gaze took command of hers, held it prisoner. "Scraped my knuckles up." His eyes darkened to a smoky gray-green.

She stepped back, feeling crowded, unable to breathe. "I think the bacon's burning." She made a little stab in the air with the fork.

"I like burned bacon." He stepped close, closed his hand over hers on the handle.

She jerked away, the fork clattered to the stove. "I— I'll be right back. I still have some of Teena's herbal salve. It will help your hands." She rushed from the room.

He stared after her, his heart sick. "She's afraid of me."

"No, she's not." Hattie rose, picked up the fork and handed it to him. "She's afraid of the way you make her feel." Her wise old eyes looked up into his. "Viola's experienced only one kind of man, Thomas. And she learned early how to protect her heart from their mean and selfish ways. But you don't fit what she's always known, and she's learnin' there ain't any way of protectin' herself from love. She don't rightly know what it is she's feelin', because she's never experienced the sharin', the givin' and receivin' kind of love. You just keep doin' what your doin'. She'll come around." She blinked her eyes, gestured toward the stove. "Now save what you can of that bacon whilst I get to work on these eggs."

"Gracious!"

"Oh!" Viola drew the needle through the velvet,

dropped the cushion to the floor and ran to open the door before the pounding woke Goldie. "Wha—"

"Ya gotta come, Miz Goddard...Miz Marsh! Ya gotta come! The church bell's here!" Matthew Harris jumped up and down, pointed down the road. "They're fixin' to hang it right now! Miz Tanner sent me to get you. I gotta get Ma!" He dashed off across the road.

Viola spun about. Hattie was on her feet, excitement brightening her faded-blue eyes, a grin deepening the wrinkles on her face. "The *bell's* here, Hattie. Get your wrap and—"

The wisps of gray hair escaping Hattie's bun fluttered with the vehement shake of her head. "You go, Viola. I'll stay here with Goldie and come along when she wakes."

"No, Hattie. This is too important an event for either one of us to miss." She whirled toward her bedroom door. "I'll wake Goldie and get her changed and ready to go. You get your wrap and grab a toy for her that I can take along. Hurry!"

"My! Everybody in town is here." Hattie looked over the crowd. "Sounds like the waterfront."

Viola listened to the hum of voices, the excited yells of children—the exclamations that rose over the pounding of hammers and clang of metal that punctuated the clamor—and nodded. She stopped, glanced around. "Maybe we should try and cut through the back lots to the school and see—"

"Viola... Hattie... Over here!"

She looked toward the voices, saw Evelyn Harris, Margie Sanders, Lucy Johnson and Mavis Goodge waving and wove a path through the spectators to them.

"Exciting, isn't it?"

She nodded in answer to Margie and looked across the road. There was a wagon backed up to the church entrance, the bell sitting at the back of the bed. Men were bent over it, attaching a rope from a block and tackle to the short, thick piece of wood the bell was fastened to.

"The bell will complete our church." Evelyn Harris beamed a smile at them all. "What a blessing we have Mack Tanner as founder of our town. He's *so* generous. That bell had to cost him a good deal of money."

"Ain't no more generous than Thomas givin' half o' them gold nuggets he found to buy the stained glass windows. Or the rest o' us donatin' what we can to help." Hattie peered up at the taller woman. "Not takin' anythin' away from Mack Tanner. Just sayin' the difference is, he gives out of his plenty, most of the rest of us give out of our just makin' it by."

A flush climbed Evelyn's neck and spread across her cheeks. "You're right, Hattie." She leaned down, gave Hattie a quick hug. "Thank you for reminding me of that. I..." She looked at the rest of the group and laughed. "Well you all know I'm too easily impressed by wealth."

"We know."

Viola joined in the laughter at Mavis's droll reply.

"Haul away!"

She snapped her gaze back across the road. Two men pulled down on a rope that rose to feed through another block and tackle, fastened to the center of a crossbeam that spanned the distance between two thick upright posts at the front corners of a platform that straddled the peak of the roof. Ed Parker and Duncan MacDougal stood on the platform looking down at the bell. The sight of them at the edge of the roof made her stomach queasy. She looked back at the bell.

The rope tightened, the block and tackle creaked and the bell lifted from the wagon bed, hung swinging from the rope.

A cheer rose from the crowd, was quickly stifled as the bell began its slow ascent.

"Why isn't it ringing, Pa?"

"They've got the clapper wrapped. It protects it while its being shipped."

She glanced at the young boy who had asked the question and smiled. "I wondered, too."

He gave her a shy smile and leaned against his father's legs.

Thomas walked up to the wagon and spoke to the driver, who nodded then drove away. Thomas moved over to stand with Mack Tanner, lifted his head to watch the bell continue its climb. Her heart warmed, fluttered. How handsome he was, with the sun gilding his sandy hair and his strong, weather-tanned features.

He straightened, turned his head and scanned the crowd, met her gaze.

Everything faded away. He smiled and her heart soared higher than the bell. She curved her lips in an answering smile. Goldie whimpered, and she switched her to her other hip, took the string of spools from her pocket and gave them to her. When she looked back, Thomas was entering the church with Mack Tanner.

"They've got 'er up there safe."

"Slide it onto the skids!"

She looked up and her heart leaped into her throat. Ed Parker and Duncan MacDougal were each holding on to a corner beam with one arm, leaning out and pulling the bell onto the platform with the other. And Frankie was standing between them. She unhooked the block and tackle and the men pushed the bell along the platform into the bell tower. A collective sigh rose from the crowd.

"Well, there's no more to see here. Time for me to get back to the boardinghouse. My roomers don't feed themselves." Mavis Goodge tugged her wrap closer about her shoulders, lifted a hand in farewell and walked away.

"And I need to go home and finish sewing those last few cushions for the pews. I'm taking them to the church tonight." She smiled at her friends and started for her cabin, Hattie beside her.

"Looks like Frankie's gonna have a bell to call folks to her nuptials."

"Yes." Thought of the wedding stole the day's luster. She must be tired from all the late-night sewing. She looked at Hattie and smiled. "That will please her."

"Folks are going to remember Frankie's weddin' forever. Her name's going to be the first one writ in the Treasure Creek Church record book." Hattie shook her head, opened the door and stepped into the cabin. "Sorta nice, Treasure Creek havin' a preacher that can perform weddin's legal and all. Saves folks havin' to travel to Skaguay to git hitched. And now we got a bell to ring and sound out the good news when the joinin's done."

Thomas would be performing the ceremony. How had she not thought of that before?

Hattie looked up at her and chuckled. "Did you see Frankie up there on that roof, a-guidin' that bell whilst the men pushed it?" She shook her head and took off her wrap. "Ain't nobody what don't see it with their own eyes going to believe that's Frankie a-wearin' that special gown you're making her. You gonna make yourself a gown like it when *you* get married?"

The words stabbed straight into her heart. "Don't talk foolishness, Hattie! I told you I will never marry." She slammed the door closed and carried Goldie to the kitchen to prepare a bottle.

Thomas stepped up onto the stoop, fisted his hand and rapped on the door. A grin tugged at his mouth. Did Viola have any idea of the conspiracy Hattie was conducting, with the help of their friends, to help him win her as his bride? Margie Sanders had tracked him down after the bell was installed this afternoon to tell him Viola was planning on bringing the finished pew cushions to the church tonight. And here he was, excuse in hand, ready to offer his services as a pack mule.

The door hinge squeaked. He wiped the grin from his face, saw Hattie grinning at him, and let it return. "Good evening, Hattie. May I come in? I have some business to discuss with Viola."

"Well, you can come on in, but Viola's a mite busy." She gave him a wink and stepped back. "She's tryin' to figure out how to get all these cushions she's made to the church tonight. They're crowdin' us out of the house."

He stepped inside, spotted Viola standing beside a pile of long red velvet pads that reached to her waist and grinned. "Looks like you've got a problem."

She shot him a perplexed look. "I was planning on hiring Matthew to carry these for me, but they are heavier than I thought they would be. But I'll manage. I'll just have to make several trips."

He crossed the room, lifted one of the pads. "You

can't carry these, Viola. They're too heavy for you. And with their length, they'd make an armful for a man. I'll carry them for you."

She wanted to refuse, he could read it in her eyes. She looked skittish, like a deer that scents a hunter and is ready to run. He frowned, not pleased with that thought.

"What about your shoulder and arm?"

"I won't use them. I'll carry the cushions on my back. Like this." He picked up the end of the top pad and twisted his good arm around as if he were putting on a cape. When he stopped, the end of the pad curved down over the top his head and the length of it hung down his back. "Got it?"

Her lips twitched. "You'd make a terrible king."

He laughed and leaned forward so she could reach his head. "Load them on."

"Well…if you're sure." She picked up the top pad and draped it over the one on his back. He opened his hands, positioned where his neck joined his shoulders, and clasped the edges of it. "I think five will be as many as I can hold on to."

She nodded, added three more pads to his load, then walked to the door and opened it. He stepped outside, waited for her to join him, then started down the road.

She giggled.

"What is it? Is something wrong?"

"Nooo, it's only—hunched over like that, you look like a big red turtle."

He laughed, gave her a sidelong look. "Is that better or worse than a terrible king?"

"I think they're about the same. Here we are." She ran up the church steps and opened the door.

He trudged up to the stoop and followed her through the entrance into the sanctuary, stopped by the first pew.

"Turn around." She slid the pads off his back, onto the seat.

He straightened and grinned down at her. "No more turtle."

"Until the next load." She gave him a cheeky grin and headed for the door.

He gritted his teeth, threw a silent plea for mercy toward the ceiling and followed.

Chapter Twenty-Four

Tomorrow was Frankie's wedding day. Viola pushed a wayward curl off her forehead, opened the kitchen door and stepped outside. Snow-cooled air, sinking off the mountain behind her cabin, touched her face and hands.

She wrapped her arms about herself and strolled through her backyard, wishing away the restlessness, the discontent that plagued her day and night of late. All of the busyness, the hard work and late nights of sewing, had not driven it away. What would she do when life returned to normal after the wedding? Caring for Goldie, holding her, playing with her only increased the dissatisfaction. Not with the baby. She was so precious, such a joy. But there was always this vague feeling that there should be more.

She picked up a small dried twig, snapped it into tiny pieces and threw them away. She had work enough... more than enough. There were so many stampeders passing through Treasure Creek daily now, she had to turn their business away. It was Thomas. The only time she was really contented now, was when she was with him. He was so kind and so thoughtful. Always ready to help her. And so…charming.

Oh, this was all his fault. He was the only man who had ever treated her as if…as if he *cared* about her. And it had put these foolish notions, these impossible dreams in her head and her heart. And Frankie's happiness over her coming marriage to Ed didn't help. It fed the dreams. She had thought them harmless, but they weren't. Love, marriage and a family were inappropriate dreams for an ex-lady of the evening. She simply had to give them up and come back to her senses. Beginning now.

She marched to the door and went inside to go to bed.

Dong…dong…dong…

Frankie twisted her head to peer out the window. "Look at all the people going into the church, Viola. Must be half the town's squeezing in there. That bell works right well at drawing them."

"It's not the bell, Frankie." Viola brushed Frankie's short black curls until they made a soft, ebony frame for her heart-shaped, freckled face. "Everyone in Treasure Creek considers you and Ed their friends."

"Not the ones we've arrested or escorted out of town because they were drunk or carrying liquor on them."

She laughed.

"What's funny?"

"Frankie, you are the only young woman I know of who would stand in her wedding dress and talk about arresting people. You are the perfect bride for Ed Parker."

"I sure hope he thinks so…when he sees me, I mean."

"He will, Frankie. You look beautiful."

A flush tinged Frankie's face, made the freckles dusted across her nose look darker.

Dong…dong…dong…

"You almost through with what you're doing, Viola? I don't want Ed wondering where I am."

She picked up the wide headband, trimmed with a cluster of roses she'd made out of the same cream-colored silk as Frankie's dress. "I'll be through in just a moment. Hold still now." She nestled the band in among the dark curls, tied the ends in a soft bow at the right temple.

"Good thing my cabin's catty-corner from the church-yard. At least I haven't got far to go when you get done. Though I don't rightly know if I can make time in this dress." She twisted her head to look over her shoulder. "That sweepy thing on the back isn't too practical. But it sure is pretty." She turned back, gasped. "Is that *me?*"

Viola nodded, tightened her grip on the large mirror she held.

"Willikers…" Frankie's voice was soft, full of awe. She ran her hands she had creamed to softness down the fitted bodice and over her tiny waist. "You did it, Viola. You made me a dress that makes me look all girly and… and…"

"Beautiful, Frankie." She swallowed hard and smiled. "You look beautiful." She leaned the mirror against the wall and lifted the train of Frankie's dress. "Now hold your skirt hems up a little to keep them clean when we cross the road and let's go get you married."

The church was abuzz with chatter when they entered. Margie and Lucy, standing by the entrance to the sanctuary whirled and started forward when they opened the door. "It's about time, Fra—" They stopped, their blue eyes widened, their rose-red lips gaped open. *"Frankie?"*

Viola smiled at the chorus of disbelief.

"Course it's me!" Frankie nodded toward the sanctuary. "Is Ed here?"

Her sisters stared, nodded, stepped forward, enveloped Frankie in a huge hug and stepped back. Margie cleared her throat. "Come on, Lucy, let's tell them she's here."

"Move over by the doorway, Frankie." Viola arranged the train of Frankie's dress. Her breath caught as the organ struck a note and the hum of conversation in the sanctuary quieted. The hymn, "Faithful and True" floated out to them. Margie stepped into the doorway and motioned for Frankie to come in.

Viola leaned close to Frankie's ear. "Don't forget to hold your hems up, so you don't trip on them." The whispered admonition finished her job. She stepped to the side, out of view, peeked around the door frame, looked at Ed's stunned expression and smiled. Frankie's wish had come true.

She ducked back, leaned against the wall and closed her tearing eyes.

Viola settled into the rocker, situated Goldie in the crook of her left arm and gave her the bottle. The chair quietly creaked out its ageless message of calm and comfort as she set it in motion. But it didn't reach the empty spot inside her.

"I ain't never seen anything like it, Viola." Hattie

looked up from her knitting, shook her head. "There wasn't a person in that church could believe that was Frankie Tucker when she come walkin' in wearin' that dress. An' Ed—" Hattie chuckled, turned her work. "Ed looked like he got kicked in the head by a mule. He couldn't take his eyes off of her when they was standin' there sayin' their vows."

"Yes. Frankie got her wish." Thomas had looked so handsome today. But she hadn't looked at him after the wedding started. She didn't want a memory of him standing beside that dress. Foolishness. She had given up her hopeless dream, so what did it matter?

"Evelyn said, from now on, every woman in Treasure Creek plannin' on gettin' married will be comin' to you to get their dresses made."

"That will be nice. I enjoy making beautiful gowns. It's more fun than mending tents or torn jackets."

"Once, when everyone was crowded around talking to Ed after the wedding, he had looked around and found Frankie and smiled. He had a wonderful smile. It made you feel…special.

"And Thomas—"

"Hattie, could we not talk any more now please?" She looked over at the older woman and sighed. "I don't mean to be rude, but I'm…tired. And I have a bit of a headache."

Hattie nodded. "You been workin' awful hard doin' for the church and for Frankie. You want me to take Goldie so you can go lay down?"

She shook her head. She didn't want to let go of Goldie. She was her one source of comfort. "No. She's almost asleep. I'll take her in to bed." She set the empty bottle aside, lifted Goldie to her shoulder and carried her to her bedroom, breathing in the sweet baby smell of her. It helped ease the empty place a bit. *Thank You, God, for giving me Goldie. Thank You for giving me a family.*

Thomas prowled through the house, too restless to read or study for Sunday's sermon. And he sure wasn't going to bed. He frowned, listened to the sound of his footsteps echoing through the empty living room and kitchen. He should give up this ridiculous waiting and buy more furniture. A man needed more than a chair and a lampstand in his living room.

Hah! Listen to him. A man who had lived in a crowded, one-room bark hut until a few weeks ago. How quickly our needs, our…wants changed. Except his want didn't change. It just kept getting bigger, deeper. He wanted Viola Goddard for his wife. And today, when he'd seen her standing in the sanctuary doorway with Frankie… Whoo!

He'd been hard put not to walk up to her, take her in his arms and declare his love right there in front of half of the town. Not that that mattered. Most of them already knew he loved her. Only Viola was oblivious to his torment. And now…

He scrubbed his hand over the nape of his neck, glanced up at the ceiling. "Lord, I'm doing my best not to envy Ed Parker tonight, but I'm not doing a very good job of it. He's got the woman he loves in his heart, in his arms and in his home for the rest of his life. I want that, Lord. I want Viola in my arms and in my home for the rest of my life. She's already in my heart."

He went to the window, stared out into the purple night. "If this love I have for Viola is Your will, Lord…

if it would be pleasing in Your sight for us to be one for the rest of our lives, then I ask You to heal Viola's heart and set her free to accept my love. Amen."

Viola stopped in the kitchen doorway, sniffed and swept her gaze over the bowls and clutter sitting on the table and hutch. "What are you doing, Hattie? Is that bread I smell baking?"

The older woman glanced up from her work. "Yep. I set me some dough to risin' last night after you went to bed. Thought I'd bake some potato bread and doughnuts. Had me a good time makin' them doughnuts the other day."

Her gray head bowed over her work again. A towel was whisked off of a large washbasin, and a plump fist punched into a mound of yeasty dough. "I left that end of the table clear for you. Gruel is ready on the stove." The dough slid from the tilted washbasin and thumped to the table, raising a cloud of flour dust. A long, sharp knife sliced through it, divided it into four parts. The towel flapped down over them.

The baby gurgled and jiggled up and down, twisted around toward the table. She laughed and kissed Goldie's warm, chubby cheek. "All right, I'll get your cereal." She sat her on the floor where she would be safely out of the way, gave her a spoon to play with and picked up her bowl.

"Milk and sugar's here on the table. Been usin' it." Hattie gave an audible sniff, turned and opened the oven door, thumped a crusty brown loaf.

The smell of the fresh-baked bread made her mouth water and her stomach remind her it had been a long time since supper. She stood back and watched as Hattie removed four loaves from the oven, then whipped off a towel covering four more loaf pans. White dough puffed up out of them, overhung the sides. She should learn to bake bread. Maybe…

Hattie stuck her knobby hand inside the oven, pulled it out and shook her head. "Too hot."

"What do you do about that?" She was learning there were tricks to the art of cooking and baking and Hattie knew them all.

"Let out some of the heat." Hattie shoved the loaves in the oven, grabbed a long, narrow stick from a crock on the warming shelf and stuck it in the side of the door near the top, holding it open about an inch.

An effective trick to remember. Viola smiled and dished up Goldie's cereal, lifted the baby onto her lap and watched Hattie dump the baked bread out of the pans and set the hot loaves on a rack spanning the woodbox to cool. Eight loaves of bread? No, *twelve* counting the four Hattie was now shaping into loaves and slapping into the emptied pans.

She frowned, spooned cereal into Goldie's sweet little mouth and looked across the table. "Hattie, we can't possibly eat this much bread. And you haven't even started on the doughnuts." She indicated the bowls sitting on the reservoir, their towel covers lifted by the dough that was rising beneath them. "What are you going to do with all of these baked goods?"

"Take them to Tanner's."

"To Lana and Mack's? What—"

"Nope. To the store."

Her mouth gaped like Goldie's.

Hattie lifted the loaf pans to the warming shelf, flopped a towel down over them.

She gave the baby another bite. "I don't understand. Why—"

"To sell them."

Her mouth gaped again.

Hattie wiped her hands on her apron and took the chair beside her. "It come to me the other day when them stampeders was buyin' our doughnuts faster'n we could make them, there ain't no one bakin' nothin' to sell in this town. So I went and talked with Mack Tanner about me startin' up a bakin' business." Her winkled face creased in a wide grin. "He said I was a genius, and he'd sell my baked goods right there in his store. Give me these here pans and supplies on credit to get me started." She chuckled, waved a hand in her direction. "You should see your face, Viola."

She made an effort to gather her wits about her. "I'm…astounded, Hattie. I had no idea…" She frowned. "Have you needs I haven't met? If so—"

"It ain't that, Viola. You're awful good to me. It's just… This idea's been a-itchin' at me ever since that day. I like bakin' and I'm good at it." Hattie chuckled, rose and lifted a towel to check on some dough. "And I kinda like the idea of gettin' my share of the gold floatin' 'round town from them stampeders. Charley would have been proud of me." She frowned and looked her way. "It could get a mite crowded and busy here in the kitchen just at the start. But I figure to add me on a bakin' kitchen when the gold starts comin' in. That all right with you, Viola?"

She nodded, her head still reeling from Hattie's news. "Of course it is, Hattie. This is your home." She jumped, looked toward the living room. "Someone's knocking."

She gave Goldie a kiss and sat her on the floor with her spoon to play with. "I'll be right back, sweetie." She smoothed down her long skirt and hurried to the door.

Chapter Twenty-Five

"I'm coming." Viola brushed a curl back off her forehead and opened the door, swept her gaze over the young man standing on the stoop. He held no clothes or packages. She glanced at the wagon out front, looked back at him. "Yes? May I help you?"

He snatched his hat off his head, nodded. "I've come for my baby girl."

Another one. She stiffened, stepped back to close and lock the door, stopped. What if he truly was Goldie's father? She looked at his eyes, saw nothing threatening and stepped outside and closed the door.

The man looked at the door, then back at her. "I've been waiting a long time to hold her again, Miss. Could we go inside and—"

"Not unless I know you are truly the baby's father." She fixed a cold look on him. "Several have already made that claim to get hold of the gold that came with her."

Anger darkened his face. He looked at the door, appeared about to crash his way through it, then looked back at her. "Who tried to claim my baby? I'll—" He swallowed, took a breath, made a visible effort to control himself. "Sorry, Miss. I've been on the trail so long I've forgotten my manners around a lady." He scowled. "It's only—I never thought about anyone else trying to claim her. I guess I was a mite too trusting before I started up the trail. Thank you for keeping her safe. I knew I could trust you."

"I know I can trust you." That's what Goldie's father had written in the note. She stared at him, her stomach uneasy. He'd never even mentioned the gold. She squared her shoulders, lifted her chin. "We have never met, sir. Why would you say you knew you could trust me?"

"Because I saw you that day in Tanner's store. The day you helped that woman with her fussing baby so she could do her shopping." He glanced at the door again, longing clear in his eyes. Eyes the same blue as Goldie's. "You were a stranger to that baby, Miss, yet you treated her like she was your own." His Adam's apple slid up and down as he swallowed. "She stopped crying and fussing while you held her. And I—" His Adam's apple slid up and down again. "I figured you would take good care of my baby. I had no one else I could leave her with. And I wanted to go and get gold. Those two nuggets my brother sent made me hungry to get enough to take care of her, give her a good life."

His brother. The queasiness in her stomach increased. That was in the note also. But the note had been seen by several people. The information could be generally known. And he could simply be a smarter, more clever kidnapper. *Please, Lord…*

"You say 'her', sir." She looked straight at him,

watched his eyes for the slightest flicker, the slightest sign of hesitation. "What is your baby's name?"

"Gretchen." The eyes softened, warmed. "I named her after my mother."

Gretchen…G C. Those were the initials embroidered on the blanket Goldie had been wrapped in the night she was left on her doorstep. She took a breath, pressed her hand to her churning stomach. "And your name, sir?" *Please, please, Lord…*

"John Carter. But what—" He stared at her, his eyes narrowing. He gave a slow nod. "You're asking because of the blanket. My wife made it, put those initials on there."

Hope faded, returned. The blanket, too, had been seen by many. His story could be a fabrication built on a few generally known facts. But there was one thing only the father would know. One thing that no one but herself had ever seen. "When Goldie—"

He frowned. "Goldie?"

She nodded. "I call her Goldie because of the nuggets, because of the initials on the blanket, and—" she swallowed back a rush of tears "—and because she is such a treasure to me."

He nodded, looked down at the hat in his hands. "I guess I didn't think about what this might mean to you." He looked back up. "I'm sorry, Miss, for causing you hurt. But could I please see Gretchen now. I—"

"One last question, Mr. Carter. If you answer this correctly, I will know beyond doubt that you are truly Goldie's father."

"What is it?"

"When Goldie was left she was in a cradle—"

"The carving! I should have thought to tell you that straight off."

He leaned toward her, whether from eagerness or earnestness she could not tell. It didn't matter, she already knew. He was Goldie's father. She would have to give her to him. Her heart splintered and bled.

"I carved a big capital C on the bottom of the cradle when I made it. Then I carved two big hearts—one each for me and my wife—and one tiny one—for our coming baby—hanging from the bottom of the capital C. Can I see my baby now, *please?*"

She nodded, blinked tears from her eyes and opened the door. "Come in, Mr. Carter. I will go…get your daughter for you." She turned and walked toward the kitchen, every step a dagger in her heart.

"'Bout time you come back. Goldie's—" Hattie straightened, peered at her. "What's wrong, Viola?"

She couldn't answer, couldn't speak. She shook her head, picked up Goldie and cuddled her close. Tears streamed from her eyes. "Goodbye, sweetie." She kissed the soft, warm baby cheek, turned and carried her into the living room.

"Here is your daughter, Mr. Carter."

"Gretchen!" He took her in his arms, cuddled her close, cupped his hand over the back of her head and swayed back and forth. "My baby girl…my baby girl…" He choked, blinked his eyes.

"I'll just…get her things…"

"I'll get them, Viola."

She spun about, looked at the tears on Hattie's cheeks and shook her head. "No, I'll do it, Hattie. You…get her bottles, please. And…and be sure to fill one." She walked to her bedroom, dragged the cradle over to the door, pulled Goldie's clothes and booties, blankets, diapers and hats from the chest, and piled them into the cradle, added her toy rattle, the string of spools, and the little bag of buttons she'd made her that she liked to shake.

Goldie hadn't cried. She kept her mind fixed on that thought, wrested what comfort she could from it. The man had taken Goldie out of her arms, and she hadn't cried. She could hear her now, gurgling her baby talk in response to his voice. Could she remember him? Did a baby that young remember? She took hold of the footboard of the packed cradle and dragged it into the living room.

John Carter rushed to her side. "I'll get the cradle, Miss—" He frowned, shook his head. "I don't know your name. Seems like I should, after all you've done for Gretchen."

"It's Goddard. Viola Goddard." She straightened, rubbed her palms down her skirt. "May I ask you a question, Mr. Carter?"

"Another one?" He gave her a sheepish grin.

"Yes." She forced an answering smile. "Why did you return? Did you find the gold you sought?"

His eyes clouded. He shook his head. "No. I never made it to the gold fields." She watched his arms tighten about his baby. "I saw so many men sickening and dying, or being maimed or killed in accidents or fights along the trail, I turned back. I didn't want Gretchen to become an orphan. I'll find work to support her. I'm a decent carpenter. I made the cradle."

He still hadn't mentioned the gold. "And you have the gold nuggets. But I don't have them here. I gave them to

Mack Tanner, the mayor of Treasure Creek and owner of Tanner's General Store for safekeeping."

"They were to pay for Gretchen's care."

"Yes. But I wanted Goldie to have them as a legacy from you if you hadn't returned. If you will meet me at the store, I will have Mr. Tanner give them to you."

He frowned. "I can't thank you enough for what you've done for my baby, Miss Goddard. And them nuggets are little enough to try and repay you. I want you to have them."

She shook her head. "Caring for Gol—Gretchen—was a privilege and a joy, Mr. Carter. I wouldn't think of accepting payment. Now—" she braced herself and held out her arms "—let me hold Gretchen while you carry her things to your wagon."

"Well, as long as Viola is satisfied you're Goldie's father, that's good enough for me, Mr. Carter." Mack Tanner cast a look her way.

She summoned up a smile, hoped it was good enough to fool him. "I am completely satisfied, Mr. Tanner. Now, as I'm no longer needed here, if you gentlemen will excuse me please, I must get back home." She touched Goldie's cheek, turned and headed for the door.

"I'll instruct my clerks to give you credit up to the value of Goldie's nuggets, Mr. Carter."

She stopped. Why would Mack Tanner be talking about the gold so freely? She could hear him all the way... Oh. She turned, glanced back at him. He caught her eye, nodded and smiled. She nodded in return, then stepped through the door a man held open for her.

The clamor of the waterfront assailed her. She hurried to the corner and turned down the road that led to the true heart of Treasure Creek—the school, the church and the homes. So she would no longer have to worry about kidnappers or robbers breaking into her cabin to steal Goldie's gold nuggets. Mack Tanner had just told an entire crowded store that the baby and the gold were no longer in her possession. The word would pass around town and the waterfront quickly. She would not need her pistol, or the shooting lessons she had put off taking. She would give the pistol to Frankie.

She looked down the road toward Ed and Frankie's cabin and stopped. Evelyn Harris and Elizabeth Dunn were coming her way and she could not face talking to anyone. She ducked behind the corner pillar of the hotel's stone wall, then ran behind the building to the school, let her feet and memory carry her beyond the cluster of cabins and past Dunkel's farm to the woods.

She stepped into the silence and suddenly realized where she was going. She blinked tears from her eyes and searched for the path, turned right and walked toward the waterfall.

The roar of water pouring over the mountain ledge told her she was near. She followed the foaming deluge of water until it turned into the creek flowing toward town, moved forward until the woods opened onto a small clearing and she could see the fence. And the gate.

She stood in the silence and looked at the tree she had hidden behind the night of Goldie's kidnapping. Her arms had been empty then, too. Just as they were empty now. But this time there was no hope of them being filled again. This time Goldie was gone from her life for good. A sob filled her throat, pressed for release.

One day. *One day,* and her life had changed forever.

This morning she had a family, people who needed her. And now Hattie was starting her own bakery business, and Goldie's father had returned and claimed his daughter. And she was glad. She was. Little girls needed fathers to protect them from all the harsh and hurtful things of this world. And Goldie would never have had a father with her. Because she would never marry. But for much different reasons than before.

She crossed the clearing to the hollowed-out tree, to the spot where Thomas had risked his life to save Goldie. She knew now it was then, at that very moment when her heart had begun to heal. It was then that the seed of truth, of the knowledge that not all men were like Dengler and Dolph and Karl, and the other men she had known, had been planted.

She lifted her hands and wiped the tears from her cheeks. It had taken her so long to understand and to believe that Thomas had risked his life to save Goldie— not for gain, but for love. It had taken her so long to understand that Thomas was a man of moral strength and integrity—a man who would never intentionally hurt or harm another. And it had taken her far too long to understand that her dream of marriage to Thomas was really the hunger of her heart. How could she have been so blind? How could she not have known how much she loved him? And how ironic that the only man she had ever wanted to love her had shown nothing but compassion and kindness toward her.

Finally, she understood the reason for her discontent. Her heart loved with no one to receive it.

Could she accept that? Could she go on day after day, accidentally meeting him about town, seeing him every Sunday. Or should she leave Treasure Creek? There was nothing to hold her here now. Her friends would understand.

Oh, Lord, show me what I am to do!

She heard a sound over the top of the whispering, rushing water of the creek at her feet and knew. Something in her heart told her Thomas was there. He was always there when she had a need. She gathered all of the emotions tearing her apart and stuffed them down behind the crumbled wall that was once her defense against the world and turned.

"Mack told me Goldie's father had returned." Thomas stopped a short distance from her, the sun streaming down through the branches of the trees revealing the concern, the caring in his eyes. "I thought I might find you here." He shoved his hands in his pockets, stepped closer. "I'm sorry for your hurt, Viola. I know how much you love Goldie. Are you all right?"

She turned, waited until she was sure the pressure in her chest wouldn't erupt in a wild bout of sobbing. "No. But…I will be."

She heard his footsteps, felt his closeness, tensed when he took a long, ragged breath. "Viola, you are the most selfless, the most loving woman I have ever known." His deep, husky voice poured over her, flooded the emptiness inside. "You are also the most beautiful, and the most frustrating."

She turned and looked up at him.

He shoved his hands deeper in his pockets, hunched his shoulders and riveted his gaze on hers. "You look at me with such questions in your eyes, Viola. Don't you know yet what high regard I have for you? Don't you realize how my heart seeks you out?" His voice grew softer, huskier. "Don't you know how much I love you and desire you for my wife?"

She pressed her hand over her heart, shook her head. "That can't be."

The gold flecks in his eyes darkened. "But it is. You just have to believe it."

"But…how—" She choked on the words, couldn't get them out. His eyes held her, wouldn't let her go. She pressed her trembling lips together, released them. Took a breath and forced out the words that would destroy her dream forever. "You are a man of God, Thomas. And I was a prostitute. It's impossible. If you married me it would destroy your ministry."

He shook his head. "Not good enough, Viola. We've already dealt with this. The people of Treasure Creek know your past. They know it *is* your past. They will fully welcome you as their pastor's wife."

"But new members…"

He shook his head. "Stop hiding, Viola. What is the real reason you're refusing me?" His chest heaved with a deep breath. "Is it that you don't love me in return?"

Tears flooded her eyes. She shook her head, rubbed her chest to relieve the horrible pressure and pain. "No it's—I'm afraid. Oh, Thomas I don't know how to…to accept your love. I don't know how…"

He cupped her face in his hands, his touch so gentle, so tender, tipped her face up to look at him. "Viola, do you trust me?"

She could barely hear his husky words. But there was no hesitation in her answer. "Yes. I do."

"Then just let your heart do what it knows how to do best—love and be loved." He lowered his head, touched her lips with his, let them remain, barely touching hers, an invitation, a promise.

The empty place inside her burst open, filled with the rich warmth of his love. She lifted her face higher, went on tiptoe, parted her lips and pressed them more fully to his, compelled by the need to return the beautiful gift of love she had received.

His strong arms slid around her, crushed her against his chest as his lips claimed her forever as his own.

Epilogue

"Gracious, it's so crowded in this yard, you'd think the church was on the waterfront. I had to search to find you here, in the middle of everyone." Hattie plunked her basket down in the center of the blanket with Viola's, Lana Tanner's and Teena Calloway's.

Dong. Dong. Dong.

Viola looked at Lana and grinned. "Which husband do you think it is, your's or mine?"

Lana laughed, shrugged her shoulders. "Who knows, they both love to ring that bell. And they're like little boys getting up to mischief when they get together." She snatched her three-year-old son off the blanket. "Oh, no you don't, young man. I said, no cookies until after we eat dinner."

"Which sounds like an excellent idea to me."

Viola turned. Mack Tanner and her husband were weaving in and out among the spread blankets to join them. She looked at Thomas and smiled. He was so tall and handsome and wonderful. Her heart did the soft, melting thing it did whenever he was near.

Thomas stepped close to her side, slid his arm around

her thickened waist. "Are you all right? You're not getting too tired are you? Because—"

She laughed and shook her head. "Stop worrying. I'm fine, Thomas. I have another month until the baby is due. You can—"

"Vi-Vi."

She grinned and turned, went to her knees on the blanket and held out her arms to Goldie, who was toddling toward her as fast as her pudgy little legs would carry her.

"Vi-Vi." Goldie climbed onto her lap as far as possible.

She lifted her over her swollen abdomen and kissed her soft baby cheek. "Hello, sweetie." Little arms slipped around her neck and hugged tight.

"Gammy."

"Here I am." Hattie leaned over and kissed Goldie's other cheek.

"I'm sorry for the interruption, everyone. But Gretchen wouldn't settle down once she spotted Mrs. Stone." John Carter bent and held out his arms. "Come on, precious. Your new mama fixed a good lunch for us." He scooped his daughter up and carried her off, her little hand waving bye-bye over his shoulder.

Mack Tanner gave a shrill whistle and held up his hands.

People all over the yard stopped flapping blankets and arranging picnic baskets. Conversations stopped. Everyone turned and looked their way.

"I just want to thank you all for coming to our celebration picnic marking Thomas Stone's first full year as pastor of Treasure Creek Church."

Cheering and clapping erupted.

Mack gave another whistle to catch their attention and laughed. "You can all tell Thomas how much you love and appreciate him after the picnic. Right now, I'm hungry." There was a laughing, whistling roar of approval from the men. He held up his hands. "Quiet while Thomas blesses our food."

Thomas stepped forward, cleared his throat. "Almighty God, we are mindful of Your mercy and love, of Your provision and care. We thank You for the daily blessings You pour out upon us here in Treasure Creek. And we thank You, Lord, for this bounty which we are about to receive. We ask You to bless this food to the health and strength of our bodies. In our Lord's name I pray. Amen."

Conversations resumed, picnic baskets were opened.

Thomas glanced at the group settling on their blankets. "Think there'll be room enough for all of us on only two blankets?" He grinned and settled down beside her. "We're taking up more space because there's practically three of us now."

She laughed and rested her hand on her distended stomach. "This little one doesn't make us three until I can see his adorable little face."

"And his red, curly hair!"

Frankie called the comment from the blankets she and Ed were sharing with Margie and Lucy and their husbands. The comment turned into a chorus from those seated around them. Everyone in town teased them about their baby being born with red curls.

Thomas leaned close. "Suits me. I'm partial to red curly hair. Especially on you." He gave her hand a squeeze that promised they'd talk more about that subject later.

Lana lifted a platter of chicken from her basket and glanced over at her sleeping baby daughter. "Well, I would highly recommend that you have a little girl like Mae. She is so much easier to raise than Georgie."

"Give her a chance to grow up and start toddlin' 'round. You might change your mind on that." Hattie chuckled, pulled the towel off her basket. Mack, Thomas and Jacob all leaned forward and grabbed one of her famous doughnuts. Mack snagged a second and held it out as a bribe to coax Georgie to eat his food.

Teena smiled and set out fish sandwiches made with some of Hattie's potato rolls. "I think the choice of son or daughter does not matter." She splayed her fingers over her abdomen in a protective gesture and looked at her husband. "Any child of ours will fill our hearts."

"And our picnic blankets next year." Jacob Calloway shook his head and grinned. "There is an epidemic of babies about to hit this town."

"We have all been abundantly blessed." Thomas looked around the group of friends, settled his gaze on his wife. "We have so much to be thankful for...each other and our coming child."

She nodded and smiled at those around them. "And good friends...and a wonderful church family."

Thomas grinned and picked up the litany again. "A warm, dry parsonage to live in..."

Everyone laughed.

Hattie jumped in. "I'm thankful for the blessin' of Viola givin' me her cabin for my own, and my bakin' business. And that I'm going to be a grandma right soon. Though it sure was hard work gettin' them two together to start with."

"Amen! I thought I was going to wear myself out

running Hattie's messages of Viola's doings to Thomas so he could *accidentally* run into her." Frankie chuckled, looked the group over. "Do you mind if we join you?"

"We carry guns."

They laughed at Ed's comment and made room on their blankets. Frankie spread the skirt of the new, blue cotton dress Viola had made her and sank slowly and gracefully to the edge of the blanket, Ed's strong hand helping her.

Jacob Calloway added tomato and cucumber from the vegetable platter Viola set out to his well-filled plate. "Well, I'm thankful for Teena loving me after the terrible, autocratic way I treated her when we first met. And for our coming child." He shifted his gaze to the mayor. "And to Mack for granting us the loan we needed to turn our small clinic into the Treasure Creek Hospital."

"We're all thankful for that." Ed Parker looked at Thomas and grinned. "Especially those of us that get shot."

Thomas grinned and lifted his fish sandwich in salute. "Amen to that."

Viola leaned against his shoulder that was at last fully healed. "I'll second that amen."

Ed Parker nodded, looked at Frankie. "And I'm thankful for the new sheriff's office, instead of the back of the smithy. And most of all for my deputy bride."

"Well, Lana and I are certainly thankful for Georgie and our newest blessing." Mack touched his infant daughter's tiny hand. "But I'm also thankful that the furor of people hunting for the buried treasure has finally stopped, thanks to the new gold strikes. Though I suppose someday, someone is going to find the map that will lead them to the buried treasure. I just hope it blesses them and provides them what they need."

Thomas swept his gaze over the group. "I'm sure we all agree, that with all the prayer that has covered that treasure, it will do just that, Mack."

Everyone nodded. "It surely will."

* * * * *

Dear Reader,

It is an odd time of mixed emotion when I finish writing a story. There is relief *Yay!— I met my deadline*—and excitement—*What is the next story going to be?*—tinged with sadness because I am leaving behind characters I have come to know so well. This time is no exception. I am going to miss Viola, Thomas, Hattie and little Goldie.

I was honored when my editor asked me to write *Gold Rush Baby,* the last book in the Alaskan Brides continuity series. I hope I lived up to her faith in me. And that I did justice to the talented authors of the first two books, *Yukon Wedding* and *Klondike Medicine Woman.* If you somehow missed reading those first two books of the series, I would highly recommend you remedy that situation. They are wonderful stories.

Thank you, dear reader, for choosing to purchase *Gold Rush Baby.* I hope you enjoyed reading Viola and Thomas's story. If you would care to share your thoughts about the story with me, I would enjoy hearing from you. I can be reached at dorothyjclark@hotmail.com or www.dorothyjclark.com.

Until next time,

Dorothy Clark

QUESTIONS FOR DISCUSSION

1. Did Viola willingly choose to become a lady of the evening? What would you have done in her shoes?

2. Do you believe God was working to lead Viola out of her lifestyle? On what do you base your opinion?

3. Why did baby Goldie's father leave her with Viola? Do you approve or disapprove of his actions? Why?

4. Why was Thomas determined not to marry again?

5. In your opinion, was Thomas right or wrong in his thinking when he made the vow to stay single? Why or why not?

6. Hattie schemed to bring Thomas and Viola together. Was she right or wrong in her actions? Why?

7. Do you believe God was working to bring Thomas and Viola together?

8. What was your opinion of Lana's plan to protect Viola?

9. The church members took "sides" when they learned of Viola's past life as a prostitute. Would you have done the same? Which side would you have chosen?

10. Do you believe God can place thoughts and desires in our hearts and minds that will bring about His desires for us? How so?

11. Can we thwart God's plans for us?

12. Do you believe God uses people to achieve His purposes?

13. Did God use Hattie? If so, how?

14. Do you think Thomas handled the situation with Viola well? Was his sermon appropriate for the situation?

15. What did you think of Frankie Tucker and her actions?

INSPIRATIONAL

Inspirational romances to warm your heart & soul.

Love Inspired
HISTORICAL

TITLES AVAILABLE NEXT MONTH

Available July 12, 2011

CALICO BRIDE
Buttons and Bobbins
Jillian Hart

FRONTIER FATHER
Dorothy Clark

SECOND CHANCE FAMILY
Winnie Griggs

HEARTS IN FLIGHT
Patty Smith Hall

LIHCNM0611